UNNATURAL DEEDS

ALSO BY CYN BALOG

Alone

UNNATURAL DEEDS

CYN BALOG

sourcebooks
fire

Published by Sourcebooks Fire, an imprint of Sourcebooks, Inc.
P.O. Box 4410, Naperville, Illinois 60567-4410
(630) 961-3900
Fax: (630) 961-2168
sourcebooks.com

The Library of Congress has cataloged the hardcover edition as follows:

Names: Balog, Cyn, author.
Title: Unnatural deeds / Cyn Balog.
Description: Naperville, Illinois : Sourcebooks Fire, [2016] | Summary:
Victoria Zell, a high school misfit coping with anxiety, is quite content
with her homeschooled, agoraphobic boyfriend until she becomes obsessed
with a charismatic new boy.
Identifiers: LCCN 2016016737 | (13 : alk. paper)
Subjects: | CYAC: Mental illness--Fiction. | Secrets--Fiction. |
Murder--Fiction. | Dating (Social customs)--Fiction.
Classification: LCC PZ7.B2138 Un 2016 | DDC [Fic]--dc23 LC record
available at https://lccn.loc.gov/2016016737

Printed and bound in the United States of America.
VP 10 9 8 7 6 5 4 3 2 1

For all the girls who can't let go.

Foul whisp'rings are abroad. Unnatural deeds
Do breed unnatural troubles. Infected minds
To their deaf pillows will discharge their secrets.

Shakespeare's *Macbeth*, Act V, Scene 1

CHAPTER 1

Duchess—Police are investigating an apparent homicide after a body was found in a wooded area early Tuesday morning. Authorities have not yet released the name of the victim or the person(s) they are questioning in connection with the investigation.

—*Central Maine Express Times*

I S THIS THING ON?

Ha-ha, I'm a laugh a minute.

Anyway, Andrew. It's me. Vic. I wanted to say I'm sorry. Sorry for... Well, where do I begin? I—

Cough, cough, cough.

Sorry. I'm losing my voice. Something bitter is stuck in my throat, and the air is so cold it's hard to breathe. This place reeks of decaying leaves, of the musty, damp rot of dead things returning to the earth.

There's something soft and wet under my head. I hope it's not brain matter. I can't raise my arms to check because of the way I'm twisted here. I think my leg is broken. Or maybe my back? Damned if I can twitch a muscle without pain screaming its way up my spine.

Somehow I managed to pry my phone out of my jacket pocket and prop it on my chest, but you know how spotty service is around Duchess. All charged up with zero bars—not that I'd be calling anyone but you. I wish I could see the background photo of you and me. It'd keep me company. You know the one. It's the picture of us at the Renaissance Faire when we were fourteen. We're both grinning like mad and you have your arm around me, claiming me as your own. It's probably the only time you were ever comfortable with yourself. With us. I miss that.

Anyway, you know how glass half-empty I am, Andrew. I wanted to record a note for you on my phone. You know, in case I don't get out of here.

Of course I'll get out of here. I wouldn't be lucky enough to die here. But maybe this'll be easier than telling you in person.

Cough, cough.

Where should I start?

It's so quiet. You must have left me, Andrew. But you'll come back. You always come back. You were scared, maybe, when you saw what you'd done. And now I'm all alone here.

I don't really know where "here" is. I think it's a drainage ditch on the side of Route 11. The last thing I remember is rushing down the road near the Kissing Woods, feeling powerful. Immortal. Like everything I wanted could be mine. For an instant, I felt like *he* could be mine.

But that's not possible now.

I know what people have said behind my back in hushed whispers. They call me delusional. But I'm not. I know what is real and what isn't.

No, wait. The last thing I remember is you with that fierce look in your eyes. You sure surprised me. Who knew that my boyfriend, quiet, unassuming Andrew Quinn, had *that* in him?

I thought I knew you inside and out, but…I was wrong.

I guess I should explain. After all, I have no other pressing engagements. And you're overdue an explanation, aren't you? The tall pines can be my witnesses. They can pass judgment as they see fit.

I'm not sure when it all began, but Lady M said it best. Hell is goddamn murky.

Whoops. Blasphemy. Yet another sin to add to my act-of-contrition list.

Looking back, you knew when I started to change, didn't you, Andrew? You know everything about me. It was that very first day of school, the day my life began and the day it began to unravel.

So here are the gory details. It won't be enough, but I'll try. You can't know it all until you've smelled that intoxicating cinnamon-and-cloves scent, read those texts that elevated even the blandest words to poetry, and seen those heart-stoppingly blue eyes.

His eyes. Even now, I can see them with perfect clarity. I've seen them in my dreams, in the sky when the sun hits the clouds just right, and in my morning breakfast cereal. It all goes back to him. Every single thought always winds *right back to him. Always. Always. Always.*

It's no use. I want him out of my head. I wish I could scrape him out of my memory. I don't want to live with him etched in the deepest part of me. I don't want to die thinking of him.

But I know I will.

CHAPTER 2

Abigail Zell of 12 Spruce Street called at 8:33 a.m. to report her daughter's disappearance. The girl, Victoria Zell, 16, a student at St. Ann's Catholic School in Bangor, was not in her bed when her mother went to wake her for school. Officer advised Mrs. Zell that missing persons report can be filed after a 24-hour waiting period.

—Duchess Police Department phone log

DO YOU REMEMBER THAT NIGHT, Andrew? Right before I started junior year? We were crouched in our hiding place, between the rosebushes at the white picket fence separating our yards, you on your side, me on mine. Just like bookends. The grass stopped growing where I used to plant my backside, but it was thick on your side, probably the result of your mom's green thumb. It was already chilly, the crickets chirruping their summer goodbye. When I was young, I used to count fireflies while we talked. That night, there were no fireflies.

"Vic," you whispered through the fence.

I giggled, lovesick. I adore your voice. It's so low and musical, even when you're not singing. If a voice made a whole person, I would be utterly, desperately in love with you. Most of the time, it's painful to watch you struggle to get the words out. Not because it bothers me, but because I know how much it bothers *you*. You've never liked yourself much, but I think you hate your wayward tongue most of all. How can something that behaves so angelically while singing music betray you so terribly the rest of the time?

You rarely stutter with me. When we were alone and darkness cloaked us, your voice was perfect. *Life* was perfect then. Stupidly, I didn't realize it.

"Y-you have fun at school tomorrow, OK?"

"Fun?"

You paused. "OK. Don't run screaming from school tomorrow. Better?"

"Much." I pushed a piece of foil-wrapped Juicy Fruit between the slats. A second later, I could hear you chewing the gum. "I wish you would be there."

I felt you push against the fence. You liked to fold the silver paper into squares and wedge them between the slats. "Save your wishes," you muttered.

It's true that wishing was useless. As if your mother would suddenly decide not to homeschool you so you could enroll at St. Ann's. As if you'd be able to enter a classroom without crumpling into a panicky mess.

"You out there still?" Your stepfather's voice boomed from the darkness.

I peered between the slats at the lit tip of his cigarette, cutting through the darkness near your back porch. Since he worked so much of the time, all I ever saw of your stepdad was that tiny orange fireball. You jumped to attention and the fence rattled. "Y-y-y-yes, sir," you said.

I poked my head up and your stepdad muttered something about me. Nothing nice, I'm sure. Your stepdad has never been the sweetest of men, which makes him the opposite of your mom. You told me the story about a thousand times, about how they married when you were seven, mostly because your dad died unexpectedly and left you two in major debt... A "marriage of convenience" you'd said, but it never seemed very convenient for you. Your mother is prim and proper and likes the finer things in life, and your stepfather, well, doesn't. Somehow though, they fit together. There's only one piece in that puzzle that never seemed to fit. You.

I told you good night, then turned to go inside. My parents had the kitchen blinds parted in a vee, squinting into the dark yard in their attempt to spy on us. "Good night, Vic," you called to me. Most people call me Victoria. People are always formal with me. They think I am oh-so-serious and uptight because I don't know them well enough to say, "Hey, let's not be formal. Vic's fine." And, well, I can't help it. "Relax" is a mantra I repeat over and over in my head. And do I ever? Nope.

Victoria is a serious name, an old name. Everything about me screams old, from the way I dress to my often-hunched posture. Even my hands look old, veined and thin and fragile.

I guess we're just two peas in a pod, Andrew: You and your

premature balding, and me and my old-lady habits. You and your agoraphobia, and me and my crippling anxiety. We belong together. And yet something in me wanted more. I am sorry to say that I wanted what I knew couldn't be. What *shouldn't* be.

And because of that, I blindly let him lead me.

CHAPTER 3

When did you realize something was off?

Off... What do you mean?

When did things start to change? Can you pinpoint when the trouble began?

Oh. It had to be that very first day he walked into the classroom. He...he infused the room with... It's hard to explain. Energy, I guess?

In a good way?

Well, yeah. Mostly. He spurred people into action, made things happen. But...I guess not all of that was good.

—Police interview with Rachel Watson,
junior at St. Ann's

I KNOW YOU CAN'T FORGIVE ME, Andrew. I fastened the collar around my own neck and handed him the leash. But some people—oh, some people are just so damn *like* that. Intoxicating. Spellbinding. You find yourself aching to belong to them, dreading freedom, thinking freedom itself is the cage.

My mom had my lunch packed and ready. She had all my pencils sharpened and supplies organized in my L. L. Bean backpack. Breakfast was lined up for me on the counter: a banana, a glass of OJ, one Effexor, and an Ativan. The Effexor was usually all I needed to control my anxiety. I only took the Ativan for super-stressful situations, and I guess my mom assumed this qualified. As I sucked down the pills, she asked me how I was doing and if I was ready for the three-thousandth time.

I swear my parents barely let me breathe on my own anymore.

Honestly, I didn't feel nervous at all. I knew the Ativan would combat any first-day-back freak-outs; it usually works like a charm.

Usually.

I felt magically good for an entire hour. Believe it or not, that morning, as I waited for the bus to school, I thought only of you. And I smiled. You've always been my constant, easily readable, black and white, like the piano keys you adore. The first day of my junior year was sure to be more of me hiding behind my books, then rushing home to complain to you, just as I'd done during my first year at St. Ann's. You always listened, no matter how much I ranted. Back then, that patch of dirt in the backyard was my haven, my sanctuary… Like you, I wanted nothing more than constancy.

The bus ride into Bangor was mostly uneventful, long as it was. Most kids in the upper grades drove or carpooled together, so I was stuck with a handful of chatty, jumper-wearing elementary-school girls. I didn't mind. I looked out the window and watched the tall pines of rural Maine as we passed.

The real nerves didn't hit me until after I sat down at my desk.

That's when I met him.

That morning I had on my uniform from last year. My old, pilled plaid skirt that I'd bought two sizes too big with hopes of scraping through senior year before it was above my knees. My Peter Pan–collared blouse was wrinkled, but it is butt-ugly even when it's nicely pressed. My knee-highs had long since lost their elasticity and had already begun to descend toward my scuffed loafers, but the right one was winning by several inches. I never cut my hair, so a ponytail was the best style my stick-straight, beige hair could manage. Activities my classmates lived for— shopping, getting a car, partying—hardly mattered to me. Little did I know, that was about to change.

When I got to my homeroom, number 46B, the junior room, all the desks were arranged in rows of five, as usual. The symmetry hit me right away. There were only twenty-nine kids in my class: fifteen girls and fourteen boys. I knew this well because last year, they'd pair up for projects and lab experiments, leaving me out in Siberia.

But now, there were thirty desks.

I hurried to my seat in the back corner. My last name always lands me at the end of everything. I put my brown-bag lunch on the desk and waited for the other students to arrive. They filtered in, sporting summer tans and crisp, new school uniforms. None of them looked at me. I was OK with that. I figured it went with the territory of being the New Kid in a class where all the other students had known each other since kindergarten.

When Z arrived, everyone stared. His body seemed to absorb the attention. He stood straighter, glowed more. Z sauntered, hands in his pockets, looking straight ahead, like nobody else existed. He didn't carry anything, as if lugging books or a bag or whatever was beneath him. He just had a pencil behind his ear, drowning in his unruly, golden mop of hair. He was tan and had nice stubble on his chin, like a full-grown man. But it was those eyes. Like a baby's eyes, they took up half his face. They made me think of billiards, even though I only watched you play, Andrew. His eyes were bluer than pool cue chalk.

In a split second I went from New Kid to…nobody.

I peeked at him for only a second. A guy like that wouldn't notice me, wouldn't even say "excuse me" if he smacked me on the head with, say, a pool cue. I watched everyone else gawk. Parker Cole ran her perfect tongue over her glossy lips and threw doe eyes his way. Her arsenal of sweet, sexy looks was as abundant as her collection of fuzzy black sweaters. She was wearing one over her uniform, which I'm sure was not regulation, but having a dad as principal has its advantages.

Even though Principal Cole's morning announcements always included a plug for going green, Parker never rode in with him. No, he had an SUV, and she commuted in from the coast in a bright-red sports car that could stop traffic from all the way over the New Hampshire state line. I'd never seen the Cole family estate, but I imagined it to be majestic and storybook perfect, with breathtaking ocean views.

I realized everyone was looking at me. Me, nothing-to-see-here, back-corner-hugging Victoria Zell. But that was because *he* was standing over me.

"I believe you're in my seat," he said.

His voice resounded like yours, Andrew, so like the voice that constantly lulls me out of my bad moods and comforts me during the worst days.

I almost looked around for you, but I shrugged, then pulled out my brand-new notebook. "Er. No. I always sit here."

"Alphabetical?" he asked.

"Yes. I'm Zell."

He thrust his hand under my nose.

"Zachary Zimmerman. People call me Z. Nice to meet you."

I shook his hand. It was smooth. I had hangnails. I'm sure he noticed.

I stood up and moved over a desk, clumsily, the way I always do. Sliding in the new seat, I already felt strange, like my world was tilting ever so slightly.

"Zell," he mused aloud. "Are you like Eminem? Liberace? Sting?"

"Excuse me?"

"You go by only one name?"

"N-no," I said, and wondered if your speech impediment was rubbing off on me. "I'm Victoria. Victoria Zell."

"Cool. Vic," he said. Just like that. I didn't have to tell him. He just knew. It was the first of many things he perceived about me.

I felt a thrill of excitement, of possibility, which I quickly tamped down. Better not to deal with disappointment. I opened my notebook to the first blank page and wondered how long it would be before he ignored me like everyone else. It was inevitable. Right now, he didn't know any better.

At least, that's what I thought until he held something out to me. Juicy Fruit. "Gum?" he asked.

"Um…" Juicy Fruit. Everyone else is into finer, fancier flavors, but he had plain old Juicy Fruit. And you know how I feel about Juicy Fruit.

I plucked the gum from his tanned fingers. "Thank you." Was this a sign? I was about to unwrap the silver foil when I realized, "Mrs. Reese doesn't let us chew gum in class." My ordinary eyes meet his brilliant blue ones.

Oh, there is nothing as intense as the way he looks at you. When he does, it's like you've been touched, maybe not by the hand of God, but by one of God's fingers. That's a whole thirteen months of Catholic school talking, Andrew. In class, our teachers spoke of saints being visited by God. You're bathed in white light, enveloped in a strange and sudden peace. Supposedly, breath and words and sane thought escape you, leaving you totally giddy without having any idea why. I never quite believed all of that, but in that moment, I got it. His mere gaze felt like an extravagant gift.

"So she's one of *those* teachers? Great." Then he smiled,

real easy, and leaned back in his chair as he fed the gum into his mouth. "I'm new. I'll tell her I didn't know." His voice never wavered, even as he chewed. He looked up at the clock, and I got a better look of that field of cinnamon stubble on his chin. He was one of few boys in the class who could probably do with a shave. "Let's see… Want to bet how long it is before she tells me to spit it out?"

I wanted to tell him no, that hell's wrath would be a mosquito bite compared to what would ensue if he kept that gum in his mouth, but I didn't have the time. The bell clanged, startling me enough that I wrote a black line across my clean page. Embarrassed, I caught him staring at me. He'd seen the whole thing.

"Jumpy, huh?"

He had no idea. You know how Mrs. Reese gave me nightmares, Andrew. She is the only late-grade English teacher at St. Ann's, so I'd have the pleasure of having her every year until I blew the joint. I wasn't the best at English, but she made even literary types want to pursue mathematical careers. She had a puckered, lemon-sucking face. She'd been at the school so long and was so comfortable in her position there that she wasn't afraid to scream bloody murder at a student for, say, putting an apostrophe in the word *its* when it wasn't needed. I'm sure I wasn't the only one who fantasized about her driving off a cliff in that smart Prius of hers.

I whispered, "I just don't like—"

"Are you talking in my class, Miss Zell?"

Mrs. Reese had only gotten louder and meaner over the

summer. I was glad I wasn't chewing that gum because I'm sure I would have choked on it and died.

She had a new haircut, more severe, but everything else was the same. The way her sensible Easy Spirits scuffed up the aisle as she neared me. The way she tapped her fingers *rat-a-tat-tat* on every desk she passed. The singular way she managed to scowl and smile at the same time, as if she enjoyed making people cry. Every head in the class turned in my direction. The next words out of her mouth would be, "I see you've learned nothing from me over the break," which she said just about any time we had a school holiday. I braced myself for it.

It was your voice that responded. Actually, not yours, but Z's. He said, "Pardon me, ma'am. But I am new and was just asking Vic a question." His voice was so smooth, so self-assured that I stared at him, marveling at the way he didn't flinch at all. Nobody spoke to Reese without flinching. Nobody. "She was kind enough to help me out."

I expected Mrs. Reese to launch lasers from her eyeballs and incinerate him. But her face softened. "You are Zachary Zimmerman?"

"Call me Z." He proceeded to fill her in on the mundane details of his life, which for some reason, I found fascinating. Z moved here from Arizona, liked baseball. As he spoke, I realized he didn't sound like you at all. His voice was too loud, *too* sure, like a radio announcer. Still, he had successfully diverted the wrath of Reese. And for that, I was grateful.

I thought that was the end of my story with Z. It was a short story, hardly worth reading. But I was wrong. Two seconds after Mrs. Reese turned toward the front of the room, as if she hadn't just yelled at me for talking in class, he leaned across the aisle, still chewing noisily on the gum, and whispered, "You should come with me."

I'd like to say that was when it began, but no. That was when it was cemented. I was a goner the second I looked into those eyes.

CHAPTER 4

You saw him often?

Yeah. He came in here weekday mornings, like once a
week. Usually with a girl.

Did you say anything to him?

Other than, "What'll you have?" No.

Did you notice anything that stood out about him?

His tips were for shit. But hey, he's a kid. I didn't expect
much.

What was your impression of him?

He was cutting school, and we don't get no cutters here.
Young people ain't our usual clientele. So the kind of
kid that goes left when everyone else is going right.

—Police interview with Brian Kelly,
owner of Kelly's Deli, Bangor, Maine

I FELT FIRE RUSHING TO MY cheeks. What could Z's invitation possibly mean? Ever since I'd transferred to St. Ann's
for sophomore year, I'd been like pavement. Wallpaper. The
thought of me hanging out with anyone was absurd.

I couldn't turn to him, wouldn't dare talk in Reese's class, so I moved my notebook to the side of my desk and scribbled, *Where?*

He didn't answer and couldn't scribble anything on his own notebook, since he hadn't brought one with him. The more time that went by, the more my cheeks ignited. He must have realized he'd made a mistake. Then I thought the mistake was mine. Maybe I'd misheard his words. As Reese went over our vocabulary list, I stuck on *illusory*. Surely I'd imagined the whole thing. Z and his Andrew-like voice were all in my head.

And then the bell rang. I got my stuff together to head off to my next class, hoping Reese wouldn't rail at me on my way out. The second I stepped into the hallway, I heard that voice: "The place, of course."

He was staring at me with those eyes. They made me think of Caribbean waters, so that's probably why my voice drowned inside me. All I could manage to choke out was, "Ehm?"

Standing next to me, he was tall. He looked over my head, down the hall toward the K–8 classrooms, with their colorful, sunshiny drawings displayed on bulletin boards. "Every school has one, right? A cutting place?"

"A…" I began, but then I panicked. He couldn't be thinking of cutting class already. That was ridiculous. It wasn't like the student body at St. Ann's was a bunch of saints—I'd heard plenty of Monday-morning chatter about wild parties that I hadn't been invited to. I know they involved drinking and maybe even drugs. I'd heard the spiel about Central Maine lacking diversion, that "kids have nothing better to do." A few kids had come to school hungover. But ditching class was impossible in our school because there were only twenty-ni—er, *thirty*—students in our class. Teachers noticed if anyone was missing. And why would Z ask me? Did I look like someone who went against authority? My parents had been spending so much time at church that they *may* have been applying for sainthood. And they expected nothing less from my behavior. "What?" I asked.

He pointed down the hall, toward the doors that backed up to the woods. Yes, some kids would go out there and smoke behind the Dumpsters, but getting caught meant detention. I guessed if one wanted to leave school unnoticed, that would be the easiest way. But no way was I going. I planted my feet despite the tingling sensation that had overcome me, the whoosh of exhilaration that had my heart beating double time.

Andrew, you know I would never do anything like that. But something about him made me queasy and breathless and unable to think. It was almost like watching a slide show. First, we were in school, my feet pointed stalwartly toward my next class. *Flash*. Another image, his hand on mine. *Flash*. A shot of us bursting through the doors and into the woods, all lush and full of life, life that didn't exist in the halls of St. Ann's.

Outside, it was like I could truly breathe for the first time. Like this whole other world existed during the day, one I knew nothing about. We followed a small path, maybe a deer trail, into the woods, and before I realized what I had done, the school was out of sight and we were completely free. I followed him in silence, trembling, still clutching my notebook to my chest, wishing I could pop that extra Ativan.

Finally, he turned around, and even the birds stopped chirping as he spoke, as if nature bowed down before him. "Don't cut much, do you?"

"What…what gave you…"

He touched my arm. "Goose bumps."

There was a sea of them on my arms, making all the fine hairs stand out like they were surging with electricity. I was clutching my notebook against me so tightly that it was bending to the curve of my body. *Relax, he's just a guy*, I told myself. Just like you, Andrew. Believe it or not, I tried to calm myself after his touch by convincing myself he was just like you.

But what a joke, Andrew. You two are nothing alike, are you?

I breathed in. Breathed out. Prayed to the Effexor gods. Tried to remember what that therapist had said last year before my parents' insurance ran out and they couldn't afford to send me. *Control. You have the control. Visualize.*

All I could visualize was my oncoming heart attack.

"We're going to get into trouble," I managed. "Mr. Cole doesn't stand for any—"

"Who's that?"

"The principal."

"Oh. Short? The bushiest eyebrows on the planet, despite having no hair on his head?"

I nodded.

He waved me on. "Taken care of."

"How?" I couldn't keep the skepticism out of my voice. Maybe he could pull whatever he'd worked on Reese and get away with it; maybe he was just one of those people. But I wasn't like him. I always attracted the wrong kind of attention. Which is why I did everything I could to stay out of it.

He grinned. "I have my ways." He took a few steps forward and then stopped. "If you pay attention, young Padawan, you may learn them."

I couldn't bring myself to laugh at his goofy Yoda impersonation. He couldn't teach me that. It would be like teaching a blind person to drive. Impossible. I mean, who was this guy? I didn't know anything about him. He could be a serial killer. And—

And I was walking through the woods with him, alone.

I stopped walking, or maybe I was still walking, but I couldn't feel my legs. My ears began to burn. My heart raced. "I-I don't know why I'm here. I don't even know you."

He walked ahead without responding and stopped to wait for me at a clearing. I heard a car horn beep. The side of a brick building appeared through the trees. Civilization! I almost lunged toward it in gratitude because I was already in far, far over my head, and this was my opportunity to escape.

Z stood in the center of the narrow path, blocking my way. He wasn't overly large, but he was broad-shouldered, formidable. And laughing at me. "Well, you might not know me, but I know you."

"You…do?"

He nodded. "You're hungry." He pointed to a sign on the brick. Kelly's Deli. "All the kids who cut go here, right?"

I really knew nothing about where the student body spent their off-hours, but Kelly's Deli looked tough, run-down. Like a hangout for prison escapees with frosted glass windows so you couldn't peek in and see what illegal things were going on inside.

My stomach dropped. Z was wrong. What else was he wrong about? He was probably wrong about Cole. Cole would suspend us without a second thought. He was probably wrong about Reese. Eventually she would get him for chewing gum in class. And he was wrong about me. I'd been a little hungry before, but not now. Now, it was Retchville, population: me. "No," I murmured. "Nobody cuts at St. Ann's. They don't. Because they'll get—"

He laughed. "Not true. We just did. And we're fine. Trust me."

We walked to the deli's crumbling asphalt parking lot, me lagging slightly behind, convinced we were about to run into a truancy officer. Inside, the deli was deserted. I wondered if the place was even open. There was nobody behind the counter and all the seats were empty. The stench of cigarettes and old bacon grease suffocated me. My breakfast of banana and juice started to fight its way back up my throat.

"Sit anywhere," a gruff, disembodied voice said from a dark-paneled wall in the rear. I was sure whoever it was probably killed squirrels in the back to transform them into lunch meat.

I thought that once Z saw how disgusting this place was, he would turn and hightail it out of there. But that's the thing about him, Andrew. That's what made it impossible to leave him. He never does what's expected. Part of me wanted to run, but the other part, the part that obviously won out, wanted to stay and see what he would do.

Z marched across the once-white speckled linoleum floor and slid into a booth like it had been reserved for him. The table was greasy and spattered with ketchup, but he didn't notice. While I tried to pluck a napkin out of the dispenser, only to find it empty, he surveyed our surroundings, drummed his fingers on the table, and whistled something that sounded like a Sousa march. "So," he said.

I spotted a hefty pile of napkins at the next table and ran a wad over the tabletop. The stains were crusted on; they were probably older than I was. I really could've used some Formula 409. "So what?"

His eyes, which were already big, widened. "Ask away."

"Ask what?"

He smiled. "You said you don't know me. Here's your chance to. Ask me anything."

I gaped. It was so forward. I would never ask anyone to ask me anything because would anyone really care for the answer? Part of me wanted to say, "I don't care about you," but already, a larger part of me *did* care. Cared and wanted to know everything about him, right down to the smallest detail.

And he knew that. The boy had me figured out from that very first day.

"Why did you ask me here?" I whispered.

He smiled. "You looked like you wanted me to buy you an omelet." He turned away to study the menu on the wall.

I raised an eyebrow. "Seriously."

He said, "I was being serious."

Looking back, if I had realized I was in danger, I might

have run. But I didn't. I suppose I was already trapped. Only I didn't know it. I thought I could make my own decisions, and my decision was to be there, with him. But I was so wrong.

Now I can see exactly why he asked me. Because when you're preparing to conquer the world, you have to start with the smallest of countries.

CHAPTER 5

Did he cut school or act out in any way?

No, he was a good student. Oh, perhaps he cut a time
  or two. But what teenager doesn't? Even our best
  and most conscientious students do from time to
  time. And his type of personality—creative, indi-
  vidual, the natural thespian—should not be boxed
  in or contained by rigid rules, but allowed the freedom to flourish.

—Police interview with Mrs. Wilma Reese,
English teacher at St. Ann's

A T THAT DINER, FOOD WAS the last thing on my mind. I
don't even like eggs. You know that, Andrew. I ordered a
bowl of Cheerios. It was the only thing I could guarantee to be
one hundred percent squirrel-free. But I knew I wouldn't eat it.
All I could do was move the cereal around in my bowl, dunking
the O's and watching them resurface. He did most, if not all, of
the talking, and I was grateful for that, because if I had to speak,
I know I would have choked on my own tongue.

He talked about his life in Arizona, how he was on the baseball team, how he was going to try out for baseball at St. Ann's because he was promised a partial scholarship to play for his grandfather's alma mater in Arizona if he kept his grades up. Was the baseball good here? I didn't know.

The thing was, it sounded as if he'd come from paradise. The weather was great. There were lots of things to do. He called his friends from back home his brothers and referred to them by name, as if I was supposed to know them too. Why, then, if his life there was so perfect, wasn't he upset about being here in boring, rural Maine?

Even though he was doing most of the talking, Z managed to polish off a ham-and-cheese omelet before I'd even scooped one spoonful of cereal into my mouth. He wiped his mouth with a napkin. "You don't talk much," he observed. "Are you one of those?"

I stared at him, confused.

"Those Catholic school girls. Prim and proper, with a naughty side?"

If I'd been eating, I would have spit everything out of my mouth in shock. "No," I said.

"You don't seem so sure." He leaned back, put his arms over his head in a luxurious stretch, and studied me, sizing me up. "Everyone has a wild side… They just need the right circumstances to unleash it. What makes you tick, Vic?" His eyes twinkled.

My face burned. I'd pretty much accepted that there are certain things in the world that people always want to know more about: The pyramids. The Loch Ness monster. People like Z. But me? Not so much. I shrugged. "Nothing. I'm boring."

He drummed his fingers on the paper place mat covered with ads for local businesses. "Nobody is boring. Everyone has a story." He leaned forward. "Do you hear me? Every. One."

He said it so seriously that I would have burst out laughing, if he hadn't been looking at me so intently. He was so weird. I was simultaneously hit with the desire to flee and the desire to never leave his side. "I don't have a story," I muttered. "Really."

"Sure you do. Like I said, everyone does. I could read every single person the second I walked into that classroom. That curly-haired girl in the front is the brain, right? She had her notebook and pens all set out, but I could tell she's nervous as hell about keeping up in math because she had a calc book open on her lap."

OK, that was Gerri.

"The guys in the back. Sports jocks. They say they're friends, but considering their competitive natures and the way they were eyeing that blond in the black sweater, something ugly's brewing."

All right, that was true too. He'd figured out in one class what had taken me weeks to learn last year. But so what? It didn't make him Sherlock.

"I make it my business to get to know people. I have everyone's number." His grin was sly. How was it that he could intrigue me with this conceited behavior that would normally disgust me? "But you? You, Vic, are the big question mark."

"Me?" I cringed. I hardly knew him, and already I hated to

disappoint him. Because that's what my story was: disappoint-ing. "I've lived in Maine my whole life. I went to public school in Duchess—that's a town about forty-five minutes north of here—until last year—"

"Duchess? Seriously? I live there too."

"Really?" I blinked, taken aback. Together we made up a good percentage of Duchess's population. "Where?"

He shrugged. "I don't know. All the roads look and sound the same." Then he started to play with the salt and pepper shakers. He couldn't keep his hands still. "You know the town was named for a legend that some exiled duchess made a home there? You could be descended from royalty."

I shook my head. "My parents moved here before I was born because they heard Maine was a great state to raise kids. Why don't you go to Duchess High?"

"Same reason as you, probably. Why don't you go?"

"Like I was saying, I did, until last year when I transferred to St. Ann's. Before you arrived, I was the new kid."

He drummed the table some more. If it had been anyone else, it would have annoyed me. "Why?"

"Why what?"

"Why did you transfer?"

I shrugged. "I don't know. My parents kept hearing horror stories about drinking and drugs at DHS. They'd rediscovered religion, and my father works in Bangor with a bunch of people who have kids at St. Ann's and liked the small, tight-knit feel of it. Plus, he thought I should get more of a religious education. My parents are really involved in the church now."

"Your parents rediscovered religion?" he asked, stroking his chin. "What, did Jesus come to them in a vision?"

Well, at least that would have lent some excitement to the story. "I think it was more about sheltering me. They're kind of protective. And…everyone at St. Ann's already knew each other, so I've kind of been…" I trail off. *On the outs. Friendless. Owner of the most pathetic backstory in the history of the world. Take your pick.*

"Gotcha. Being new sucks. Been there," he said with a grin, as if being new had happened to him years ago. I couldn't believe it. Back in class, he'd seemed to revel in being the new kid. He laughed, making me even more self-conscious. "What you do is make it a point to talk to as many people as possible. Put yourself out there."

Oh sure. He made it sound so easy. If I'd felt comfortable with him, I would have rolled my eyes.

That's the thing about Z though. I'd soon learn that you couldn't present him with a dilemma that he wouldn't try to solve for you, all the while stirring up a hurricane of new problems, problems he was completely oblivious to. Sometimes it was infuriating. He wasn't a shoulder to lean on because he never stood still.

"Um…well… I don't really *want* to do anything…extra-curricular." I was blushing more now because I had just pronounced it *extra-curler*, like I was drunk.

And maybe I was. Remember the time you and I swiped that bottle of champagne from my parents' twentieth-anniversary party and drank the whole thing in the backyard? What were we, thirteen? I remember it like it was yesterday, Andrew. I'd felt like a study in contradictions, shivery and yet perfectly warm at the same time. I'd felt completely content when you put your arm around me, but anxious, wanting more. It was the first time you got up the courage to kiss me. For the record, I liked it. I liked everything you did with me. I would have let you do a lot more, but you were so respectful.

So yes, here I was, thinking of you and our kiss, but looking into the beautiful eyes of someone who seemed interested in me. In *only* me, as if nothing else in the world mattered. You can maybe understand how I was a goner from the start, right?

Z leaned forward and tapped his fingers on the greasy table between us. "So what *do* you want?"

My eyes widened. What a weird question. How did he expect me to answer that?

I guess he didn't. He'd already moved on. I always got the feeling he was five full steps ahead of me. "Hand it over."

"What?"

"Your schedule."

"Oh." I reached into my notebook. My class schedule was pressed between the cover and that first page, where I'd written my reply to Z earlier. He took a square of paper from the pocket of his chinos. It was folded over and over. He straightened it out and compared the two.

"Unbelievable."

My stomach sunk because I thought I'd done something wrong. "What?"

"We have all the same classes. Well, except you have art

and I have debate for seventh. And I get early release, and you have…honors math?"

It wasn't hard for me to believe we were in most of the same classes. St. Ann's is small. I'd been in the same classes with most of the sophomores last year. The only classes that were more varied were our electives, which we shared with other grades. I'd decided on art because it was the only thing that didn't completely bore me. Debate? That sounded worse than death.

Z wiped his mouth with a napkin again and started to get up. "Guess we'd better get back then, you not-so-naughty girl." He said it in a singsong tone, his eyebrows rising, as if he was challenging me.

I reached into my bag for my change purse, but he already had the check. "Allow me. It's the least I can do, since I kid-napped you."

I muttered a thank-you as he went to the front counter while I put my wallet back in my bag. He came back a minute later with a toothpick hanging lazily from the corner of his mouth. He had one of those red-and-white-striped pepper-mints, which he pushed across the table to me. I popped it in my mouth, half sure I'd swallow the thing whole by accident, and then stood up and followed him out the door.

Outside, I breathed in the late-summer air. While suffo-cating and hot, it was still fresher than the heavy smell of grease and cigarettes in that dive. I sucked on the mint as I pulled my books to my chest and hoped I didn't have food in between my teeth, which was completely ridiculous considering I hadn't eaten more than three Cheerios. As we stepped from the rickety wooden porch, I noticed he was moving a little faster than before.

"We might want to run," he said.

"Why? Are we going to be late for next period?"

He didn't answer. He booked it into the woods, and I followed. He didn't slow down until we'd left the deli far behind. By then I was breathing hard and could feel sweat sliding down my sides. Finally, he slowed to a saunter and smiled. "And you said you're not a naughty one."

"What do you mean?"

"Well, where I come from, skipping out on paying for your food is a punishable offense."

I stared at him. "What! I thought you—"

"Relax," he said.

I turned around. I had to go back and pay. My mother, my dad... If they found out, you know how they would be, Andrew. You remember how upset I was when I accidentally walked out of Uncle Sam's Five and Ten with eleven pieces of penny candy instead of ten. I couldn't eat for a week. I was so afraid the shop owner would see me in church and come after me, and I'd spend the rest of my life rotting away in some prison cell over a freaking gumdrop.

I'd taken five steps when I felt his hand on my arm. He had the smoothest hands, just the right temperature. Not clammy, despite the heat and the little jog we'd just taken. They were sublime. I couldn't even think of wrenching myself free at that moment.

"Relax," he said again. The touch of his hand was like a blanket on a cold day. I leaned in, wanting more. "It's under control, Vic. Look at me."

I looked into his eyes as he repeated, again and again, that it was under control. You know I don't believe in witchcraft or hocus-pocus or junk like that. But in that moment, I knew that magic existed. Those eyes could make me believe anything. Anything. The world is flat? OK. Have a bridge for sale? Sign me up.

Finally, I whispered, "All right," and said an act of contrition in my head.

We walked a little farther, and he reached into his pocket and pulled out a crumpled white paper, which he smoothed and handed to me. A receipt. "I was kidding."

I crumpled it, wanting to throw it at him. My cheeks burned. "That was—"

"You went along with it. See? You *are* naughty."

I stared after him. Now that I think about it, I should have hated him for playing that trick. Instead, I felt something else welling inside me. Excitement? Maybe. I could tell he was proud of himself for bringing out a side of me no one else knew existed. And it had brought us closer.

We sneaked in through the side door, just as the bell signaling the end of second period began to ring. He grinned at me and put a finger to his lips, and I felt warm all over. Here we were, sharing a secret. Students filed into the hallways, and we simply filtered in with them. People stared at him, not because he had broken the rules, but because he was Z.

He had a way of making things that were so wrong seem all right. He did it as easily as he blinked. And though I should have walked back into school feeling ashamed of myself, I felt as if I'd been on the most exciting adventure of my life.

And I already couldn't wait for the next one.

CHAPTER 6

You went to school with Z in Arizona?

Yeah.

And were you friends with him?

Who wasn't? When his grandmother died, I swear, half the people who went to the funeral didn't know her. They were friends who'd gone to support him. When the school found out that Z was moving to live with other relatives, it was like a national day of mourning.

So he had a profound effect on people. Why do you think that was?

Well, you have to understand something about Z. He was interested in everyone. He made it his job. You'd start off talking about the weather, and two seconds later you'd be telling him your life story. He asked questions... They weren't intrusive, really. More like the questions you wished someone would ask about you. If you had a problem, he'd try to work it out for you.

He had this knack for bringing out the best
in everyone.

So he had a lot of close friends?

Weirdly, no. More like admirers. I mean, you'd come
out of a conversation loving him, but later you'd
realize you knew absolutely nothing about him.
He rarely talked about himself.

—Police interview with Rolly Vine, senior at
Southwest High School, Phoenix, Arizona

THE NEXT ADVENTURE DIDN'T COME right away. Z had
a knack for timing. He'd wait until you were begging for
attention and then spring something on you. But only a little.
He'd never give you enough to satisfy you because that would
give you control.

Oh no, he always had control. I see that now, Andrew.

But then? I'd only known him a few hours, and already I'd
been struck blind. The rest of that day was like all the others
that had come before it. The only difference was that instead of
paying attention to my studies, I was paying attention to him.
I'd peer at him out of the corner of my eye or bend down to get
a pencil out of my bag, letting my hair fall in my eyes, and check
to see what he was doing.

I won't bore you with the details, but watching him was
anything *but* boring. You know how people buy magazines
with pictures of famous people just walking down the street or
whatever, doing their own thing? Watching him was like that,
somehow fascinating.

History and trig went by—boring, boring, boring—and I thought he would lean over and whisper something funny, like "When will it end?" or "Kill me now, this is so dull," or maybe just ask to borrow a sheet of notebook paper, but no.

During lunch, I sat at my lonely spot in the corner of the cafeteria, thinking he might join me, but he sat with a bunch of popular jocks. Baseball players.

In gym, I sat on the bleachers by myself, waiting for Ms. Phelps to call my name to be assigned a locker. Z tipped an imaginary hat at Parker Cole and Rachel Watson as they sat huddled together, discussing something riveting like nail polish colors, but he walked right past me.

Putting himself out there, I guess. Isn't that what he'd said? Getting to know everyone so he wouldn't be a ghost like me. By chemistry, he'd morphed into just another one of the kids at school. I started to wonder if our morning excursion together had been a dream. *Illusory*. When the bell signaling early release rang, Z slid out of his seat and disappeared without so much as a "See you."

On the bus ride home, I'd pretty much accepted that my breakfast with Z would never be repeated. I wasn't deflated though. I'd started to think it was better that way. I didn't need any distractions. My mind cleared, and I began to think of you again. When the bus dropped me off on the corner of Spruce Street and I walked past your house, I could hear you practicing your Chopin. It was hot, and the front door was open to catch the breeze, so I just walked in and sat beside you. Without skipping a beat, you broke into "Chopsticks" for me, and I filled in the "Heart and Soul."

After our duet ended, you said, "So fill me in. Gory details."

I shrugged and told you it was the same old story. But you knew I was lying. I was trying not to make anything out of cutting class with Z—because surely it *was* nothing—but the more I tried to ignore it, the more my mind replayed what had happened. You didn't have to pry it out of me. The news just slipped out. "There was a new kid at school."

"Oh yeah?" You were busy studying your sheet music. The light streamed in through the blinds, and I could see that you'd really been going to town on the side of your head. The hair was plucked clean in a large, round patch behind your ear, leaving red, raw scalp. "Is he hot?"

"I didn't say he was a he."

You didn't look at me. Your long fingers grazed the keys. "I can tell by your voice."

"What?"

"It went up an octave. You're pretending like it's no big deal, but you think he's hot."

I both love and hate how you know me so well. I thought about denying it, but I knew you wouldn't believe me, so I told you that he was kind of cute, which you probably knew was the understatement of the century. You sighed, the same sigh I'd heard a zillion times before when you wished we could go to school together.

"How were things here?" I asked.

"Same old, same old."

But for you, I knew it was. Your mother had your routine down to a science. Caring for you was your mother's vocation, what filled her days with purpose. I don't recall a single day that I've come home from school and not found you at your piano. Piano practice was from one to three. Which was probably why I knew she'd come in with iced chamomile tea and homemade sugar-free cookies. Snack time.

"Oh, hi, Victoria!" She usually prefaced everything she said with an "Oh," as if seeing me there was a surprise, which it totally wasn't. She handed me a glass with a swirly, twirly straw. Mrs. Quinn didn't want to accept that you were too old for such things, and I loved that you never argued. You just let her go on with her delusion.

You never faulted your mother for anything. Just yourself.

I hated that about you.

"Hi, Mrs. Quinn. Thanks," I said, taking a cookie from the plate. I bit into it, and when she offered me another, I shook my head. I know your mother was strict about your diabetes because she had to be, but damn, her cookies have the texture of cardboard.

Then she just stood there and stared at us.

You cleared your throat, hoping she'd get the hint, but she didn't. She said very carefully, "Did you have a nice day at school, Victoria?"

I nodded.

"First day, right?"

"Yep. I was just filling your son in on all the excitement," I said in a hushed voice, so maybe she'd get the idea that our conversation was private.

Her smile faded. "Oh. Right."

I remember that lingering look you gave her, long after she'd left. You just kept staring at the doorway to the kitchen, guilt evident on your face. You always thought you were your mother's ball and chain, her biggest nuisance, didn't you?

You swung back to the piano and started to play for me. You know all my favorite songs. Frank Sinatra has nothing on you. *Someday, when I'm old and gray…*

"Those aren't the right words," I whispered.

You grinned, that way you do when you're poking fun at me for being a know-it-all. Then you started from the beginning, screwing up the lyrics again. I cringed as tears started to fill my eyes. I don't know why; I guess I'm always emotional on the first day of school. "Stop it."

You stopped, took my hand, and kissed every fingertip in apology. Then you wrapped my hand in your own and squeezed. Your hands were warm too. I loved them—so graceful. I loved watching your long fingers glide across the keys. And your singing…oh, your singing. Sometimes I would dream of you performing in a big, packed concert hall, like Carnegie Hall. You'd have gotten me front-row tickets, and I'd have a pile of crumpled tissues in my lap from crying my eyes out. Even the funny songs you played made emotions ball up inside me, pushing their way out as tears.

We sat down on your couch, that ugly, flowered one, under your giant family picture. The walls of that room are covered in every picture of you ever taken, framed, and matted, from the day of your birth right on up, like a shrine to the Only Quinn Child. But that family portrait…wow. The Picture from

Hell. That's what you called it, right? Your mom is smiling like a debutante; your eyes are bulging like a deer caught in headlights; and your stepdad's mouth is set in a straight line, like he'd rather be anywhere else. Your mom blew it up extra big because she's weird like that. There were other, better pictures, but your mom liked that one because "it shows our souls."

I always wondered what my soul would look like if I were in that picture. Now, I think it would be entirely black because of the things I've done to hurt you.

"Got your meeting with Leary tomorrow?" you asked me.

I winced at the thought. "At three," I grumbled, thinking of Father Leary, the unofficial guidance counselor at school. He was quite the jokester, so most students loved him. I wasn't one of them. My once-a-week meetings started when I began at St. Ann's, to "ease the transition into a new school," but nothing about meeting with him had made the transition easy. Even though I complained every week that the sessions were worthless, my parents still thought they were beneficial. "Necessary," my dad had said, but that didn't change my opinion.

Your stepdad always came home at four thirty. You ushered me out before then. You were at your weakest when he was around, and you didn't like me seeing that. We made plans to meet that evening at our place in the backyard.

I was late that night because I'd been covering all my textbooks with contact paper. There were still no fireflies.

"Want to do something with me for my birthday?" you murmured in the darkness when I'd slid down against the fence.

"Of course. I'll have to check my busy social schedule though."

You chuckled softly. Back then, *we* were each other's social schedule. "Murray Perahia. You in?"

"At the Center for the Arts? You know it," I said right away. I'd seen the ad in the *Central Maine Express Times*, and you'd been talking about those tickets for months. You were willing to brave Bangor for the concert, which shows how much it meant to you. Perahia was your God. Me? Music lost its allure when you weren't the one playing it.

You said something then like, "That is, if you haven't dumped me for your Hot New Student." I laughed at the preposterousness of that idea.

Except now, when I think about it, Andrew, I see that you knew it was destined to happen all along.

CHAPTER 7

This is a story of desire, madness, and murder.
—St. Ann's theater company program, on
their autumn production of *Macbeth*

THE NEXT DAY, THE FAINT glimmer of hope that Z would talk to me again ignited into a burning wildfire when I dropped my backpack beside my desk. He was already sitting in his seat, hunched over his phone. He was so beautiful that it seemed a sin for him to be surrounded by so much dullness. I slid into my seat with my newly covered vocabulary and grammar textbooks and began fishing around for a pencil.

The next thing I knew, he thrust his phone in front of me. I looked over at him, wondering why he needed to spread himself out over two desks.

He said, "I got home and realized I didn't have your number."

I startled. "You...want to call me?"

"Text, mostly," he said, wiggling his thumbs. "I'm big on texting."

"Oh," I said. I took his phone in my hands and tried to

remember my phone number. Keying it in was as hard as input-
ting a random string of nine numbers that had been recited to
me once. It took three tries. Finally, I handed his phone back,
sure I'd greased the screen with my sweaty fingertips.

He looked at the screen and nodded, then stuffed the phone
in his pocket. "Want mine?"

"Uh, OK," I said. I rifled around in my bag for what felt
like four hours because my cell phone was at the very bottom.
Before, the only people who called me on it were my parents.
Your mom wouldn't let you have one, so I only used mine in
case of emergency. And really, Duchess is the safest town in the
world. Nobody texted me, so I sucked at texting. I had no idea
how to use most of the features, and I wasn't sure how to enter
a new name into the contact list.

I stared at the screen, pressed a few buttons, and found my
contacts list. My very empty, very pathetic contact list. "Um…"

My phone dinged with a notification. He'd texted it
to me.

Just then, Reese walked in. I swallowed and wished I'd
taken an Ativan. My face began to overheat. Z had to have
noticed because he whispered, "Let me guess. Cell phones are
a big no too?"

I nodded and slid mine into my bag.

He leaned over, picked up my pencil, and wrote RELAX
on the cover of my notebook. Really big, so I wouldn't miss
it. So that every time I went through my bag, there it was.
Unavoidable. Unforgettable.

Not that it helped.

I never could have predicted how much this seemingly innocent exchange would come to mean. It quickly snowballed into the Affair of the Cell Phone. I went from barely caring about my phone to checking it casually—and then to checking it four thousand times a day. I would spend every moment in the shower in absolute torture, wondering if I'd missed a beep signaling a new message. Whenever you played your piano, I'd hear that beep mingling with the notes. And whenever I was faced with a blank screen, I'd wonder what Z was up to. It was just the first of many ropes he'd throw around my neck, tying me to him.

Mrs. Reese turned her scowl toward the board and scrawled something with chalk. When she stepped away, she had written *Jorge Luis Borges*. "Today, we're going to study two short stories by Borges," she announced. "Turn to page two-twenty-seven."

We all opened our textbooks. Except Z. His stayed closed on his desk. I looked at him from the corner of my eye. He was leaning back, phone in his lap, thumbs working furiously.

He was texting. In Mrs. Reese's class.

She started talking about Borges's life in Argentina or Bolivia, or wherever he was from, and walking down the aisle, tapping on desks as she went, as usual. Every tap echoed my heart in my rib cage because she was getting closer and closer to Z. I'm not sure why I cared so much, why I wanted to protect him, but I did. But did he glance up? Did he care about Reese? No. He just kept thumbing away.

I shouldn't have worried. Of course he didn't get caught. Though all eyes always seemed to be on him, for some reason, at the moment he was doing wrong, Reese had turned and started down a different aisle. His luck was impeccable.

"Does anyone know what the Aleph is?" Reese asked.

As I'd expected, the room was completely silent. Noses buried in textbooks, people were doing their best not to be called on. Even Gerri O'Donnell, our resident Harvard-bound genius, looked perplexed. As you might have expected, Andrew, I thought the Aleph was an artifact Indiana Jones found on one of his adventures, but I wasn't about to volunteer that.

Z's hand poked up. He was still holding his cell phone in his other hand. Reese had to have noticed it. But despite her hatred of such technology, Mrs. Reese beamed at him. Beamed. Her beam turned fluorescent when he said rather unenthusiastically, as if it were common knowledge, "The Aleph is a point that contains all other points. Anyone who looks at it can see everything else in the universe from every angle at once."

A moment of stunned silence followed, during which every person in the room surely realized the inequity of it all. Z was not only gifted physically, but mentally as well! The notion sucked the air out of the room. Gerri's once-superior brain was no longer. Her dark-blond corkscrews quivered as her face contorted with anger. Parker licked her lips and smiled at Z again.

The rest of the period went along as usual, with Reese talking about the symbolism of whatsit and the cultural implications of whoosit, while I stared at her, trying my best to listen. My thoughts kept going back to the intellectual giant beside me who was, infuriatingly, still toying with his phone. How could he skip classes, pay zero attention, text like a madman, and have known

what an Aleph is? I never missed a class and wrote down practically every word the teacher said, afraid I might miss an important
study point, and yet I didn't even know how to *spell* Aleph.

Five minutes before class ended, Mrs. Reese had us all close
our books. My head was still swimming with questions about Z.

Mrs. Reese said, "I wanted to call your attention to the
flyers you might have seen around school this morning."

I had seen them. They were red with MACBETH printed
big on top. I'd stopped reading there. As you know, Andrew,
tryouts for the school play were of no interest to me. Back
then, I had an equal abhorrence for the stage and for anything
Shakespeare. The thought of being in front of an audience made
my insides turn to jelly. Add in Reese as the play's director, and
I found it about as fascinating as influenza.

"We had a poor showing last year for our production of
Oliver," she said.

That was no shocker. No one wanted to be near Reese
for longer than forty-five minutes every day. The only person
who could stand her was Quincy Laughlin, a senior. He'd been
Oliver, George Gibbs, Daddy Warbucks…pretty much all the
male leads since eighth grade. When he graduated, future theat-
rical productions at St. Ann's would be screwed. Tryouts were
merely perfunctory for him; this year, he'd be Macbeth.

"This time, we're giving you plenty of notice so that you
can think it over and practice your auditions. We're doing
something new this year," Reese continued. "Anyone who is
awarded a major part in this year's production will get extra
credit worth one entire grade on his or her final average."

Everyone started whispering. The concept was definitely gossip-worthy. Reese never gave out As. Never. I could see visions of that elusive four-point-oh dancing in Gerri O'Donnell's big, fat brain. Her hand shot into the air. Gerri was also the class interrogator. Most teachers knew that if they were going to give an assignment, they needed to leave plenty of time for questions, all of which would be asked by Gerri. I think she did us a disservice for later in life. None of us even bothered to think of questions because we all knew she'd take care of them. "To clarify, what do you mean by 'major' part?"

As much as I disliked Reese, she had come up with an ingenious way of shutting down Gerri's quizzing. She always answered with a question of her own. "Well, Geraldine, you read *Macbeth* last year. Can you answer that?"

"*Macbeth*?" Ian Cummings, the resident joker, quipped as Gerri opened her mouth to speak. She cast a glare in his direction. Gerri started listing all the main characters, but I really wasn't paying attention. If Gerri wanted to be Lady Macbeth and make out with Quincy Laughlin for an A in English, Godspeed. Quincy was about three inches tall and spoke like a jaunty English fellow, using words like *hence* and *thusly* in normal conversation. Once I'd seen him at the mall wearing a dorky bowling shirt with a hamburger print, Keds, and white sport socks pulled up to his knees. Strangely enough, he was still popular at St. Ann's, mostly because he didn't really care what anyone thought of him.

The bell rang. Finally. I opened my bag to put away my books and found the display on my phone glowing. I pulled it out, wondering and knowing at the same time. The text said: Eat lunch with me. Have something to ask you.

I turned to Z. He was staring at me.

"Um, you could have just asked me that," I said.

He grinned. "I'm shy."

"Yeah, right."

"No, really. What if you said no? My whole day would be ruined."

The idea of his day being shot to hell because I told him I couldn't eat lunch with him was ridiculous. There was no possible way *anyone* could say no to him. He got what he asked for. End of story.

"Fine." I tried to say it like I was doing him a favor.

You might not realize this, Andrew, but eating alone in a packed cafeteria? It sucks. The thought of being seen eating with someone, *anyone*, thrilled me to no end.

And what did he have to ask me? Concentration during the rest of my morning classes was blown. I came up with every scenario, from Z wanting to go out with me to wanting to borrow my chemistry notes. That is, If I *had* chemistry notes. We'd only had one class, and much of our time had been spent taking attendance, getting books, and reviewing lab safety. So by the time lunch rolled around, I was flummoxed, which is what, I now realize, Z wanted. He's a master at making people wonder about him for hours on end.

I took my brown bag lunch with me to the cafeteria, wishing I'd brought something cooler. Tuna fish was gross. It smelled, and the presentation was less than stunning. I was sure that Z would probably buy lunch, and I was right. Somehow, his shriveled gray burger and soggy french fries managed to look more glamorous than my lunch. I waited for him at the end of the lunch line, and he grabbed a seat at a table with a bunch of other random kids, not even scoping out whether it was OK to sit. I guess you don't have to worry about that when your mere presence *makes* a place cool. He motioned for me to sit next to him.

"Look, what I'm going to say to you is really hard," he started. He looked around surreptitiously, then leaned forward and lowered his voice. "Can I trust you to keep this a secret?"

As I'd sat down, I'd noticed how every set of eyes in the cafeteria was trained on us. The strange girl and the new, hot guy. On the surface, we made an odd couple. People must have thought he was talking to me on a dare. I confess, the thought had crossed my mind too. But when he spoke, all of that fell away, and we were the only two people in the room. I leaned forward instinctively, and the word came out as barely a breath: "Yes."

He swallowed. "I–I have three months to live."

There he was, joking again. But the longer he kept his gaze on mine, the more I thought that maybe he wasn't pulling my leg. All he had to do was catch my eyes, and even the improbable seemed possible.

Then he smiled. "Kidding."

"Oh…kay."

As annoying as his "kidding" would have been from anyone else, why was I still fastened to the seat across from him with absolutely no inclination to move? He was used to getting his own way, so I should have walked away. Simple. Looking back, I could have stopped everything *so easily*. Instead, I stupidly hung on his every word. Because Z was offering something I'd never had: a chance to belong. With Z, up became down and right became wrong.

"No, look, here's the thing," he said, gnawing on a french fry. "What's the deal with this Lincoln dude? I'm getting the feeling he's the kind of guy who will screw me over."

"Lincoln? You mean chemistry?"

He nodded. "Yeah. I'm getting a vibe from him."

Mr. Lincoln's nice and kind of cute. A little goofy, but cute. He's only twenty-five or so. Last year in biology, most girls in class developed crushes on him. I was no exception. He'd been my favorite teacher. There's something charming about a guy who can make goggles and a lab coat look good. He's the epitome of geek chic. And he liked me a lot too because he'd recommended me—and only me—for science camp last summer at USM. Remember that, Andrew? It didn't work out because my parents didn't want to send me to Portland on my own for a week, but it was supposedly a big honor to be accepted, and you were very proud of me. "What kind of vibe?" I asked.

He looked from side to side again. "Inappropriate relationship vibe."

My jaw dropped in horror. "What? Lincoln would never—"

"Kidding again," he said, still grinning. As irritating as it was, he was a kidder. If I wanted to spend time with him, I'd best get used to it. "But you *do* think he's hot, don't you?" His stare weighed on me.

"What? No!"

"Listen. Lincoln won't pair us by the roster or whatever. He'll let us choose our own lab partners, right?"

"Right," I answered, remembering last year, when everyone else had paired up, leaving me alone. I'd had to sit with Parker and her best friend, Rachel, who gabbed about how far they'd gone with their boyfriends while giving me the honor of doing the entire frog dissection on my own.

"So. You. Me. Partners?" he asked.

I coughed. What did that mean? Did that mean we were *friends*? "Really?"

"You seem like a sciency girl," he said. "I suck at chem, and I really need at least a B if I'm going to haul my ass to college with a scholarship and make something of myself."

Oh right. I was good at science. Of course he'd want to buddy up with the girl who could get him an A. Still, it was loads better than listening to Parker and Rachel drone on about the wild parties they went to. "OK."

"Awesome." He looked down at the unopened brown bag in front of me. "You eating?"

I shrugged. "Not hungry."

And I wasn't. Remember how you mentioned a few weeks later that you thought I was losing weight? Remember how I had to use that massive safety pin so my skirt wouldn't puddle at my ankles? I'd always been kind of round and soft, with breasts that seemed to disappear into my body and no distinguishable hips or waist. I liked to eat, and I wasn't keen on exercise. But the more time I spent with Z, the less of an appetite I had.

So later in the afternoon when Lincoln asked us to partner up, I didn't have to shrink down in my seat in embarrassment. Z and I just looked at each other, and the deal was done.

It was the first of many deals that I wish I'd never made.

CHAPTER 8

What can you tell us about your daughter?

Victoria's a good kid. Shy, but a good student.

Has she ever had any trouble?

Trouble? As in… She can be high-strung and anxious, tends to obsess at times. She's always been that way.

Always?

When she was a child, sometimes I would tell her to get changed, and a few minutes later, I'd find her in her room naked and trying to solve a word-search puzzle. She gets so wrapped up in the details that she fails to see the big picture. But I understand a lot of kids are like that.

You transferred her to St. Ann's last year. Why?

More demands were put on her in high school. The coursework was harder, and she was worried about getting into college. Her grades were fine, but Duchess High is large and impersonal. The social aspect wasn't doing her any favors. We felt it was inhibiting her ability to learn. We'd heard good things about St. Ann's and thought she might be more focused at a smaller school. She doesn't do well in large group situations, and we thought the lower student-teacher ratio would benefit her. We were just trying to protect her.

—Police interview with Abigail Zell,
mother of Victoria Zell

A FTER SCHOOL I HAD MY meeting with Leary. As usual, when I showed up at his dusty office, which had probably once been a closet, he gave me a pitying smile. Then he shooed a bunch of other kids out so we could talk.

Leary's old enough to be a grandfather, yet acts like a kid. His desk is crowded with Batman figurines and smiley-face pencils. He always bakes—cookies and pastries and stuff—and he brings them in to share, so his office usually smells of cinnamon. Still, it always kind of freaked me out that he's, you know, a *man of God*. Other students didn't seem to censor themselves around him, but I always felt like I had to watch what I said or he'd strike me down with his divine power. It was the same thing, week after week. He asked me question after question, to which I would provide the shortest and vaguest answers possible.

When I sat down in my usual chair, farthest away from him, he offered me a plate of sugar cookies and asked, "So, Victoria, how was your summer?"

I told him it was uneventful, as my summers usually were.

"Good, good," he replied. He's big on repeating positives. "How have things been going for you this year?"

"Fine," I told him, staring at the crucifix on the wall behind him. Even Jesus looked like he was rolling his eyes at Father. "I'm good."

"Well, that's good. You're fitting in OK? Classes good?"

I smiled. "Everything's great."

"Friends?"

I nodded. "I have a few."

He leaned forward. "Tell me, do you keep in touch with your friends from your old school?"

"No," I told him. I had a couple of acquaintances at Duchess High, but no one worth keeping in touch with. From the way he grimaced, I knew it was the wrong answer. "I don't need a bazillion friends though. I mean, I have Andrew."

Leary didn't look at me. He was busy plucking some dust off the knee of his black slacks. "Tell me about Andrew."

I sighed so deeply that Father Leary's gaze rose to mine. But seriously, had he forgotten? I talked about you nonstop last year, since you're not only my boyfriend, you're my best friend. I swear, I've probably told him your favorite color and what you eat for breakfast, like, twice. I think Jesus groaned behind him. "What do you want to know?"

He frowned. "What would you like to share?"

"There's nothing to tell. He still lives next door, still is studying his music."

And on and on we went, having the same conversation that we'd had every week last year. As if asking incessant questions about my life and making me repeat myself time and again is supposed to be therapeutic. I mean, isn't that the definition of insanity, repeating oneself and expecting different results? This is probably why I checked the clock on the wall about twice a minute and rocketed out of my seat as soon as the minute hand hit the six. Thank God I had to catch the late bus.

Of course, when I got home, to further me on the road to insanity, my parents made me repeat everything we'd discussed. I set the table in the kitchen, and there they were, helicoptering around me as I set down each utensil, wanting to know exactly what had transpired in the meeting.

Sometimes, Andrew, I swear I feel less like a person and more like a hamster on one of those wheels.

Maybe that's why all this happened. Maybe I just wanted to escape the wheel.

CHAPTER 9

Why was Victoria Zell seeing you on a weekly basis?
Her parents had asked me to. She was new to the
   school and had a few anxiety issues that they
   were concerned about.
Did she ever talk about her relationship with Z?
Yes, she did.
Was she having problems where Z was concerned?
I'm sorry. That's confidential. But I will tell you
   that Victoria didn't discuss any of her prob-
   lems willingly.
And why is that?
Simply put, she didn't think they were problems.

—Police interview with Father Ryan Leary,
guidance counselor at St. Ann's

THE REST OF THE WEEK was mostly uneventful. Z went
off with the jocks, leaving me to eat lunch alone again.
The way he laughed with them, commanding their attention
as they hung on his every word, you'd think he'd been part

of their group since birth. And they'd implicitly appointed him leader.

I'd talk to him between classes, but only briefly. I'd like to say I got to know Z in lab, but I really didn't. He had a way of talking about himself—and he talked about himself constantly—without revealing any personal details. He'd say, "If I could live anywhere, it would be in Key West," or, "I wish my name was Gus." Many times I wasn't sure if he was being serious. By the end of the week all I really knew about him was that he was from Arizona, played baseball, and liked to joke around. So pretty much all I'd learned on the first day.

I hadn't gotten much more comfortable around him either. He was still too beautiful to look at directly. The goggles amplified his eyes, so while I looked like even more of a doofus, he managed to look even hotter. This did nothing to help my nerves. During our first experiment, I kept dropping the stainless steel scoop, and my hands were shaking so much that I nearly spilled hydrochloric acid on him. He noticed too, and from that point on, I was our designated note-taker. Very embarrassing.

I was frustrated. I thought being lab partners would give me insight into Z, the most-talked-about person in the school, but I had nothing. I had no idea what his family was like, where he lived, what he liked to do in his spare time…nothing.

Friday, as he set up the Bunsen burner, he said, "I wish I had a can of hair spray. I should have warned you that I'm kind of a pyromaniac."

I didn't even raise an eyebrow.

He continued, "Tip: When you're with me, always scope out the nearest fire exit."

I leaned over my notebook and waited for him to start adding the next element.

"You know that song? 'The Roof Is on Fire'? That's my favorite song. For obvious—"

"Can you just do the experiment and stop talking?" I grumbled.

He smiled. "If you would talk once in a while, maybe I wouldn't have to."

"I don't have anything to say. We're supposed to be doing this experiment."

"And we can't engage in witty banter at the same time? It's called multitasking. A very good exercise, mind you, should you choose to enter the corporate world," he said. He *tsk*ed with his tongue and tossed his blond curls from his forehead. "It's obvious who will climb the corporate ladder, and who will be uni-tasking her whole life."

Now, that detail had potential. I asked, "So you're going to go into business?"

He leaned over and studied the concoction we were heating. "Is it supposed to be blue like that?"

I looked around. Everyone else's test tube was blue. "I guess."

He shrugged and placed our test tube over the burner, then started adding compound to it. We were supposed to note the reaction, but I was infuriated by his lack of response. After a moment he said, "I'm going into the family business."

"What's that?" I asked, a little too eager.

"Prostitution," he deadpanned. He added more compound.

I couldn't take it. I threw my notebook down as foam began to erupt from our test tube. It oozed over the sides, frothing and hissing. Z stood like a statue, holding the scoop with an amused smile on his face. "Wild," he said.

Lincoln came flying down the aisle. He extinguished the burner and dumped the test tube in the sink.

"Slowly, guys. *Slowly*," Lincoln said, looking at me and only me. "What happened, Victoria?"

Lincoln's disappointment was palpable. I was his star student, failing him for the first time ever. Twenty-eight goggled faces stared at us. Ian snickered and muttered something that made everyone around him crack up. My face burned. "Sorry, I…" *I hadn't read all of the instructions because I was too captivated by my dumbass lab partner?*

Lincoln was already walking away and gesturing at the clock. "You don't have time to start over. Clean up, and then observe with Parker and Rachel."

Great. I got some paper towels to mop up the foam that was still frothing all over the table. When we were done, we migrated over to the lab bench in front of us. I did so reluctantly, standing at the very corner, while Z sandwiched himself between the two girls like peanut butter.

"Easy with that Scoopula, boy," Parker said in her low, sexy voice. "You might get us in trouble."

Rachel snickered. She lived for adoring Parker, as evidenced by her slightly upturned nose, perfect for brownnosing. Z smiled, clearly enjoying their attention. I fought back vomit.

Parker spent the rest of the class standing so close to Z that molecules of O_2 couldn't pass between them, or across from him, bending over to "observe" so he'd have a perfect view down her blouse at her ravine-like cleavage. Even though it was a foursome, I was definitely a fifth wheel. I stood to the side, wondering if they'd notice if I set my hair on fire.

Two minutes before class let out, Z helped the girls clean up while I finished my notes. Back at our stools, he started copying my notes with his right hand and checking his phone with his left. I snuck a peek at his screen. *You have 16 new text messages.* Holy cow. He was a texting addict. Was that from one class period? I'd had my phone for more than a year, and I had precisely two texts. Both from Z.

To my embarrassment, he caught me staring. He wiggled his fingers. "You never seen anyone multitask like this before? You are amazed?"

"Yes, that will be very useful in your family business of… prostitution," I could barely manage the word without blushing. I shoved my books into my bag and watched the red second hand on the clock sweep toward freedom. *A few more periods*, I thought, *and it will be the weekend, and I will be with Andrew.* Yes, I was thinking of you.

So that's why I couldn't be sure I heard Z correctly when he muttered under his breath, "Except I don't have any family."

CHAPTER 10

Out again?

Yup. Sick.

Want me to get your homework for you?

Nope. Under control.

Think you'll be in tomorrow?

Why? Miss me that much?

Miss you too, Precious.

Just got in trouble with Lincoln because your lab
report is exactly the same as mine. How did that
happen?

I heard a rumor about you.

U ok?

—Cell phone records, courtesy of the
Duchess Police Department

I KNEW WHAT YOUR STEPDAD WAS doing to you, Andrew.
I've always known.

You didn't fault me for not trying to stop it. I think you
loved me more because I stayed out of it, because I turned a

blind eye to the cigarette burns on your neck and pretended not to hear when he called you a little faggot. You didn't want anyone to know how pathetic your stepdad thought you were. You liked music, not hunting, beer, and porn. His anger is because you are gentle and soft-spoken and nothing like him. He saw that as weakness, but here's what I should have told you a long time ago: There was never anything wrong with you, Andrew. None of this was your fault.

It was mine.

Friday night, you were upset. Having to wake up at four the next morning would do that to anyone. Deer season was starting. That meant spending two hours driving in your stepdad's pickup to his favorite hunting spot, then another two hours on the drive back, listening the whole time to the twangy country music you detested. You said he'd gotten a new bow for his birthday and couldn't wait to try it out. I think you joked that you wanted me, wanted anyone, to shoot you with it.

I'm sorry that I wasn't paying better attention. A few minutes before I met you at our spot, I'd been rifling through my purse for my Juicy Fruit and was surprised to find a message from Z.

Want to do something tomorrow?

I checked the time on the text. He'd sent it right after school, before dinner. I wondered if he'd sent it to the wrong person. Maybe his phone had autocorrected his message and he'd really meant to say something else. He didn't really want to hang out with me, did he?

I was so lost in my head that I nearly tripped over my own two feet crossing the lawn to our place at the fence. You were focused on your stepdad, wondering if he would permanently excuse you from hunting excursions if you accidentally shot an arrow through your foot. You laughed about it, but I know you were scared. Every time you came back from a trip with him, you always looked a little smaller, a little more wounded.

I tittered along with you, all the while thinking of how to respond to Z.

Sure, sounds good.

Let me check my schedule and get back to you.

Are you serious?

I'm sorry, did you mean to send that to me?

Then you said, "Are you still there?" which broke me out of my reverie.

"Um, yeah."

"Thought I lost you for a second." I looked over my shoulder and could see the porch light reflected in your eyes as you peered at me through the slats in the fence. "Are you all right?"

"I'm fine. Tired, I guess."

"School was OK?"

"Yeah. Same old thing."

"What are your plans for tomorrow?"

Up until Z's text, I didn't have any. I liked not doing anything on weekends but lazing around and watching television. My parents preferred that because it made keeping tabs on me easier. Tomorrow, they'd be prepping the gymnasium at St. Ann's for a spaghetti dinner to raise funds for a new church organ. "Same old thing," I said again. Right then, it was the truth.

You started to speak, and I wish I could take back what I did right then. I scratched my shoulder against the fence and wiggled to a standing position. "I'd better go. I'm getting destroyed by mosquitoes."

It was early. We usually stayed out together longer. Your voice was a little hoarse when you replied, "Oh. OK. See you, Vic." You stood up and made a lame attempt at cracking a joke, "See you…if I survive tomorrow."

I'm not even sure I said anything back. Before I knew it, I was inside. All my surroundings melted away except that one little sentence on my phone display. I took a few deep breaths and typed in: Like what?

Then I began counting the seconds, waiting for Z's response. My mother and father were in the kitchen, busily counting boxes of spaghetti and loaves of garlic bread and doing their best to pretend they hadn't just been spying on me in the backyard. Why do they always have to spy? I don't know if they think you and I are having dirty, nasty sex in the rosebushes or what. It's not like you or I have ever done anything even remotely depraved. I mean, we've known each other since we were seven. Your family had moved in, and you showed up on my back porch with a red ball and asked me if I wanted to play. We ended up pretending to be royalty, and the bushes were our fortress. We'd hide out there for hours every afternoon, and guess what? Shockingly, we'd both managed to keep hold of our virginities.

When my phone dinged, my parents turned and stared as if it had announced that the house was on fire. "What's that, Victoria?" my father asked.

"It's a device for communicating with people," I snapped, heading to my room as I checked the display. I slammed the door behind me before my parents could ask the inevitable follow-ups.

Torture animals?

I should have known he'd joke around. I responded quickly with Ew and spent the next few moments wondering if that made me seem like I was three. I expected him to say that he just wanted to go over our trig homework together. That was the kind of invitation I was used to. I was an "early afternoon girl." Parker, now, she was a Saturday night girl. She probably hadn't had a free Saturday since fifth grade, considering that her line of ex-boyfriends stretched across the state. And I knew from the way she'd been showing him her goodies in chem lab that all Z had to do was ask her out. So why was he texting *me*, if not to ask for math help? But a few minutes later, the response came back:

Like

???

Do people do movies around here?

I swallowed. He wanted to do fun things with me?

When?

One?

OK, so I was still an early afternoon girl. He probably had some big party or date set up for later. But still, it was my first social engagement that didn't involve you, Andrew. Of course, the second I thought about you, I felt guilty. But we were just going to hang out. Early afternoon hanging out. Surely, other people would be there. Guys and girls could hang out together in a group without it meaning anything. All of this reasoning played in my head as I typed.

OK.

The second I did, my heart started thudding in my chest. I was going to hang out with Z for fun. *I was going to hang out with Z for fun!* And other people too, but this was an invitation to a new world. One I knew you'd want me to accept. Right, Andrew? I mean, you ached along with me whenever I told you how alone I was at school, and above all, you wanted me to be happy. I was both thrilled and terrified as Z wrote back with: Pick you up at your place? Where?

He was going to drive me. Like a date. But not a real date. Just hanging out. With other people. I thumbed in the address carefully, realizing that since you didn't drive, this was the first time I'd be in a guy's car, ever.

I mentally dissected my closet, wondering what I should wear. Z had only seen me in my uniform. You pride yourself upon being a fashion victim (yes, I'm thinking of those jeans that are two sizes too small and that lumberjack shirt, Andrew), so I never had to "dress to impress" with you. And because I didn't have any social life other than spending time with you, my wardrobe was limited. I started rifling through my drawers and found one pair of jeans and a nice blouse. But I thought the blouse might be trying too hard, so I found that pink T-shirt you bought me from the Renaissance Faire. It was enormous then, but now it fit me fine. I went back and forth… Blouse? T-shirt? Blouse? T-shirt? I finally settled on the T-shirt. I laid them on my bed and found my flip-flops, then realized I had to paint my toenails, so I gave myself a quick pedicure.

I hadn't slept at all, so when you left at four in the morning, I was awake to see you leave. Stiff and yawning, I tilted the blinds and watched you load the cooler into the back of the pickup. You hefted your blue backpack on your bony shoulder and looked up at my window—as if you were hoping I'd jump out of it and save you—then climbed listlessly into the cab.

If I'd been a better person, maybe I would've come out and saved you. If I could go back and do any one thing different, *anything*, Andrew…please know I would have tried.

CHAPTER 11

What sort of person was Z?

The best. Cool dude. Always the life of the party. Always willing to help a friend. Everyone liked him. Everyone. That's why I really can't understand what happened. I think about it and...it's just insane. I can't get it through my head.

So there was nothing that seemed off about him?

No. He kept to himself a lot. And he was unpredictable, I guess. You couldn't really pin him down.

You'd heard the rumors about him then?

Which ones? That he was a drug dealer, or that he was an heir to an oil fortune, or that he was a transvestite stripper on weekends? Yeah, the kid was a rumor magnet, but he took them all the same way—with a shrug. So even if the stories were true, you wouldn't know by his reaction.

—Police interview with Ian Cummings, junior at St. Ann's

Z DIDN'T COME TO PICK ME up at one.

I waited faithfully by the window, like some one-eyed dog at the animal shelter that nobody wants to adopt. At first I thought that he had other people to pick up and that was taking longer than he expected. I sat there, hope pulsating in my heart every time I heard the sound of tires approaching on the asphalt.

My parents were busy worker bees, moving from room to room. The first time my dad passed me, he said, "Hey, kiddo, what's up?" I told him I was going out with friends, to which he replied "Friends? Cool!" in a surprised way. He was clearly excited for me because if I didn't count you, Andrew, I hadn't been out with friends before, ever.

"Who?" my mother piped up.

I shrugged. "From school."

My mother wandered into the hallway, wiping her hands on a dishrag. "Should we meet these friends? Who's driving? Is she safe?"

I shook my head. "Mom, that would be embarrassing."

She and my father exchanged worried glances. "Victoria," she said, "what's a little embarrassment if it saves you from getting wrapped around a tree because your friend decided to text while driving?"

My father studied the growing panic on my face and said, "Oh, Abby. Let her go. She's happy." He squeezed my side.

I felt a surge of love for my dad. He was obviously as ecstatic as I was that I had friends to spend the day with. But by two, my father's elation had dissolved into concern that bordered on pity. My parents kept giving me wary, sideways glances, probably waiting for me to break down in tears. My dad asked me to help load the car with supplies for the dinner, and I did so reluctantly, hoping I wouldn't get all sweaty. They were close to enlisting my help with rolling meatballs, which I knew would make me smell like garlic, when Z showed up in a battered black Honda Civic. I flew out of the house as if shot from a gun.

As I neared the car, I saw there was nobody else in it. I swallowed. I'd expected to be sandwiched in the back of the car with a bunch of jocks, but instead, I climbed into the front passenger seat.

Z managed to make St. Ann's gray slacks and a burgundy polo shirt look nice, but words can't express how he looked in regular clothes. He was wearing a wrinkled T-shirt and loose cargo shorts, exposing his tanned, athletic forearms and calves. He'd probably taken three seconds to select his wardrobe, as opposed to my three hours. I just stared and stared and stared, until he motioned at the open door and I realized I had to close it if we wanted to make it out of the driveway.

He didn't apologize for being late. He just said "Hey," took a sip from a giant travel mug, and threw the car in reverse. He must have seen my confusion because he asked, "What's wrong?"

I shook my head. "Who are you picking up next?"

"Next?" he asked. Then he grinned. "What? Are you afraid to be alone with all this manliness?" He gestured at himself.

Yes, I was afraid. I mean, this wasn't, like, a date, was it? No, of course it wasn't. We were friends, and I had you, Andrew. I mumbled something incoherent about thinking it was a group thing. Then I shrugged. "No big deal."

He didn't know where the movie theater was, so I gave him directions as best I could since I'd only been there a handful of times. I'm sure in Arizona they have one of those mega-cineplexes that shows twenty movies at one time. Our old theater was built early last century and was the only entertainment here in Duchess. The Forum was playing only one movie, a comedy with a bunch of old actors who were way past their prime and making fun of how they each had one foot in the grave.

Z's face leaked no emotion as he parallel parked across from the theater. "I was going to ask you what kind of movie you like," he said, "but it doesn't look like we have a choice."

That the movie had started thirty minutes ago didn't faze him. The tickets were only two dollars and he bought mine, which both excited and terrified me. How chivalrous! But did he think this was a date? I itched like crazy to see inside his mind.

We crept into the darkened theater. It was easy to find seats. There were only a couple gray-haired people in the audience illuminated by the light from the screen. We sat in the back, in the very center of the row.

The seats in that old theater are really close together. I let him have the armrest to be nice because he's bigger. I kept my hands in my lap and tried to concentrate on the movie, even though I had no interest in the story and no idea what was going on, since we arrived late. Mostly I concentrated on filling my lungs with air because although I'd popped my trusty Ativan earlier, Z made me so nervous that even breathing was hard. I had a small heart attack when his hand snaked over the armrest and found mine. Mine was hot and sweaty; his, warm and nice. He played with my bony, knobby-knuckled fingers and then started stroking my palm.

Mayday, Mayday! This was quickly progressing from friendship to something else. Something I'd convinced myself wouldn't happen. For a second, I just stared at his hand on mine, hardly able to believe this was happening to me. Finally, I got up the courage to slide my hand out from under his, run it through my hair, and place it back on my thigh. *No, sir, I'm not available like that.*

But two seconds later, his hand landed on my knee. Breathing about a mile a minute, I angled my knees as far as I could get them away from him without changing seats, but he kept his hand there. Obviously, Z did not get the hint. So swallowing, I leaned over and whispered, "I-I don't…"

He looked at me with a blank expression, as if he had no idea what was going on. As if he was completely innocent in this.

"Your hand," I whispered. "I didn't know… You see, I have a sort of…um…boyfriend."

He looked down at his hand, almost surprised to see it on my knee. He said, "I have a girlfriend."

"Oh," I said, feeling dumb. *Wait, he has a girlfriend? But…*

"Does this scare you?"

Yes, it scared me. But maybe it shouldn't have. Maybe it was normal for friends to touch each other's knees. I mean, it wasn't like he'd grabbed my boob. I didn't answer because he'd already moved his hand. We watched the rest of the movie in silence and without touching. I spent those twenty-three hundred tortured breaths wondering what he'd say to me after the credits rolled. When they finally did, he stood up, and I followed him out of the theater.

We didn't speak again until we were back in his car. He started the ignition. "Weird. I thought half the people in that movie were already dead."

That was that. We were just going to forget about the whole hand-holding incident. Great, I could do that. I relaxed. "I did too."

I thought he would drive me home. I was OK with that because, really, I'd had enough being social to last me a year. Keeping my anxiety in check so I didn't act like a total loser was exhausting. My heart was about to give out.

Instead, Z said, "I'm hungry. Let's get food." I didn't have to agree. It wasn't a question. He was just going to do it, and I suppose if I was against it, I'd have to jump out at a stoplight. I was kind of against getting something to eat because I knew you would be home soon, and if you saw me being dropped off by Z, I wasn't sure if I could explain. But I couldn't bring myself to tell Z that. After all, it *was* innocent. I needed to chill.

He said, "Just got to stop at my house first."

I suppose I thought that anyone as perfect as Z would have an equally perfect house. Say, a pristine, white house with Greek columns and manicured landscaping and a butler waving to us from the front door. Nope. Z lived in a run-down mobile home down on Route 11 by the recycling drop-off about three miles past my house.

Andrew, you've probably driven by it a thousand times and

not noticed because it's half shrouded in overgrowth and shade trees, and the other half is speckled with greenish-black mold. There were gnomes with faded paint and wooden silhouettes of dogs and a boy fishing in the overgrown weeds. The lawn hadn't been mown in ages. There was a Ford Festiva in the driveway that was so dirty its original color was a mystery, and a rotting, metal swing-set carcass peeked out from the backyard.

Maybe his house should have been my first clue that something was off with Z. I know, Andrew, our duplex is nothing great. I've always been a little embarrassed by it. But Z wasn't embarrassed at all by the trailer. "Come on in," he offered, searching his key ring.

I got out and started to follow him, but then I saw the Beware of Dog sign on the door. I stopped. "I'm allergic to dogs," I told him. I lied because I was embarrassed to tell him the truth—that I was afraid of dogs. Ever since one jumped on me at my aunt's picnic when I was five, even cute and cuddly dogs scare me to death. Andrew, you're the only one I've ever told about that.

See, Andrew? There are still some things only you know about me.

Z tilted his head, looking at me, looking *through* me. I think he knew it was a lie. "Really? OK. Wait out here." He ran inside, and no sooner had the door shut than I heard a voice.

"Zacky?"

From my position, I could just see around the back of the mobile home. Ten toes, painted in bright-pink polish, were waving in the air. I craned my neck to look. A girl was lying on her stomach on a towel in the middle of the weeds. By "girl," I mean the most beautiful creature I'd ever seen. She was blond and light, her skin gleaming porcelain, her lips bright and red like one of those fifties pinup models. Her body was perfectly proportioned and wearing the tiniest pink bikini I'd ever seen. I shifted my stare toward the ground because it seemed wrong to look at anyone wearing so little. She turned over, leaned forward, and removed her movie-star sunglasses to inspect me. "Who are you?" she asked, frowning. "Where's Zach?"

"I'm Victoria," I began dumbly.

I thought she would introduce herself, but she just rolled her eyes as the screen door in front slammed. The girl called to him again, but he tugged on the sleeve of my T-shirt and motioned for me to follow.

After we got into his car and pulled away, he said, "Sorry. I didn't know *she* was going to be there." There was a hint of disdain in his voice, but then he flashed a smile.

"Who is she?"

He pulled his dark sunglasses over his eyes as he drove. "My aunt."

"Your...*aunt*?" That young, pink vixen looked nothing like an aunt. I was hoping he'd explain further, but he didn't. "Um...you two don't get along?"

He shrugged. "Rarely. She's supposed to be working today. And obviously *that's* not happening." He seemed to shake off his mood when he put on the radio. It was "Dope Hit" by the Young Freaks. He said, "I like this song. Who sings it?"

I told him. "Yeah, I like it too," I agreed.

We listened until we pulled up at the Duchess Diner, which has only slightly better food than Kelly's Deli. We have a lot more dives in Maine than respectable restaurants. I'd been at the diner once with my parents, and we'd never gone back because they ruined our grilled cheeses. How hard is it to make a grilled cheese?

We went in and got a booth. I opened the menu, looking for something other than grilled cheese. Z folded his hands over his menu, leaned forward, and stared at me. "So, what about this boyfriend of yours?"

I nearly choked. "What about him?"

"I want details."

Andrew, I foolishly thought that talking about you would make me completely yours. So I did. I told him all about you, how we've known each other since we were seven, how you are homeschooled, how your stepdad works at the paper mill, and how you go on hunting trips with him every month, but what you really love to do is play music. But the funny thing was, the more I said, the more it felt like I was betraying you. Z knew everything about you, and you knew nothing about him.

Z listened intently. Then he said, "I need to meet this guy."

I raised my eyebrows. He'd tried to hold my hand in the theater, and now he wanted to meet you? Maybe that was a friendly gesture. After all, his tone made him sound like a dad. Or a brother. Maybe that's what he wanted to be, my protective brother type. "OK."

"So he plays the piano?"

"He plays pretty much every instrument," I said proudly.

"But he's best at the piano. He wants to study music, to be a teacher."

He scratched his chin. "Julliard?"

"No," I said, trying to think of a way to talk about you and your condition so that you didn't sound like a weirdo. "Andrew is...sheltered." I bit my tongue. I didn't want to say more. I didn't want to tell him your secret, your biggest shame. Agoraphobia. Your constant need for routine, for refuge from the outside world. I guarded those details as if they were my own. But Z has a way of prying things out with only a look. I said, "He's more of a small-town boy. He wouldn't last a day in the city. He also doesn't like being in front of large groups of people. It...frightens him."

"Frightens?"

I winced. I didn't mean to make you sound weak.

"Well, it makes him uncomfortable. So he'll study music around here and tutor local kids. He'll be happy doing that."

"But he has the talent to...um...play Carnegie Hall?"

"Oh yes. He's amazing. Anyone who hears him says so. They say it's a shame to keep his talent a secret. If he could just get over his fears, he could write his own ticket. He's really the best."

Z nodded. "That's impressive, but...can he play knick knack on his shoe? Because I can. Really well."

I laughed. "He probably can't do that as well as you can," I acknowledged.

Z propped his chin on his hand. "Great. Now I'm jealous. You have a fabulously gifted boyfriend. He's probably handsome and debonair too, huh?"

"He's not bad," I offered humbly. He was joking, obviously. "And you have a girlfriend. Tell me about her."

His phone dinged. He looked at the display and said, "She's in Arizona. And she has a worse texting habit than I do. Today she had eggs for breakfast." He rolled his eyes. "So you see? I'm all alone here. And you have a fabulously gifted boyfriend."

I stared at him as he pouted in front of me. Was he serious? He had *everything*. How could he be jealous of me? "You said before you had no family…"

For the first time, his face darkened. "Yeah."

"But your…your aunt…"

He was silent. He looked down at his menu and opened it. The waitress came. I ordered french fries. He asked if he could share mine. So we got a huge plate of fries. When the waitress left, he said, "She's not really my aunt."

Well, duh. "Oh really?"

"She… Long story," he said, prepping me.

"I'm listening." I was actually on the edge of my seat. Was he going to tell me something genuine?

"My mother had me when she was young," he whispered, his eyes never leaving mine. "Really young. Thirteen. So my grandparents raised me. But they both died last year within a couple of months of each other, and by that time my mother had gone off to Mexico with a new husband who's, like, old enough to be her grandfather. I've never met my stepdad, and my mom's not exactly the most loving mother on earth, so I sure as hell wasn't going to live with them in Mexico. So rather than put me in foster care, they arranged to have me move here to live with his first wife's youngest sister, Bethany. Who you met. She's my aunt. Kind of. Step-aunt, I guess."

My mouth dropped open, and an "oh" came out. Suddenly, the big cloud of mystery that had been hovering over Z's head lifted. No wonder he made a joke of everything. He hadn't had the easiest life. "That's…"

"Messed up, I know."

"But you have family. They're just—"

"I don't consider any of them my family. Not my mom. Not my stepdad. Bethany is just someone I'm living with until I'm legal. And then I'm out of there, quick as that." He snapped his fingers. "Every one of them will use you until you're no longer useful and then throw you away. Anyway, I don't talk about that. To anyone."

But he'd chosen to tell me. That meant something. He was the one person in school everyone wanted to know, and yet I knew him best. I shivered at the thought. We could be *real* friends. I could have an ally at St. Ann's, instead of walking the halls desperately alone. I wanted that. I tried to think of something to say, something that showed I understood, that I was there for him. Something meaningful.

Before I could, his grin returned. In a flash, the vulnerable Z disappeared. "It's all good. Now, what about your parents? You get along well?"

I told him about my mom and dad, the boringest story ever told. How my parents met in college and fell in love. How they were into two things—church and me. I cut it short though because I was sure Z didn't want to hear that my parents loved me so much they nearly smothered me, when his were the opposite.

Leave it to Z to find the common link in our childhood stories. "You're an only child too," he observed. "That means we're both used to getting our own way. Am I right, Vic?"

I'd laughed, buoyed by the thought: *A real friend at St. Ann's.*

But now I see it much more clearly. Z wasn't interested in friendship so much as followers. And he always got his way. Anything else was unacceptable.

CHAPTER 12

Suxamethonium chloride (INN), also known as
suxamethonium or succinylcholine, is a nicotinic
acetylcholine receptor agonist used to induce
muscle relaxation and short-term paralysis.

—*Narcotics and Their Proper Usage*

Z DROPPED ME OFF AT MY house a little after five. By that
time your stepdad's Ford F-150 was back in the driveway,
but I didn't care anymore if you happened to see me leaving a
strange boy's car. I was in a state of bliss. Z and I were *friends*.
Our relationship was defined, and it was everything I wanted. I
was friends with the most interesting guy at school. And I had a
caring, talented boyfriend too. Life was good.

The garage door was open. Your dad had strung a scrawny
deer carcass from the rafters. There were two black holes in its
backside, and blood dripped from them into a green bucket.
You sat deep inside your garage, on the concrete stairs going
into your house, with your elbows on your knees, watching
the deer like it'd been your best friend. But you managed to

force the corners of your mouth into a smile when you saw me. Your voice was monotone. "Behold the spoils of our latest hunting excursion."

You started to untie your boots as I stepped into the darkness of the garage, being extra careful to stay as far away from the deer as possible. The stench of your stepdad's cigarette smoke hung in the air. I fought back the urge to gag. As I got closer, I noticed your jeans were covered in blood and tufts of wispy white fur. "It looks like a baby."

You pulled off a boot. Your sock had a hole. You grimaced. You said, "It is. My stepdad got pissed he couldn't find a buck, so he took it out."

"Isn't that illegal or something?" I asked, but I knew what you were thinking. *Better it than me.*

"In the words of my stepfather, 'it's only illegal if you get caught.'" You threw your boots on the ground beside the stairs, and dried mud flaked off them.

Just then the door swung open. It was your mom. She took a step back when she saw me. "Oh, hi, Victoria," she said, wringing her hands and wincing at the sight of the deer behind me. "What are you doing in here?"

I gave your mom a smile. "I wanted to see how the hunting expedition went. Venison stew this week?"

She returned the smile slowly. "That's right. Well, I guess I'll just leave you." She tentatively started to close the door and then said, "Don't stay out here too long. It's almost dinnertime. And be careful with all these…things lying around." She nodded toward the gear strewn on the floor.

"I'll take care of it." You got up and started going through your stepdad's camo-and-fluorescent-orange gear, which he'd left for you to sort out. You started hanging each piece on its respective hook. You've always thrived on organization, so most of your life has been cleaning up your dad's messes.

I leaned over to help you but stopped when I saw blood crusted on one of the arrows. "Gross," I said.

"Who's anyone kidding? No one likes venison stew but my dad," you said, picking up an arrow with a head that looked different.

"What is that one for? Bigger deer?"

You shook your head and showed it to me. "These have a compartment for poison. A spring-loaded release injects it into the bloodstream when the arrowhead pierces the deer."

I studied it. "Why do you need to poison a deer? Isn't shooting it with an arrow enough?"

"Deer run when they're hit, and sometimes they run a long way before they die. This is a muscle relaxant that basically paralyzes and kills them on the spot," you said. "It's also illegal, in case you were wondering. Bambi didn't stand a chance."

You pulled out a small, brown glass bottle. The label said *succinylcholine chloride*. Just looking at that vial, my hands began to shake. "Is that what you used for..."

He nodded. "It didn't hurt."

Oh, it hurt all right. How could it not? Our gazes trailed over to the deer. From this angle, I could see its lifeless black eyes. I gagged. Time to change the subject. "Did you and your dad bond?"

You looked at me like I had three heads. "What do you think?"

It was a dumb question. Your dad probably drank a thermos of coffee laced with something extra the whole time, until he was so sloshed he couldn't remember his own name. You probably had to carry the deer back to the car for him and spent the whole harrowing ride home digging your fingernails into the armrests. I could just imagine your dad passed out on that ugly, flowered sofa in your living room, with his dirty-socked feet propped on the arm.

That was better than what could've happened, what happened before. You know the time I'm talking about. There'd been a big buck and you'd missed it. On purpose? I don't know. But your dad was pissed. That was a given. You never told me the details, but your hair didn't hide the sore on the back of your head or the brown stain that stretched from the collar of your jacket down your sleeve. He'd hit you. Probably with the end of his bow. In my mind, that's how I saw it: him coming after you, rage distorting his face. You'd spent a good chunk of your savings on another bow for his birthday. He'd hit you with his bow, but he blamed your hard head for breaking it.

"How was your day?" you asked, inspecting me. "Why are you all red?"

I felt my face. "Am I?"

"You're all dressed up. Did you go somewhere?"

I looked down at my jeans and T-shirt. "*This* is dressed up?"

"Your hair is down. You never wear it down." I opened my mouth to explain, but you shrugged and said, "Looks pretty.

I mean, you always look pretty, but you're even prettier with it down."

I blushed, not so much from the compliment but because it suddenly felt like deception, wearing my hair in a "pretty" way for someone else. I didn't mean it that way, you know. "Thanks. I went to a movie with a friend."

You didn't look at me. "Hot new student?"

"He's a *friend*," I reminded you. "And I didn't know it was just going to be the two of us. I told him all about you. He has a girlfriend too."

You nodded, and we finished cleaning up the rest of the mess in silence. The whole time though, I knew you were still thinking about your stepdad. You always got that tired, dead-eyed expression whenever you spent time with him. You told me you were feeling faint and needed to get your insulin and lie down, but then said something about maybe hanging out tomorrow.

As I walked back to my front door, my thoughts were on you. On how unfair it was that you were so wonderful and brilliant and being suffocated by that horrible man. Then my phone dinged. I read the message from Z.

Thanks for listening.

And then…oh God. I'm sorry, Andrew. My thoughts turned right back to Z, where they stayed for the rest of the weekend.

CHAPTER 13

What were your impressions of your classmate Z?

A clown. Never took anything seriously. He was always
   in a good mood. That's why everyone gravitated
   to him. He had no shortage of friends.

In your opinion, was he a poor student?

No, he was smart. If he concentrated and did the work,
   he probably would have been one of the best students in class. But he had other things on his mind.

Like?

No clue. There was a rumor he was dealing, but I don't
   do drugs, so how would I know?

So he wasn't one to devote time to his studies.

No. He was the kind of guy who probably didn't have to.
   Things came easily to him, no matter what he did.

Such as what?

Such as...everything.

—Police interview with Gerri O'Donnell,
junior at St. Ann's

I CAN'T EXPLAIN HOW THE ATMOSPHERE at St. Ann's shifted, but I saw change everywhere. Nobody talked about it, of course. But I knew the cause. Z affected everyone in the school. It was as if all the people he'd come in contact with had become the movie-star versions of themselves.

Brainy Gerri never wore anything other than the school's regulation pink blouse, buttoned to the very top. Today though, her two top buttons were undone. Parker Cole came in with a brand-new haircut and dye job. She and Rachel were wearing bright-red lipstick and black eyeliner, which they had to remove after homeroom since it was against school policy. Some of the guys had taken to chewing gum. During morning prayers, instead of kneeling straight, people would kneel with their butts propped against their seats. Reese, the hardest of the hard-asses, seemed to smile more. It was like the whole uptight school had suddenly let out the breath it was holding.

And it was all because of Z.

Even I have to admit that I took more care in my appearance. I'd never been athletic, but early that morning, I went for a run. Just a short, half-mile jaunt around the block, but I felt better about myself. I wasn't about to test school policy by wearing makeup, but I curled my hair, rather than sweeping it into the standard ponytail. I made a conscious decision to stop biting my nails. I wore earrings—though nothing too fancy. When I gazed at myself in the mirror, I practiced standing straighter with my chin up so I didn't look as much like an arthritic old lady. Before Z arrived, it took me minutes to get ready for school.

Now it took me an hour. I think his mere presence gave us a reason to try to be our better selves.

My parents noticed. Father Leary noticed. They were glad that I was feeling good, exercising, making an effort with my appearance.

Z didn't notice any of it. Or maybe he was so used to having that effect on people that he didn't care. He breezed into Reese's class on Monday—as I was practicing keeping my shoulders back and pushing my chest out—and said, "Hey, Precious."

"Precious?" I wrinkled my nose, even though I liked the attention. I'd never had much of a reason to think I was precious to anyone.

"You have a good rest-of-the-weekend?"

I nodded and noted the way everyone in the room seemed to turn to face him, like flowers tilting toward the sun. Parker flipped her hair and batted her eyelashes, pouting when Z ignored her. I smiled. She wanted his attention, but he was friends with me. He'd chosen to let *me* into his life, not her.

Which was probably why I'd spent all of Sunday thinking of him. Even at church, while Father delivered a stirring homily on God's forgiveness, I thought of Z. Prayed for him. He prayed right along with everyone during school masses, but I'd never seen him at church. I had to wonder how he spent his Sundays.

He smacked his gum and took a bright-red square of paper out of his back pocket and started unfolding it. It was a poster for *Macbeth*. "I'm doing this," he said surely.

I said, "You are?" but of course he would. He was outspoken

and attracted attention the way most people only dreamed of. He was made for the stage. Me, however? Never!

I bristled. He already had baseball, which I couldn't pretend to be into. Now he'd have *another* activity without me. Soon he'd be so busy with the jocks and the thespians that he wouldn't be mine anymore.

But he isn't really yours, I scolded myself. How could such a silly thought be in my head? He was sure to go off and find cooler people to hang out with, and then I wouldn't be Precious anymore. I wouldn't be anyone. My voice was soft when I acknowledged, "I guess you'd be a good actor."

He nodded at the crumpled sheet of paper. "Yeah. I would rock this Shakespeare thing. 'Tomorrow and tomorrow and tomorrow.'"

Reese strode into the classroom and didn't zero in on the gum in Z's mouth, but on the red poster in his hands. She said, "Are you thinking of auditioning, Z?"

"That I am," he answered, which made her clap her hands together. "Wonderful!" Probably the last time she'd found something wonderful was in 1976.

The bell rang, and Reese launched into a discussion of Borges's "The Zahir." Have you read it, Andrew? The Zahir was a coin that the narrator received as change, and somehow, that seemingly innocent object consumed all of his thoughts. He became obsessed with it, unable to think of anything else.

Once again, Z seemed to know everything about the short story. Reese nearly bent over and kissed him on the top of his golden mop. When class was over, I asked him, "How do you know all this?"

He put his finger to his temple and whispered, "I have a good memory."

"That will help you remember your lines," I observed. "For the play, I mean."

"You should do *Macbeth* too," he said. "Ever fancy yourself an actress?"

"That's not... I'd be terrible."

"Why?" he asked, as if the answer wasn't totally obvious. I'm *not* someone people watch for enjoyment. But he was still staring at me, waiting, so I had to answer.

"My voice is too quiet. No one would hear me."

After that, he dropped the subject, but I kept thinking about it. What would it be like to be onstage with all eyes on me? I daydreamed about wearing a beautiful costume and standing beside Z. He performed miracles every day. Maybe he could make me watchable. Maybe his friendship was all I needed to be someone other than meek, forgettable Victoria Zell.

At lunch, I ate by myself, trying to reread "The Zahir" but constantly sneaking looks in Z's direction. Every day, he sat with the other baseball jocks. They were insulated in their own little shell, oblivious to the world around them. So I was surprised to see him crack a joke, and then, while the rest of the guys burst into fits of laughter, look over at me. *Was he making jokes about me?*

I tried to look away, but I couldn't. He palmed his phone,

one thumb moving expertly over it. A second later, my phone dinged. I'd made the ringer extra loud so I wouldn't miss another text from him. I tried to act nonchalant, but I was dying to know what was going on. My fingers fumbled on the zipper as I pulled open my purse. The message said: Look inside your locker for a surprise.

I looked up. He was smiling at me. I wrinkled my brow and mouthed, "What?" My palms had already begun to sweat.

His thumb started going again. My phone dinged.

Can't tell you. You have to look. Go. Now.

I got up, told the lunch monitor I had to use the bathroom, and walked out of the cafeteria at as leisurely a pace as possible. Once I got away from the doors, I slipped into a run.

My locker? How had he gotten my locker combination? What was he up to? Was I the butt of some stupid jock joke? I got the combination right on the second try, lifted the latch, and pulled open the door. On the top shelf, just at eye level, was a bag of candy kisses.

My heart thrummed and my cheeks burned as I hugged them to my chest. Then, I pulled out my phone and texted: How did you know my locker combination?

Ten seconds later, the text came back: I have my ways.

He must've looked over my shoulder to figure it out because he wanted to surprise me, to make me feel special. And I did. No one at school had ever made a gesture like that for me. I was about to respond when he sent me another text: You are too sweet to be corrupted by someone like me.

Z corrupted people? With what, his adorable smile and

chocolate kisses? Smiling, I texted back: Yes, you are very evil... You and your bad candy.

I smiled at my wittiness. Look at that. I was getting *comfortable* around him. I felt a little like I did around you, Andrew. Like this was the beginning of a great and lasting relationship.

Stupid, stupid me.

CHAPTER 14

*His junior year, Z was an otherwise good student.
Can you explain how he ended up with a failing
midterm progress report in your class?*

He didn't do the work. He fooled around, and he
thought he could use other students' work to
help him pass. Some teachers might accept that,
but I don't.

By other students, you mean…

Victoria Zell. She was his lab partner. It was unfortunate she ended up with him, but being rather new
to the school, she was the only student without
a long-standing lab partner. Ms. Zell is incredibly
smart, but also, well…naive and trusting. She's a
teenage girl. She wants to fit in. I can't blame her
for succumbing to his charming ways.

—Police interview with Jeffrey Lincoln,
chemistry teacher at St. Ann's

EARY NOTICED THE CHANGE IN me right away. "I have a friend at St. Ann's," I said. It was the first time I'd volunteered information.

He nodded. "Z."

I thought he'd be happy, but instead, he looked concerned. His eyes narrowed at the package of candy that was peeking out of my bag. I stuffed it down and made a vow never to offer any information to him again. I sighed.

"What does Andrew have to say about your new friend?"

"Andrew," I murmured, confused. "What do you mean? Why does it matter?"

He shrugged. "I was just asking. Andrew has been such an important part of your life for so long."

"Z and I are friends," I told Leary matter-of-factly, not really liking what he was insinuating. "So Andrew is happy I'm fitting in better. He wants me to be happy. Same thing I want for him."

"So he knew the struggle you had adjusting last year?"

"He knows everything about me. I mean, I coped fine. It wasn't much of a struggle."

Leary smiled. "Then, this is a good thing. I'm glad you're starting to find your way at St. Ann's." It felt like an ending. Like he was finally admitting I didn't need him anymore. I waited for him to say something to that effect, to hand me a diploma and tell me I'd officially graduated from his maddening hamster wheel of emotions. Instead he said, "Take it slow and steady, OK?"

I nearly snorted out loud in annoyance. This was friendship, not a stupid obstacle course. I might not have much experience with friends, but I figured I could handle it. Real friends want the best for each other, like you and me, Andrew. And I thought that's what Z wanted for me. "Right. Of course," I murmured. The sooner I agreed, hopefully the sooner I could leave.

When it was time to catch the late bus, Father walked me out and gave me a cheerful wink, a departure from the quiet pity that usually dripped from his puffy jowls.

I skipped down the stairs, shaking my head at how stupid his advice was. Take it slow and steady? Why? Things were getting better. Why have them do that slowly and steadily when they could go fast and furious?

CHAPTER 15

Z's attendance record was less than stellar.

Yes, that is correct.

Reason?

I can only speculate.

And would that speculation involve potentially illicit activities?

I wouldn't go so far as to say that. He was a good student. But life was difficult for him at home. Considering that, I think he managed remarkably well.

—Police interview with Edward Cole, principal at St. Ann's

THE NEXT FEW DAYS SPED by in a blissful haze.

Every so often, I'd find a surprise in my locker. Always small gifts, like stickers or jelly beans or a plastic spider ring. I'd immediately arrange the stickers on the front of my notebooks, or slip the ring on and admire it, making sure to thank Z loudly so that Parker and the others could hear. He'd always just shrug and say, "No problem, Precious." I know they'd all heard him call me that.

I wanted to believe I was *his* Precious. You know, like the ring in *The Hobbit*. *His* Zahir.

After the first few gifts, I asked him again how he got my locker combination, and he winked and said, "It isn't exactly a matter of national security." So I let it slide. Of course, that made going to my locker a new obsession. Before, I used to visit my locker once or twice a day to change my books. Now I visited after every class.

Then, a few days before the auditions for *Macbeth*, everything came to a standstill.

The bell rang, and Z's desk remained empty. When Reese took attendance, she seemed shocked by the lack of Z's enthusiastic "Here!" You could hear a pin drop in the silence.

By the end of that first day without Z, the whole school fell into a general malaise. Students moved through the halls slower and didn't smile as much. Everyone looked doubly hard at Z's desk, as if staring could will him back. He was the sun, and his disappearance had sent us all out of orbit. And so, as the planet closest to him, I felt even more purposeless.

On the second day of his absence, I wanted to call in sick too. The minutes ticked by like years. Is this how school had been before Z arrived? So lifeless and dull? Had the classrooms' lighting always been so gray and depressing? How had I managed to exist in such a state of utter boredom? I stopped checking my locker for gifts between periods and began checking my phone for texts. Surely he would text me about the homework he was missing.

But my phone remained quiet. Then, in the middle of English, as Reese droned on about "The Zahir," it hit me.

I could text *him*.

My body quivered as I turned the thought over in my head. Could I be so bold? What would I say? Maybe he was bored stiff, lying in bed with whatever illness he had, waiting for contact with the outside world.

By the time English came to an end, my resolve had strengthened, and I'd formulated a message. I reached into my bag for my phone and typed: Out again?

Ten seconds later: Yup. Sick.

I thought about what a friend would say. What I would want a friend to say to me. Want me to get your homework for you?

Nope. Under control.

I blushed, feeling stupid. His answers were short, terse, as if he didn't want to talk to me. Maybe he was at death's door, but it felt more like a blow-off. I reminded myself that I was his Precious, the one he left locker gifts for, right? He couldn't hate me. So I tried again.

Think you'll be in tomorrow?

Why? Miss me that much?

My cheeks burned. I was about to lie and tell him that no, I didn't miss him, when he came back with:

Miss you too, Precious.

I smiled like an idiot for the rest of the day. Nothing had the power to erase that smile from my face, even during chemistry, when Lincoln made me work with Parker and Rachel because I didn't have a lab partner. They both looked at me as if I were from an alien planet, and whenever I talked, they looked at me as if I were speaking Alienese. I had the urge to shove Z's texts under Parker's nose, to show them that I was somebody, that I was *precious*, not the piece of dog crap their disgusted looks seemed to imply. But I zipped my mouth shut and wrote notes, stopping every few seconds to check the clock and see if I could break free yet.

Ten minutes into the experiment, Parker removed her goggles from her head, being cautious not to disturb her perfectly coiffed hairdo. "So…"

She was looking at me. Addressing me. For the first time ever.

"Where's your lab partner?" she asked like she didn't know his name, but I was wise to that game.

I said, "Home. Sick."

She grinned as if she knew more than me. "Riiiight." Rachel rolled her eyes and grinned too.

Normally I cared nothing for their secret whisperings, but knowing they were talking about Z, I itched to be in on it. Maybe Parker knew something I didn't. Her dad was principal, and she knew more about the school and its students than most. "What does that mean?"

"Nothing." Then she and Rachel burst into giggles. I wanted to lunge across the table, grab her glossy mane, and thrust it into the blue light of the Bunsen burner. "I'm sure he's home getting chicken soup from his mommy," she said in a baby voice.

"His aunt," I corrected.

She laughed. "Whatever. You really think *that* is his aunt?"

My insides were starting to boil. She'd seen Bethany. How had she seen Bethany? Z didn't discuss his background with just anyone. What right did Parker have to ridicule people who didn't have all her advantages? Indignant, I said, "Not everyone's life is as perfect as yours. Mind your own business."

She studied her nonregulation nail polish undeterred and shrugged before giggling more at Rachel. The bell rang, and I let out the breath I'd been holding, relieved. Lincoln told everyone to have a good afternoon and, as I was packing up my books, said, "Victoria, hold back a sec, OK?"

I cringed. Mr. Lincoln stood at the front of the classroom, a vaguely disappointed look on his face. I hunched over as I approached his desk, my face already burning. Parker's whispers and giggles faded into the hallway, leaving the lab eerily silent. I muttered, "I'm sorry," before he had a chance to speak.

"Hold on," he said, motioning to the stool next to his desk. "How do you even know what this is about?"

"I don't. Sorry."

"Then hold on to those apologies," he said, shuffling through some papers on his desk. He arranged them in a neat pile and then sat on the stool next to me so that our knees were almost touching.

For some reason, the whole *inappropriate relationship vibe* that Z had joked about stuck in my head. Ridiculous. And yet... why did the things Z said to me always take root and grow in my mind? Was it because I rehashed them over and over again, like a favorite song on my iPod? I squirmed, putting some distance between me and my teacher and hoping I wouldn't fall off the stool.

"I wanted to discuss your lab reports…"

"What about them? They're not good?"

"They're great. They're typical Victoria Zell quality. But I've been observing, and you've been doing the majority of the heavy lifting." He had one of my recent labs in front of him. He picked it up. "This one, for example."

"We have a division of labor. Z does most of the lab work, since I'm a little clumsy," I explained. "I take notes."

He pulled out another sheet of paper. I recognized Z's light scrawl. He placed it beside mine. I wasn't sure what he was getting at until I started to compare the two. My eyes darted back and forth between the two sheets, faster and faster. I'd done my reports alone in my bedroom after school. And yet…

His report was, word for word, the same.

"I don't understand," I said. This had to be a mistake. The product of two people being so in tune that they produced the same work. Two peas, same pod. We'd worked off the same notes. It was possible. Besides, my chemistry notebook was with me, in my backpack until I got to school. Then I put it into my locker until chemistry class.

My locker.

"Did you let Z copy your work?" he asked.

"No, I, um…" My throat constricted as it all became clear. Those Hershey's kisses, the little tokens…they were not gifts. They were payment. I swallowed to get my voice back. "It's just a coincidence. We worked off the same notes. And..." I saw his eyes narrow in disbelief, so I lied: "we...sometimes do our homework together."

He looked at me intently for a moment, then said, "OK, Victoria. If you say so."

I exhaled deeply. He'd bought it. I was his star student, after all. "Yes."

"All right." He smiled. I relaxed. Then he leaned forward, and I knew what was coming. "How are things with you otherwise?"

"Fine," I answered.

"No problems at home? Problems with friends?"

Great. As if I hadn't heard it enough from Father Leary and my parents. Now I had to answer to my science teacher? I knew if I spoke up, anything that came out of my mouth would reek of bitterness, so I pressed my lips together and shook my head.

"Well, that's good. It's not easy, being the new kid."

Or so everyone liked to remind me. Somehow, I didn't think Z had the same problem. "It's all right. I'm not all that social. I actually prefer to be alone."

"And there's nothing wrong with that." He gave me one of his signature shoulder squeezes and motioned to the door with his head. "Now get on out of here."

When I got into the hall, I pulled out my phone. Quickly, I texted: Just got in trouble with Lincoln because your lab report is exactly the same as mine. How did that happen?

Two seconds later, my phone rang. It was Z. Two minutes before next class. I rushed into the bathroom and answered it. Before I could say hello, he said, "Because I borrowed your report."

"Borrowed?" I challenged.

"OK, stole?"

"That's more like it, since you didn't ask me," I muttered. "Couldn't you have changed a word or two? I mean, duh."

"Sorry, Precious. I was busy the night before it was due. I thought that since we're friends…"

"You could have asked me. I would have let you look at mine. I would have helped you."

"I know. But this way, you're innocent. You knew nothing about it. Plus, there's no reason for Lincoln to be pissed because we *did* use the same notes. So obviously our work would be the same. Did he give you hell?"

"No. I told him that we did our homework together."

"Right. That's my girl."

His girl. I liked that. But still, I was mad at him. Really mad. For…why again? For a flash, I couldn't remember, and then it came back to me. "He's going to give *you* hell if it happens again."

I expected him to say that it wouldn't, but instead, he said, "Don't worry. I've got that all under control."

"Maybe you should stop going into my locker too," I suggested weakly.

"You don't like the gifts?"

I couldn't tell him the truth: I loved the gifts. They brightened my time at St. Ann's like nothing else. I felt dumb for even suggesting that he stop. "No, I do, but… Forget it."

I could sense he was smiling. "Forgotten. And Lincoln won't be giving me hell, or I'll give it right back to him. You see?"

I didn't. Anyone who challenged a teacher like that would be in major trouble. Fear knotted in my throat. "You want to be expelled?"

"Vic. Calm," he said, laughing, as I remembered that he was out sick. He didn't sound sick. His voice wasn't gravelly or strained, and he hadn't coughed once. I started to ask how he was feeling when the bell rang. It echoed in the small, tiled space, and I jumped.

Oh shit. I was late. "Got to go," I said, hanging up the phone and running for the door. By the time I made it to my next class, I'd decided to use stomach cramps as an excuse. The teacher just nodded, and I slipped into my seat, feeling weirdly thrilled and exhilarated, like I was part of something bigger than anything that could be found inside the walls of St. Ann's. You know I'd never been one to fudge excuses with teachers, Andrew. But I was surprised at how easily the lies had come.

CHAPTER 16

I watch over him the best I can—but I'm not his mother. It's hard. I work for a living. I'm not around a lot. And it's not like watching a toddler. A seventeen-year-old is nearly a man. What was I going to do? Spank him for going out after curfew?
—Radio interview with Bethany Montez, family member who resided with Z at the time of the murder

THE FOLLOWING DAY, Z WAS out again, and I had to sit with Parker and Rachel in chem. I wanted to stab my eye out with my pen listening to them talk about their current boyfriends, and eventually, the conversation swung to Z.

Just ignore, just ignore, just ignore, I told myself. That lasted about three seconds, until Rachel piped in with: "Auntie must be very good at *taking care* of him."

"What?" I snapped, disgust in my voice.

Parker ignored me. "You can't expect Victoria to understand, Rachel. She didn't see them in the parking lot."

"Didn't see what?" I asked.

"I guess we should fill her in." Parker leaned in really close, like she was going to share her deepest secrets. "According to one of the ladies who work in attendance, his *aunt* came to register him for school. She was high or drunk and wearing this little next-to-nothing outfit. Her writing was barely legible, and she nearly fell over as she was leaving. And then—" She stopped and winked at Rachel. I didn't want to hear any more. "Then she got into Z's car—he was driving—and they started going at it. Right in the school parking lot."

"Going at it," I repeated, sure there must be some other definition for that phrase. When it didn't come to me, I said, "What do you mean?"

She rolled her eyes. "He was making out with his *aunt*, dummy. She climbed into his lap and they were getting dirty, right in the parking lot, for everyone—"

"You're lying," I spat out.

She shrugged. "I'm just telling you what Beth in attendance said."

My voice rose. "She's telling lies about the students?" This was not just wrong; she should lose her job. I needed to tell someone, to complain. Z would never do anything so stupid with the "aunt" he didn't even get along with—and in broad daylight! I slammed my notebook shut. "It's not true. Why would you believe that bunch of fat gossip whores?"

I don't think I'd ever said the word *whore* in my life. But I didn't stop there. It all poured out. I told them everything Z had told me—about his mom giving birth to him when she was thirteen, and how his grandparents had died and he'd ended up living with Bethany. I said, "So maybe you should stop being so judgy."

Parker and Rachel stared at me, their smirks totally gone. Then I realized that pretty much everyone else was staring at me too. Including Mr. Lincoln.

I had to stay after class *again*. Obviously for the display I'd made. What had gotten into me? Just like before, there were disappointed creases in his forehead. I apologized again.

He laughed. "You really need to stop apologizing before you know what you're apologizing for."

I bit back the "sorry" in my throat. "But I know this time."

He nodded. "That behavior was...surprising, Victoria. You want to tell me what set you off?"

"They were telling lies about my lab partner," I said. "Really vicious ones."

He nodded like he'd known that all along. "And you felt the need to defend him?"

"Well, yes," I answered. As if there was any other option.

"Because he's your friend."

"Right."

"I see," he said, looking down at his desk. He seemed to be choosing his words carefully. What? Was defending a friend's honor the wrong thing to do?

"Look, Victoria. You know you're one of my very favorite students. You are very talented. So I don't want to see you being taken advantage of."

"I'm not," I answered immediately. "Z doesn't... It isn't like that. He's a friend. We do homework together sometimes."

He studied me for a moment, as if trying to figure out a complex puzzle. "Well, OK then. If you have anything you want to talk about, I'm always here."

"I know," I said, shoving off the stool and out the door. I was beginning to hate how he was *always* there, witnessing everything that went on between me and Z. Because it's annoying when someone perceives more about you than you do.

And yet, I didn't mind when that person was Z.

CHAPTER 17

Though Zimmerman's happy-go-lucky personality was well-known, witnesses recalled seeing him uncharacteristically agitated on the night of a school dance the Saturday prior to the murder.
—From an article in the *Central Maine Express Times*

THE RUMORS ABOUT Z AND Bethany were flat-out ridiculous. She was at least five years older than he was. And his aunt, sort of. Plus, he had a girlfriend in Arizona. Still, I kept replaying everything I knew about her in my head. Physically, she was perfect, no doubt the object of many a teen kid's fantasies. He'd said he was only living with her until he was old enough to go off on his own. Late that night, I gave up on trying to unravel the mystery and eventually drifted off to sleep.

The next morning, he swept into class and sat down. He looked tan and healthy, not like he was recovering from a cold. He had his nose buried in his phone, so he was completely oblivious to all the questioning eyes on him. He was used to being the center of attention, but I wondered if he knew that everyone's fascination had shifted. He was no longer a Hollywood movie star, more the shocking tabloid headline.

In that moment, I resolved to tell him. He needed to know.

He grunted and slammed his phone on the table, his face dark. Everyone stared.

He looked up and smiled when he saw me. "Hey, Precious."

Maybe he'd already heard the rumors. "Are you OK?"

He waved a hand at his phone. "Yeah, relationship troubles. Brianna can be a little…possessive. We all can't have perfect significant others like you do." He grinned.

"Oh. Um…I need to talk to you. At lunch?"

He raised his eyebrow. "Something wrong?"

I nodded.

"Chemistry?"

I shook my head. "Lunch?"

"Can't. I have to leave early. Doctor's appointment."

"What's wrong with you?"

"It's a follow-up. Can it wait?"

I wasn't sure how to convey the importance of it without telling him outright. And I never quite knew how he'd react. Maybe he'd say it was "under control" like he usually did. "I'm not sure."

Some of his darkness returned. "Tell me now."

I looked around and whispered, "It's…private."

He wiggled his fingers. "Text me."

"But…"

"Just the basics."

"OK." I pulled out my phone. I heard a rumor about you.

He looked at his phone, then turned to me and raised his eyebrows in concern.

Whatever answer he was looking for was already in the expression on my face. Without warning, he grabbed me by the wrist and pulled me out of my desk. I followed him to the door, where he nearly careened into Reese. "Vic is taking me to the nurse," he muttered. "I'm not feeling well," which was ridiculous, since wherever we were going, *he* was clearly taking me. He didn't wait for her approval, and Reese didn't challenge him. I'm not sure even drama-geek Quincy could've pulled that off. Z dragged me to the other side of the school, well past the nurse's office to the always-deserted band wing. "Spill," he said.

"I know it's not true," I prefaced to make the medicine easier to take. He moved his hand in small, impatient circles, trying to draw out the information. "But I was sitting in lab with Parker and Rachel, and they said that the attendance ladies saw you and your aunt in your car…um…"

His brow wrinkled.

"You were…" I felt like a three-year-old. I couldn't bring myself to say *going at it* or *making out* or any of the things they were possibly doing. Not around Z. "You know…"

"I don't," he said, and then his eyes widened as understanding dawned on him. "You mean me and *Bethany*?"

The way that he said it, I knew without a doubt that it wasn't true. No one could be that convincing a liar. I had the urge to put a comforting arm around him, but he went ballistic. He balled his fist and slammed it into a locker. Then he kicked the locker again and again, mumbling, "Fuck, fuck, fuck." I'd never seen him so emotional. Frankly, he scared me.

He stopped and rubbed his eyes. "You heard this from Parker and Rachel?"

I nodded.

"So that means everyone knows." He exhaled slowly, then growled. "Shit!"

He leaned against a locker, gulping air like I always did during my anxiety attacks. I wondered if I should get him some water. Slowly though, his breathing returned to normal.

Gently, I repeated, "I know it's not true."

That didn't seem to comfort him as much as I would have liked. In fact, it offered no comfort at all. He worked his jaw, gnawing the inside of his cheek. "But *they* don't. They all think I'm… Shit, shit, shit." He jammed his hands in his pockets and looked at me. "What do I do, Vic?"

"You ignore them," I said.

He didn't say anything after that, retreating deep inside himself for a minute. I stood there awkwardly, wondering what else I could do to make this better for him. Finally, I said, "I'm sorry. I thought you should know."

He startled, as if surprised to see me there. "No, I'm glad you told me."

Gratitude flashed on his face for a split second, but it was gone before I could bask in it.

"I'm nice to everyone, and *this* is how they repay me," he murmured, almost to himself. He swallowed, then composed himself. "I can fix this. Tryouts next Monday. You ready?"

"What?" Truthfully I hadn't thought of *Macbeth* for weeks. There was no way in hell I was trying out. "I'm not—"

"You *are*," he said. "One hundred percent."

"I-I can't." I stammered.

He said, "Look. I'll be Macbeth. You do Lady Macbeth. You can help me with my lines."

I stared at him, incredulous. "You can't be Macbeth. Quincy is always the lead."

Z said, "That's OK. He can play Banquo or one of the three witches or something."

You had to admire his confidence, especially not five minutes after learning the whole school was spreading rumors behind his back. "But—"

"Competition is healthy." He grinned. "That's why I really need help practicing my lines. Can you help me? Today. After school. In the gym. I'll drive you home."

I nodded instinctively. The idea of helping him, of basking in his gratitude... Even then, I craved his adoration like a drug. I don't know when it became something I'd betray you for, Andrew.

CHAPTER 18

*So who would you say was his best friend? Who
    knew Z best?*
No one. As friendly as he was, he only let people
    in so far. He was still an outsider, the subject
    of rumors.
So he had secrets?
Yeah. He didn't talk about himself a lot. When he did,
    you never knew if he was being serious or not.
*So it's possible he had a whole other life you
    knew nothing about?*
More than possible. It was assumed.

—Police interview with Rachel Watson,
junior at St. Ann's

THAT AFTERNOON, INSTEAD OF RUNNING for the bus, I
ran to the gym, which is also St. Ann's theater. I hadn't seen
Z since his doctor's appointment. It had only been three hours,
and yet my chest ached with anticipation. I knew that feeling
wasn't familiar, but I thought maybe that was how all friends are

supposed to feel. Maybe it was normal to ache for someone you cared about.

Maybe I had never really cared enough before.

But I didn't know. I mean, I cared about you, Andrew. So why did everything feel so different?

The gym was mostly dark when I sat, dangling my feet off the stage. I pulled out a copy of *Macbeth* that I'd taken from English class and opened it to one of Lady Macbeth's parts, reading it in the dim light.

> *Come, you spirits*
> *That tend on mortal thoughts, unsex me here,*
> *And fill me from the crown to the toe top-full*
> *Of direst cruelty.*

For a moment I imagined myself on that stage, in a velvet gown and with all eyes on me. I imagined my words, unusually loud and fraught with emotion, cutting through the silence of the theater. I imagined myself bringing the audience to tears with my performance. Z and me, arm in arm, bowing countless times in response to the standing ovation, and when the curtain finally swung closed, him turning to me with a look of awe and saying, "Wow, Vic. You were phenomenal."

Yeah. Like that would ever happen.

I repeated Lady Macbeth's Act One soliloquy over and over until the words were more mine than hers. Until I thought that maybe, just maybe, I could be her.

The wheels on the janitor's trash can squealed. I looked up

just as he turned out the lights in the auditorium, throwing me into darkness.

I checked the display on my phone. It was three forty-five. Z was later than he'd been for the movie.

I barely made the late bus home. Otherwise I would've had to call my dad to pick me up on his way home from work and spend a maddening forty-five-minute ride home enduring a parental inquisition.

Maybe I should have felt used or upset, but I worried about Z. Had everything gone OK at the doctor's? Was he still stewing over the rumors about him?

When I got home, my mom had dinner waiting, tuna pockets she got from the school's latest fund-raiser. The three of us said our prayers and then my mom asked, "How'd your meeting go with Father Leary?"

Dread settled over me. "Oh, I forgot," I mumbled, head down.

"Forgot?" The word exploded out of my mom's mouth. I didn't have to look to know my parents were exchanging worried glances.

"I…" I tried to think of an excuse but had nothing.

"Where were you?" my mother pushed.

"I was helping a friend rehearse for *Macbeth* tryouts. Sorry."

"I'll call Father Leary tonight," my dad said. "Maybe he can fit you in tomorrow."

I sighed. "Can't I skip this week? I'm fine. I have nothing to talk about." I forced a smile to show them how fine I was.

Again, a tennis match of worried glances. Silence. I'd won.

Mom and Dad started to talk about some fund-raiser at the church, and I smiled and nodded and said yes and no at all the appropriate moments, even though I had no clue what we were talking about.

I wondered if I should text Z. Everything else seemed so inconsequential, considering he could be in major trouble. Maybe he would text me when he could, to apologize for not showing.

I really don't know what we talked about when I met you at our spot, Andrew, and I'm sorry for that. I was preoccupied with my phone that was sitting on the grass beside me. It was silent, though I tried willing the screen to light up with his text.

The more time that passed, the more frustrated I got. When it finally began to drizzle, I told you I had to go and ran inside. I hadn't said more than five words. I could've told you I was worried about him, but I was afraid you'd take my concern the wrong way.

Funny, back then, I kept Z a secret from you because I wanted to protect you from feeling hurt. But who was I really protecting?

When I got to my room, I texted Z. I wanted to yell at him for blowing me off, but he'd had a hard day. He didn't need me giving him more crap. So I finally wrote: You OK?

I turned up the volume extra-loud.

No response.

The rest of the evening I kept my phone in my hand. I even told my parents to turn down the *Family Feud* rerun they were watching on television because there were entirely too many sounds in it that sounded like an incoming text.

My father looked up from the television. "Is everything OK?"

"Yes, why wouldn't it be?" I snapped.

He swallowed. Then he leaned over, dipping the blinds and looking into the backyard. "Why were you outside before? Is everything all right?"

I peered through the window beside him. You were still out there, standing in your yard now, watching our back door. I'd been inside for at least a half hour. I rolled my eyes and lied, "Andrew and I just had a fight."

He looked at me, then my mother. "About what?"

"Nothing." He turned off the television and set down the remote. My mother set down her romance novel. The silence was deafening. They stood up and moved to the kitchen table, pulling out my chair, getting ready for *a talk*. That was so *not* what I needed right then. I backed away.

My father said, "Can you talk to us? We're worried that this thing with Andrew might be getting serious."

Serious? I nearly laughed. They knew you. We'd known each other for almost a decade, and *now* things were getting serious?

"Dad." I forced my voice to be extra-cheerful so he'd quit with the third degree. "It's not serious. Believe me. We're fine."

I yawned and told them I needed to crash. But I didn't. Well, I went to bed, but I don't think I slept at all. I kept my phone on the pillow beside me, right near my hand so I could grab it the second a message came through.

But Z didn't respond.

CHAPTER 19

Is it possible he was engaging in illicit activities?

Like…

Drugs, for instance. A secret relationship. That sort of thing.

Nah. Not Z. We played ball together, so he knew we'd get random drug tests. And the ball schedule is nuts. We didn't have time for any kind of real relationship. Add in *Macbeth*… No, man. He wouldn't have time for illicit shit.

You know that for sure?

Nothing's for sure with Z. Good guy, the best, but hell, he's an actor. You never could quite tell what was fact and what was fiction.

—Police interview with Roger Falcon,
junior at St. Ann's

Z DIDN'T SHOW UP TO SCHOOL on Friday either.

I sent him another text that morning, trying to force away the feelings of desperation and helplessness that clawed at me. It was normal for friends to text each other, right? To see how they're doing?

By lunch, there was still no answer.

At prayer, I prayed for him. I imagined thousands of different scenarios for why he hadn't texted me back, many involving his injury or death. After all, he was attached to his phone, a texting addict. Why else wouldn't he respond?

Maybe he'd lost his phone. Maybe he didn't have the money to get a new one. I wanted to believe that was more likely than him being dead. I replayed our last conversation over and over in my head so I could dissect the words. He'd been upset over the rumors. Was he lying in a sloppy heap in his bed, depressed and unable to face the world? No. That wasn't Z.

He'd been on his way to the doctor. Maybe he'd learned he had three months to live. If it had been anyone else, I probably wouldn't have cared. After all, he'd only been silent a day. Instead, I tore apart every word, every gesture, trying to come up with an explanation. When chemistry came around, I had to pair up with you-know-who for another lab.

"Z's not here again," Parker mused. "Where could he be?"

I ignored her and continued to write in my notebook.

She sat down beside me and leaned in so close that I could smell her perfume. It smelled like cake but somehow nauseated me. "You mean, you don't know? I thought you two were besties."

I tried to ignore her. "I have no idea."

She stood up and sashayed around the table in her four-inch, completely not-regulation heels. "That is shocking," she said, pretending to fan herself. "Wait, did you get angry when you found out he was doing his aunt? Did you think he was your boyfriend?"

I couldn't stop myself. I threw down my pen. "He's not doing anything with his aunt, OK? And he's not my boyfriend. He's been sick."

Parker rested her chin in her hands. "Too sick for school. Not too sick to bowl?" She gave Rachel a questioning look.

"What," I said.

"We saw him at the bowling alley last night," she said, checking her manicure. "He looked fine."

I stared at her. Z was at the bowling alley last night? It was one thing if she'd seen him at the mall. He could have been picking up cough syrup at the pharmacy. But I could think of no reason why he'd blow me off to go to the bowling alley. There had to be an explanation. *Had to.*

I waited, but it didn't come to me.

I reached for my purse and swung it over my shoulder, then hurried to the front of the room. Mr. Lincoln watched me as I grabbed the bathroom pass. "Everything OK?"

I mumbled a response and raced to the lavatory. *Bowling.* I'd been worried he was lying dead somewhere, and all the while, he'd been *bowling.* He hadn't told me, hadn't asked me if I wanted to go. He hadn't even had the courtesy to tell me, his Precious, that he was OK. Sure, maybe his phone was lost or broken, but I wouldn't be able to ask him because now I wouldn't see him again until Monday. If then. The weekend seemed to stretch before me, dull and endless.

I'd never been so unhappy that it was Friday.

CHAPTER 20

Someone mentioned Victoria changed during her junior year. What was your daughter's motivation for her self-improvement?

She was feeling better about herself. Gaining friends and self-esteem. We were happy for her. She was feeling good about herself, becoming less anxious.

Was she on anxiety medication?

Yes. She was jittery in certain situations and took pills occasionally to help combat it, but as the fall semester went on, she was taking fewer and fewer of them. We hadn't had to fill her prescription in more than a month.

Do you know why she was feeling better?

No, but she talked about her friends. We thought it was probably her new boyfriend.

Z?

Yes.

And how did you feel about her dating?

We were so happy she was finally being accepted. We
   wanted her to bring him home for dinner.

And did she?

No.

Why?

She always said he was too busy.

Did she talk about him a lot?

Victoria never was one to discuss things openly with
   us, even before Z came into the picture. She tried
   to avoid our questions, typical teenager behavior.

Has Victoria ever been a typical teenager though?

No, no she hasn't. But even atypical teenagers don't
   often have heart-to-hearts with their parents.

—Police interview with Eric Zell,
father of Victoria Zell

Saturday morning, I went for a run all the way
down Route 11. I'd thought about jogging past Z's house,
but that was nearly three miles away. I'd be a sweaty mess by the
time I got there, so I ran to near the Kissing Woods and back,
which is more like two miles each way.

I hate the Kissing Woods, or the Killing Woods, as they're
better known now. When I was a kid, I thought it was a romantic place, and it probably used to be. That's how it got its name
after all. People used to go there to hook up. At night it's eerie
and dark, even on the most moonlit nights, and noises echo like
the moans of the dead. Or so the stories go. Like the one about
a girl who'd been murdered there when we were nine or ten?

Remember that ghost story we used to tell each other whenever we'd camp in the backyard, Andrew? She'd been stabbed to death and dismembered, her identity still a mystery. It's no wonder I didn't like going by those woods, even during the day.

You'd never been afraid of that place, but everyone else sure was.

I'd started running every morning after I went to the movies with Z and had already lost ten pounds, not that anyone had noticed. Usually, running made me feel good. I hoped those exercise endorphins would kick in and help me forget that I hadn't heard from Z since Thursday, but they never did. After my run, I huddled under my covers for the rest of the day. Of course, my phone stayed within arm's reach because I still had a tiny glimmer of hope that he'd get a new phone and text me.

It wouldn't have taken much to deliver me out of my deep funk. An I'm fine would have done it.

But he didn't text.

I cursed him for not thinking enough of me to take the time to let me know he was OK. Then I cursed myself for putting so much importance on a text. Then I popped two more Ativan, hoping they would numb the part of my brain that missed him, but they just numbed everything else.

On Sunday morning, I told my parents I was sick. My mother pressed her hand against my forehead like she usually did and pursed her lips. "You don't feel warm. Is it…" She looked around the room, as if I'd left the explanation on the night table.

"I feel like I'm going to throw up," I explained.

They left for church without me. After they'd gone, I heard your dad yelling and throwing things. Because our duplexes share a wall, I hear almost too much of what happens in your house. Your mother was crying again too, desperate sobs that floated into my open window on the crisp autumn air. Minutes later, you rapped on my door, two short knocks and a long one. I ran into the hallway, stood at the top of the staircase, and peered out the semicircle window at the top of the door. All I could see from that angle were the top of your head and your ears, which were red. The blood always rushes to your ears whenever you're upset or embarrassed.

You'd sometimes escape to my house when your dad got into one of his moods. We'd never talk about it—we'd just play Sorry! or Clue and wait for him to calm down. Sometimes you'd talk about running away, but whenever we talked about where or how, you cringed as if you were swallowing nails. Even so, several times it'd gotten so bad that we'd started down Route 11 together. But we never got far. You'd start thinking in practical terms of the wide, cruel world and how it would most likely chew up and spit out a kid like you. An hour later, you'd go home and the storm would've blown over.

I was your sanctuary. But that Sunday, you found no sanctuary. I wasn't there for you.

I flattened myself against the wall so you wouldn't peer in the window and see me. You probably thought I was out with my parents. Instead, I was wallowing in my own misery, feeling sorry for myself, like a bratty kid.

I wanted a sanctuary too. It used to be you, Andrew. And

now…now things were different. You no longer had that magic ability to make everything all right. I realized, as I sat there praying you'd go away, that all the things that used to make me happy didn't work anymore. I needed something more, with a desire I couldn't explain or control.

And I was fucking scared.

I'm sorry to use that language. But I was.

By evening, I'd spent ninety percent of the day lying in bed with my head under a pillow, coming down only for bowls of cereal. During that time, my mother followed me around, peppering me with questions to diagnose my mysterious illness. I was hot, restless, uncomfortable. I went to bed early, knowing the sooner I did, the sooner I'd see Z at school the next day.

And then I heard a noise outside.

You know how I always keep my window open at least a crack. In the summers it's because we don't have air-conditioning, and in the winters, our heating system turns my room into a furnace. I thought it was a branch scraping against the cedar shingles. There it was again. By the third time I heard it, I knew it was my name.

Someone was whispering my name.

I checked my clock. Ten thirty-seven.

I thought it was you, Andrew. After all, who else would it be? I got the shock of a lifetime when I peeked between the blinds and saw Z standing in my backyard, on the patio below my window.

I opened the window carefully, so it wouldn't squeak and

wake my parents, and asked him what he was doing at my house in the middle of the night.

He said, "Is ten o'clock the middle of the night to you?"

Embarrassed, I started to explain that it was ten *thirty-seven*, but he was already climbing on top of the grill underneath my window. "Wait. What are you doing?"

"I need to talk to you."

I didn't think it was possible that anyone could climb up to my window. First of all, I'm not exactly Juliet, so guys don't do that on a regular basis. Second, I don't have a trellis, which would make scaling the walls of my house easier. But from the top of the grill, he latched on to the gutter drain and kicked his way up the pipe.

When it was clear he was coming in, I surveyed my room in the darkness. It was a total embarrassment. It was reasonably clean, but pink with posters of kittens and unicorns that I'd had since I was a kid and never gotten around to taking down. My dirty clothes were scattered on the floor. I was wearing my old sweats, the same ones I'd been wearing since Friday night. I probably smelled bad. Perfect.

He pulled himself in through my window, as if he'd been climbing into girls' rooms all his life. He slid in feetfirst and then just sat on the windowsill, not looking at me. I knew something was wrong. He wasn't smiling, and his breathing was uneven.

"What's going on with you?" I asked, my words coming out in a tumble. "Where have you been?"

He said very softly, "I'm sorry I missed you on Thursday. I had something else."

"Bowling?"

His eyes snapped to mine. "What?"

"Parker told me she saw you there."

He shook his head. "Yeah. It was a thing I had to do."

"Meaning what?"

He shut his lips tight.

"Why can't you tell me?"

He exhaled again. "Here's the thing. You work your whole life to be a certain person…and then circumstances force you to be someone else. Someone ugly. Someone you hate. I'm only dragging you down."

"But you don't just stand up a girl like that," I persisted. "I told you, I never believed—"

"I know. I just… Hear me out." He ran his hands through his hair. "Everywhere I go, it's the same. Nobody gets me."

It was a chilly night, and he was only wearing a T-shirt. He was trembling a little—from the cold? From anger?

"I get it," I said. "You're unpredictable so people won't figure you out. That's your big fear, isn't it? You don't want anyone too close to you. Because the people closest to you have all let you down. And you're afraid of being let down again."

Z looked into my eyes. "See? You…you get me."

I nodded. I was glad it was dark because I was sure I had tears in my eyes. "Yeah. People have a knack for disappointing."

He smiled, a faint, barely there smile. "You're the only one I trust."

The only one he trusts. My heart swelled. I opened my mouth to say something meaningful. Instead it just slipped out:

"It's better not to trust anyone."

He looked at me, surprised. "You have issues with that too, huh? You don't even trust that talented boyfriend of yours?"

I hated it when he brought you up in such a teasing way. I opened my mouth to tell him that it was none of his business, but he reached out and touched my arm, sending a shock straight to my heart. I took a step back.

He said, "See you, Precious," swung his legs out my window, and disappeared into the darkness without as much as a thud when he hit the ground, leaving me to wonder if it was all a dream.

The truth was, I was far from figuring Z out. Maybe I'd peeled back one of his layers, but I knew there were many more. He was as frustrating as a necklace with a knot, the kind that the more you try to figure it out, the more hopelessly tangled it becomes.

CHAPTER 21

The body of a teenaged male was found in a wooded area near Route 11 in Duchess. A needle was found in the woods near the victim. Victim died from acute heart failure brought on by injection of lethal substance(s), possibly self-inflicted. Full toxicology analysis to come.

—Coroner's report

I SPENT THE NEXT TWENTY-FOUR HOURS in a haze. My thoughts centered around Z and me, acting out every scene from every buddy movie ever made. Us together in a dizzying montage—holding colorful umbrellas and jumping through puddles, eating ice cream cones, him pushing me in a shopping cart through the parking lot at Shaw's, my arms spread in a victorious V above me… The whole time we'd be laughing like we'd been sniffing glue.

I would be lying if I said that my mind didn't wander toward what it would be like to kiss him. Would his lips feel like yours? But I figured that was simply an unfortunate, unavoidable side effect of being friends with a good-looking guy. And that's what this was: a platonic, noble friendship of the highest mutual respect. I felt so happy and grateful to have him in my life, my one true friend at St. Ann's.

When school ended on Monday, he pulled on my sleeve as I hitched my backpack onto my shoulder. "Let's go."

I liked that he was so familiar with me, that he didn't have to invite me somewhere, but just assumed we'd be together. "Where?" I asked, my insides whirring at the thought of another adventure.

He reached into his back pocket and pulled out a worn copy of *Macbeth*. "Did you forget?"

My stomach lurched. Very few obstacles would've stopped me from following him. This was one of them. "No. No, no, no," I said, my lower lip quivering.

"Yes. Yes, yes, yes," he mimicked, clamping his hand over my shoulder and steering me toward the auditorium.

"You don't understand. I didn't rehearse. At all." OK, that was a lie. I knew much of that soliloquy from the hour I'd spent waiting for him to show the week before. The truth was, I could pop Ativan until the end of time, and I still wouldn't be OK with taking the stage. "I really can't."

I expected him to argue, but he shrugged and said, "OK. Come and cheer me on."

That I was OK with. Relieved, I walked with him to the gymnasium, which had been set up with those uncomfortable metal chairs. The place was packed. I'd never been to an audition before, but I knew that they usually weren't a big draw.

Reese's offer to raise the grades of any performers had really done the trick.

We sat together, and I thought Z would rehearse his lines. He didn't. He just sat there, leaning back in his chair, as comfortable and relaxed as ever. Reese started with the main parts, so Macbeth was first.

She called Quincy. He got up in front of everyone, and wow. He read the part like he'd been practicing it all his life. He didn't falter, and his voice was fraught with emotion. As he spoke, I kept sneaking glances at Z to see if sweat had begun to appear on his forehead. But Z just watched, his composure never melting. When the audition ended, the cavernous room erupted into applause. Who knew there were so many Quincy groupies? Quincy bowed, smiling widely, and jumped from the stage, giving the people nearest the center aisle high fives. He sat in the back row with a bunch of his thespian friends, basking in his win.

I don't think Quincy knew someone else was vying for his role. Nobody had ever challenged the great Quincy Laughlin before. The kid was an acting machine. Like, you knew he probably had posters of great performances on his bedroom walls, and when he dreamed, he did it in scenes. He was the one person at St. Ann's who'd probably be suicidal over not having the lead in the school play. So when Mrs. Reese called Z's name, Quincy's smile faded. He watched Z climb onto the stage. Quincy's face turned pink, and his lips moved slightly. He was probably chanting to himself, *I'm still the best. I'm still the best. No one can beat me.*

And maybe he believed it…until Z opened his mouth. I knew

the soliloquy—who didn't? It was the famous "Is this a dagger I see before me?" speech from the second act. His voice took on such uncharacteristic weakness and indecision that my eyes welled unexpectedly. As he went on, every movement, every breath Z took, convinced me that he was Macbeth, even though he was still wearing his St. Ann's polo and gray slacks. Z finished the scene on his knees, his fists clenched in agony. This was the guy the entire school had been spreading horrible rumors about—and what a way to sock it to them! To laugh in their faces!

My chest swelled as he looked up at the audience and loosened his posture. An unprecedented silence filled the room. Even the noisy clock seemed to stop ticking. I looked around, and just about everyone was sitting there stunned, their jaws hanging slightly open.

Then the applause came. It was a thunderous sound that room might never have heard in all its sixty years.

Z jumped from the stage and sauntered back to me. "Was that OK?" he asked.

"Um. Yeah," I mumbled, barely coherent. He had to have noticed the tears in my eyes. "I mean, whoa. You're good. Have you acted before?"

He shook his head. "Why?"

The entire room was abuzz over his magnificent performance. People turned to look at him, maybe wondering if it was too premature to ask him for his autograph. Quincy's face was now completely red—he looked as if he'd just seen the curtain go down on his life's purpose.

Nobody else dared audition for the role of Macbeth after

that. I was still in a daze when Reese said, "Now let's move on to the auditions for Lady Macbeth. Victoria?" And then she turned to me.

Everyone did.

Oh hell…

I looked at Z. "You didn't."

He batted his eyelashes innocently.

"I *can't*," I growled.

This time, instead of being easygoing, he grabbed me by the shoulders, stood me up, and nudged me into the center aisle.

Apparently, I get vicious when pushed to the point of certain humiliation. Panic overtook me. I lost control of my body and voice. "I will kill you," I whispered to him, but he just grinned in that way that made it impossible to hate him. The stage started to go blurry before me. I attempted to step in its direction, but instead took a step backward. My lips felt like Jell-O. How would I get them to form actual words? Then I noticed Parker and Rachel in the front of the auditorium, heads together, snickering.

They were laughing at me.

I felt like someone had launched a cannonball at my chest. I couldn't breathe. The urge to flee grabbed me with both hands, and I turned on my heel and rushed out of the gymnasium and into the girls' bathroom.

In a stall, I wiped my forehead with a wad of toilet paper and took some deep breaths. Stupid me. Z was probably out there with his adoring audience in all his thespian glory, thinking how sad and pathetic and unworthy I was. I stared at myself in the mirror, wondering why I had to be so weird. Then I summoned my courage and made the decision to tell Z that it wasn't possible, that my body just couldn't do the many magnificent things his could, and I was so sorry if it meant we could no longer be friends.

I stepped into the hallway. Z was there. "What happened?" he asked.

"I-I don't *do* that, you understand?" I snarled at him. "I don't like people looking at me like that."

"OK, easy," he said, trying to calm me. "You...actually *like* being on the sidelines? Seriously?"

He said it as if it just occurred to him, like he was just realizing for the first time that I wasn't the outgoing person he was. I nodded.

Z snapped his fingers and said, "That's too bad. We could have made the ultimate dysfunctional couple."

Couple? My mind stuck on that word. Me and Z, a couple? I glanced through the open gymnasium doors from my spot in the hallway as Parker Cole took the stage and began to speak the part of Lady Macbeth.

I crept toward the gymnasium, listening. Compared to Z, she was awful. Anyone else would have paled in comparison, but she *really* paled. She missed an entire line in the soliloquy. (It was the one I'd practiced, so I knew it well.) She had to check her lines twice. I think she was chewing gum. She kept sweeping her hair out of her eyes and stood as stiff as a board the whole time.

How dare she? Auditioning for a role that would put her

close to Z? Of course, that's what she was after. Not the grade, not the adoration. She certainly wasn't in love with the stage like Quincy. The vulture wanted Z.

When it was over, Parker's admirers applauded, and she curtsied with great flourish and blew kisses. And then…

Then, she looked straight back to the gymnasium doors, right at Z, and licked her lips.

That was it. I was done for.

"Is anyone else interested in auditioning for Lady Macbeth?" Reese asked, looking around the room.

I could have just walked out, gone home, given up, resolved to experience *Macbeth* from the comfort of the audience. But as I watched ethereal Parker Cole flounce back to her chair and give a double thumbs-up to Rachel, a fire ignited in me. She always got everything and everyone she wanted. And if I wasn't careful, she would probably dig her talons into Z too. She'd chew him up and spit him out the way she'd done to a hundred other boys.

I pushed past Z. "Here!" I shouted so loudly that everyone turned.

I went up to the stage. My knees wobbled, and sweat broke out in places I never knew could perspire. By the time I got to the stage's stairs, I was a shaky, sweaty mess. I climbed them slowly. I hated that everyone was watching me. And yet, here I was.

I'm saving Z, I told myself. *He'll thank me for this.*

The next three minutes were a blur. I muttered the soliloquy I'd practiced in a soft monotone, and meanwhile, people in the chairs talked, did homework, went on with their lives. I did not hold anyone's rapt attention like Z had. I stuttered several words. But I didn't forget the lines. And when I finished, the world didn't end. As I left the stage, some people clapped politely.

Z clapped too, and he wasn't ashamed to be seen with me after my performance, which was a plus. He smiled. "See, you are a natural. You'll get it for sure."

I said, "You think so? You don't think Parker was better?"

He leaned back and yawned. "No way." He grinned and patted my head. "Oh, Vic. My innocent little starlet. I refuse to let fame corrupt you."

I adored him so completely then. My heart was beating so loud that I could barely hear my own voice. But inside, it'd already begun to dawn on me. I'd done what I'd previously thought was impossible—without dying and without my magical anxiety pills. A new sense of power surged through my veins. I'd transformed into a determined beast. I *would* get that part. Or…I don't know what. But at that moment, I'd never been so sure I wanted something and was willing to do anything to get it.

Z tapped me on the knee. "Let's get out of here," he said. "They won't announce who got the roles until tomorrow. I'll drive you home."

I nodded and followed him, feeling an unfamiliar sense of power at having stepped out of my comfort zone. But even my euphoria couldn't stop me from glancing around for Parker. I didn't see her, but I would have liked to think she was watching me, for once wishing she could trade places with me.

"I can't believe I did that," I murmured numbly as we stepped into the dusky, warm afternoon.

Z just laughed as we walked across the lot to his Honda Civic. "You're going to be famous."

I shook my head. Not possible. People at school barely knew my name.

He unlocked the door with his remote, and we both climbed into his car. "You don't think so? Why not?"

"Because I'm not like that. I'm more of a behind-the-scenes person."

He screwed up his face. He was always the center of attention, so I knew he had no idea what that was like. "Well, that's no fun."

"I'm OK with it," I said.

"Probably because you're just used to it. Playing it safe." He pretended to snore.

I'd only been in his car a handful of times, but I'd already begun to adjust to Z's way of driving. He'd be going a leisurely pace, and the next moment, he'd be up the ass of the car in front of him. At first I hated it…never knowing whether to lean back and relax or brace myself. But this time I was prepared. Like I'd gotten comfortable with being uncomfortable.

He said, "Maybe you'd like being center stage."

"I don't think so."

"You've never tried," he singsonged. "Have you?"

I didn't answer. He already knew what my reply would be.

We stopped at a light. He took his hand off the gearshift and plopped it right on my knee.

His hand was warm on my bare skin. I froze. "Um. What are you doing?"

His big eyes widened. He didn't move his hand. "What? Nothing."

"Your hand?"

He began to massage my knee, moving up to the hem of my skirt. This was more dangerous than the movie theater incident because I was wearing my too-short, pleated St. Ann's skirt. I wanted to tell him not to, but all the same, I thought, *It's just my knee. A knee is like an elbow. There's nothing remotely wrong about touching someone's elbow.* And I liked it. I liked the way his hand felt on my bare skin. It felt protective.

"So, why have you never tried to be center stage?" he murmured. "You're nervous, is that it? You think there's something wrong with you?"

I didn't answer. I mean, obviously. And not only that— what the hell were we talking about? I couldn't even think.

"Vic, calm down. Relax, all right? You're perfect." He let out a tortured kind of groan. I didn't know I could have that effect on anyone, much less him. "*This* is perfect."

Perfect. Yeah. As scary as it was, he was right. Being with him was also strangely perfect. He let his fingers trail circles on my skin, which was a field of goose bumps. Then he had to downshift. Before the warmth from his hand had faded, his hand was back, even higher on my leg this time.

Over the whip of the wind and roar of the engine, I heard a whisper float from his mouth. I would have recognized it anywhere, but his playful tone threw me off. *Oh my God, I am heartily sorry for having offended Thee, and I detest all my sins because I dread the loss of Heaven and the pains of Hell.*

He pulled into my driveway, nearly rear-ending my parents' SUV, then removed his hand and looked at me over the rims of his dark sunglasses. "Amen. See you, Lady M."

I shivered as I opened the door. I mean, way to jinx things. I didn't even have the part yet, and I wasn't even sure I wanted it. "Stop it."

He leaned over to look at me as I got out. "Now why would I do that, Vic?"

I meant to slam the door, but the way he was looking at me so seriously, I nearly missed the door as I bumped it with my hip. It closed with a soft thud. "Huh?" I said through the open window.

"I have no intention of stopping, Precious," he said as he threw the car into reverse, "because I think you'd like being center stage. And I believe it's my mission to get you to try it."

CHAPTER 22

You were in the play, correct? The Friday before the incident?

Yep.

Z was there.

He had the lead role. Turns out he was quite the thespian.

You sound bitter.

Oh no. I enjoy some healthy competition now and then.

Did he get along with everyone in the cast?

It's hard to imagine him not getting along with anyone.

And what about Victoria Zell?

Victoria? Oh, you mean Lady Macbeth.

Yes. What was their relationship outside of the play?

None.

None?

Quite honestly, I don't know. That girl was a bit of an enigma. We thespians have a few screws loose, for certain. So she probably could've fit in. But she kept to herself.

*So they didn't have a relationship, or you didn't know
    about it?*

Well, it wouldn't be the first time Z surprised me. I
    think he quite liked to surprise people.

—Police interview with Quincy Laughlin,

senior at St. Ann's

THE THOUGHT OF GETTING THE part of Lady Macbeth both thrilled and terrified me. I was scared stiff at the thought of performing in front of an audience, but at the same time, I could imagine a scene where, in the heat of the moment, Macbeth pulls Lady Macbeth into an embrace and delivers a passionate kiss. I wondered how Z kissed, if he did it perfectly, the way he did everything else. I knew that would be my only way to experience it—on the stage, as part of a performance, since we were both attached to other people.

Andrew, I knew you wouldn't mind, as a fan of the stage. And I also knew that Parker and a slew of other girls at school would probably jump at the chance to be kissed by Z. They'd all be so jealous! Still, my palms got all sweaty because kissing a person was scary enough—but kissing Z? In front of all those people? Then I started to wonder... *Was* there even a make-out scene in *Macbeth*? Maybe I was spending all this time worrying about it for nothing.

For the rest of the night, I kept thinking of his hand on my knee. How nice it felt, in a protective, big brother way. I wondered if he liked it too. I went to sleep repeating his last words over and over to myself: *I think you'd like being center stage, and it's my mission to get you to try it.* I tried to get the play out of my head, but couldn't. In my nightmares, Parker got the part, and I had to watch her making out with Z.

So a combination of emotions flooded me the next morning when I walked past the gymnasium doors and saw my name posted on the very top of the page, right under Z's. Relief. Excitement. Fear.

I'd gotten the part.

I was going to play Lady Macbeth, and Z would be playing my husband.

I walked to class that morning in a daze. For once in my life, I'd topped Parker. For once in her life, the principal's perfect daughter wouldn't be getting everything she wanted. I couldn't believe it.

Z was uncharacteristically early. When I arrived in the classroom, he was already there. Usually I was the one waiting for him. I beamed at him. "I can't believe it," I said, still numb.

For some reason, Z looked nervous. "I can. I told you. I knew you'd get it," he said in a monotone, staring at his phone.

I'd assumed that after he'd earned the lead, he'd be a little happier. "Congratulations to you too," I said.

He kept thumbing his phone and murmured, "On what?" Then his mouth opened and he looked up. "Oh, right. Thanks."

"You're not happy? Quincy's probably crying into his breakfast somewhere."

He looked up. "It's hardly worth getting worked up over, either way. It's a fucking school play."

"Oh." My excitement fizzled. Right. It was just a stupid school play. It wasn't Broadway. "Then why'd you try out?"

He shrugged, looking back at his phone. "Why not?"

What had happened to the playful and flirtatious Z who had dropped me off the night before? *I think you'd like it better center stage.*

As if he could read my thoughts, he smiled. "Ah, little Vic. Sorry. I don't mean to be an asshole. Just…" He tapped his phone. "There is so much of the wide world you know nothing about."

My cheeks reddened. I thought about what he'd said: *It's my mission to get you to try it.* Try what? Why did he have to be so cryptic? "You could maybe fill me in," I suggested.

He opened his mouth to reply, but the bell rang.

Reese glided into the room. She said, "I'm sure the news is all over the school, but in case you haven't heard, Z and Victoria will be playing Macbeth and Lady Macbeth in the play!" She'd never sounded quite so excited before. I doubted the news was all over the school. Maybe in her warped world it would have been, but aside from Quincy and a few others, the vast majority of students at St. Ann's could give a rat's ass about drama. Reese clapped her hands together and extended her hands, presenting us like we were refrigerators on *The Price is Right.* "Congratulate them!"

The class turned and mumbled halfhearted congratulations. Most of them looked at Z, not me. Roger Falcon, a baseball jock, high-fived Z. A girl in the front of the room cheered, "Go, Z!" The only person who really paid any attention to me was Parker. Her glare lingered on me for what seemed like hours.

Reese went on and on about what a performance it was going to be, and how talented this year's cast was, and—for a split second—I thought that things might be different between us. That Reese might treat me the way she treated Z.

That didn't last. A few minutes into the lesson, she called on me to define *eleemosynary* and gave me a glare that rivaled Parker's when I drew a complete blank.

Somehow, I'd thought that being Z's friend would make me visible. That being next to him would finally put me on the map and make people who once detested or ignored me give me a second chance.

So far, that was not the case.

Now, instead of liking me because *he* liked me, they were almost more wary of me.

But that was OK. They were just jealous. Like Parker.

I was prepared for more icy glares from her during chemistry. And I got them. But I ignored them. What I didn't understand though was when she leaned over at the end of class while I was gathering my books and whispered, "He bought Reese."

Before I could ask Parker what that meant, she was gone.

CHAPTER 23

Let's talk about the incident that happened at the theater during dress rehearsals. What was the atmosphere like?

It was tense. Some of the cast were sour about the selections for the main roles. There was talk of roles being bought.

Bought? From Mrs. Reese?

It was no secret Reese played favorites. But why she chose Victoria Zell as Lady Macbeth was pretty much beyond anyone's guess.

Victoria was not a favorite of Mrs. Reese?

Not really. There was a core group of us who lived for the stage, and she wasn't part of that.

Was Z?

No...but his tryout was singular. No one thought he bought his way in, but they certainly thought she might have.

—Police interview with Quincy Laughlin,
senior at St. Ann's

I T WAS THE WEEK BEFORE Halloween, and my mother had put purple lights all over the fence on our side of the duplex. They cast an eerie, supernatural glow on the yard. My dad had taken to putting the trash cans where I always put my backside, but I moved them out of the way and slid down into my place against the fence. Then I told you I'd gotten the part.

You, of course, were shocked. It was like the Little Mermaid going out for track. You stuttered, "W-why?"

I told you that it was for the grade. I told you that I needed all the help I could get in English, which was true. "I can't believe I got it though," I said. "Parker auditioned, and I even beat her out."

"Parker *Cole*? The principal's kid?" you asked. You'd heard me complaining about how perfect she was, how the entire world revolved around her. Usually when I did, you would try to boost my mood with compliments. But this time, you just went, "Huh."

The shock in your voice kind of annoyed me. "What?" I snapped, chewing on my Juicy Fruit.

"It's just so unlike you, Vic," you said. "You don't usually step out like that."

I said, "Well, maybe I wanted to try something different." I shoved my hands into my pockets. "And it turns out I'm good at acting."

You were silent for a long time, taking it in, I guess. "Wow, my girlfriend. The actress." Another long silence passed. Then you said, "Of course you're good at it, Vic."

We stood up. I came around the side of the fence and you

hugged me. That's when you said, "Is that why you're running every morning?"

"What?" I didn't think you'd noticed. But you must have seen me from your bedroom window, leaving the house early each morning.

"To try something different." You leaned against the picket fence, the little twinkling, purple lights casting an unnatural glow on your pale face as you scratched at your temple. "Because correct me if I'm wrong, but I seem to remember you telling me that the only reason to run is when something with pointy teeth is chasing you."

I laughed. You were right. I had said that.

You took me by the hand and made me twirl like a dancer as you inspected me. I'd lost maybe fifteen pounds by then. "Trying new things is *definitely* working for you."

"Thanks," I said, blushing. "I actually like running. I'm lifting weights too. I like not feeling weak."

I made a bicep and you felt it. "Impressive. Let's face it. I have a hot girlfriend."

Hot. I'd never imagined I'd be described as that.

You smiled, but there was a hint of sadness in your eyes. Like you knew I was growing apart from you, and there was nothing you could do to bring me back.

CHAPTER 24

Two Duchess residents were arrested for possession
of crystal meth.

William Blanchette, 30, and Bethany Lynn Montez,
26, are being charged with possession of a
controlled substance. The two were taken into
custody on Tuesday as part of an ongoing investigation, according to Piscataquis County Sheriff
Van Elkins.

Elkins said a search warrant was executed for
Blanchette's and Montez's residence, 1465
Maine Highway 11, Duchess. "We seized 15
grams of ice, or crystal methamphetamine, and
two firearms," Thomas said. "One was a 45mm
pistol. The second was a 12-gauge shotgun.
Various other drug production paraphernalia
was obtained."

—*Central Maine Express Times*

THE NEXT WEEK, WE HAD play rehearsals after school.

Since Z had fall ball to think about, I asked him if he would be there for all of our scheduled rehearsals, and he said that he would. He said something about being there with bells on, *all* over his body, and then winked suggestively.

But he never showed.

Sure, it was exasperating, never knowing what to expect from him. But at the same time, that was part of his appeal. And he knew it. He liked making people guess.

We all sat on the edge of the stage as Mrs. Reese introduced each of us and the parts we would be playing. A lot of us kept glancing at the door, waiting for the last, all-important actor to show.

When Mrs. Reese got to the end of introductions, she looked up and around. "Where's Z?" she asked over her bifocals, tapping her script.

We all shrugged. Then Mrs. Reese shrugged and muttered, "Well, that's not good," and marked something on her clipboard.

Without him there, I was out-of-my-mind nervous. The confidence boost I'd gotten from beating out Parker had already faded, and I'd spent every evening since the casting announcement memorizing my lines in my room. I thought about asking Z to practice with me, but his mind was on fall ball. Most of his free time was spent huddled with the other jocks.

In the afternoons, I'd see him heading out in his baseball uniform, shirt opened and untucked over a clean, white undershirt that clung nicely to his defined chest, while he effortlessly tossed the ball into his glove. The uniform and baseball hat made him look, in Parker's words, "infinitely lickable," whatever that meant. I'm sure seeing him in action on the field would make him even more so. But I needed to practice my lines.

And he evidently didn't.

And now he wasn't even at rehearsal. I wondered if Reese would make a fuss and replace him with Quincy, who was already rolling his eyes at the disgrace of Z's absence. Instead, Reese just clapped her hands and had us practice the first scene, which didn't include Macbeth. And that was that.

Quincy had been given the part of MacDuff, Macbeth's main antagonist and killer, and though Parker didn't get a part— she was my understudy, which was a nice way of saying "better luck next year"—her best friend Rachel did. She was the gentle-woman, Lady Macbeth's caretaker, so we were in a lot of scenes together. I cringed whenever she walked near me because the looks she gave me were no nicer than the ones Parker kept shooting me from the wings. Part of the scene included Rachel pretending to powder my nose, and the first time, she punched me in the face as I was saying my line.

"Ow!" I shouted, pushing her arm away.

"My mistake," she said with a shrug. Then she did it again.

"Ow!" I said again.

Gentlewoman, my ass.

Reese was oblivious. "Victoria, *ow* is not in any of your lines."

I glared at Rachel and we started again. By the time we finished the scene, Rachel had shoved me once and elbowed me three times. My body ached. This was no way for the lead

actress to be treated. When Reese dismissed us, I went to the
water fountain. As I straightened after taking a gulp, Rachel was
standing beside me. "Where's Z?" she snapped.

I shrugged and tried to walk away, but she grabbed me by
the arm.

"He's going to ruin the play."

In many situations, I found myself wondering how Z would
react, what he would say. This time, I knew exactly how he would
respond. I rolled my eyes. "It's only a fucking school play."

Her eyes narrowed. "Why did you even try out for it
then?" she huffed. Then she smiled. "Oh, that's right. You're
his little right-hand girl."

I rolled my eyes again and started to push past her, but she
stopped me.

"Stop it with the high-and-mighty smirk. You don't really
think you got the part because you're so talented, do you?"

Really, I didn't think I was talented at all, but I'd beaten
Parker, fair and square. "I'm more talented than Parker, obviously."

"Because Reese picked you? Don't flatter yourself. Z got
her to choose you," she spat out.

I burst out laughing. "What? Is he sleeping with her too?"

"Fine. Don't believe me. Whatever," she said, walking away.

I wanted to be like Z and rise above the gossip, but for the
rest of the night, Rachel's words were all I could think of. In
fact, I missed meeting up with you because after I got home, I
had to rush and do my chemistry homework, then spent the rest
of the night staring at my dog-eared copy of *Macbeth* and wondering if Z *had* arranged for me to get the role. He'd been so

sure I was going to get it. He hadn't been surprised at all by the posting. That was typical of him, to be so cocky and sure, but... had he done something to ensure I got the part? Was it even possible to put a teacher—particularly a hard-nosed old lady like Reese—in his back pocket?

No, that was ridiculous.

But then I thought of the way Reese would smile at him.

I thought of Parker sneering at me earlier. *He bought her.* OK, yes, he did have an uncanny ability to make everyone a little giddy whenever he passed by. He had incited the whole school into a rumor-spreading frenzy, trying to figure out what made him tick. But his influence stopped there. It certainly didn't spread to teachers, and most definitely not to Reese.

Right?

I wasn't sleeping when pebbles tapped against my window that night. It was a moonless night, and I had to blink a few times to make sure it was not my imagination. But there he was, standing in my yard. Since his last visit, I'd taken to wearing nicer pajamas and not gunking white cream on my zits, just in case.

I checked my clock. 2:00 a.m. It really was the middle of the night this time. Turning on my bedside lamp, I checked my door—closed and locked.

When he climbed up, I started to say, "Where were you?" but his eyes were red-rimmed, like he'd been awake for hours upon hours. "What's going on?" I whispered.

"You ever just want to tell everyone to go to hell?" he muttered, looking at the ground.

"Why?"

"They're at it again, aren't they, spreading rumors about me that aren't true?"

"Well…"

He snorted. "I'm not a fucking sorcerer. I can't make people do things. And I didn't *make* Reese give you that part. They're out of their minds."

I relaxed and started to agree with him, that it was all a stupid misunderstanding, that they were just jealous of us for landing the lead roles. But he kept going, talking so fast I couldn't get a word in.

He said, "I told Reese that as an actor, I'd be more comfortable with you, and she agreed that was important. She was salivating to have me in the play, so I told her we were a package deal. I told her I wouldn't do it unless you were my Lady Macbeth, and she caved."

"Wait. What?"

He said, "You're not angry at me too? I mean, I did it for you. I think this will be good for you."

I cringed at the way he looked at me, like I was a defenseless three-year-old and he was my doting parent. "Because it'll get me *out there*?"

"Well, yeah. And because you told me English was your worst subject. Now you're guaranteed a good grade."

The heat rose to my cheeks.

"You're mad?" He threw up his hands. "Fuck."

"No, I'm not," I assured him. I wasn't mad. More like deflated. Embarrassed. What Rachel had told me was essentially true. I wasn't a great actress. Z had arranged the part for me. But looking at him with his eyes pleading, my heart softened. He'd done it for me. Because he wanted me to be happy. Did the rest even matter? "I… You didn't have to do that. I mean, thank you."

"Sorry I missed the first rehearsal. I was, you know…dealing with a bunch of shit you don't want to know about." He balled his hands into fists, then slowly uncurled them. "Part of me doesn't even want to be Macbeth if people think I bought my way in."

"You didn't buy *your* way in," I murmured. "Just mine."

"Oh, fuck it," he muttered. "The only reason Parker would have gotten the role is because her daddy pays Reese's salary. She blew and you knew it."

"I kind of…um…blew too."

"No, you were fine. She couldn't even remember a few lines. You deserved that part. No one should be getting worked up. I mean, it's a fucking school play." He waved his hand dismissively. He got up from his perch on the windowsill and walked to my bed, where the wrinkled sheets told the story of the restless night I'd had. He sat down on the corner of my bed, leaned back on his palms, and surveyed the walls. I'd already gotten rid of all my unicorn posters, so the walls were mostly bare—with little pinpoints where the tacks once were. "Nice room," he said.

"Thanks," I whispered.

He leaned over and picked up my weekly medication organizer. "What're these for?"

"Oh, I…" I tensed. Z wouldn't understand anxiety. He'd likely never had a nervous day in his life. "I take them for…

Sometimes I'm…" *Sometimes I need to take a shitload of pills to deal with the ordinary stress of everyday life that most people have no problem handling.* I bit my tongue.

He set the pill box down and waited. When I didn't say more, he said, "Sometimes you're what? Adorable?"

I blinked, shocked, and started to blush again. Did he really think that? "No, I…"

He grinned. "You are. Especially when you do that."

I covered my hot cheeks with my hands. This was not happening, was it? Maybe it was a dream.

I think Z could tell I was freaked out by him sitting on my bed. I mean, a guy on my bed? My parents would have loved that one. He stood up. "So, we're good?" he asked, hunching over a little to stare into my eyes. For some reason, I couldn't raise my chin from my chest. *He was on my bed.*

I nodded. "Are *you* OK though?"

"Yeah. Now that I've seen you," he said with a wink. "Thanks."

He tried to move around me. In the cramped space between the bed and the window, we wound up doing an awkward, close-but-not-touching dance until I slipped on one of my throw pillows. He caught me to steady me. So embarrassing.

"Whoa. Been drinking?" he teased.

"Um, been sleeping, actually."

"Oh. Right. Hey, I just remembered," he said, still holding on to one of my elbows as he snapped his fingers and reached into his back pocket. "I have something for you. Close your eyes and count to three."

I smiled. *Candy*, I thought. Another gift like he'd left in my locker. I closed my eyes and counted silently.

And then I felt his lips on mine.

I opened my eyes, startled. "What was that?"

His face turned a warm shade of red, a color he wore impeccably well, though I'd never seen him embarrassed before. "I... well... How about them Sox?" He gave me a *Well, that didn't go like I'd planned it* shrug. So he'd been planning on kissing me all this time? "I'd better go."

Instinctively, desperately, I reached out and grabbed the front of his shirt. "No, I mean, obviously, I know what that was. But why?"

He put his palms up. "I just thought, why not?"

"I wasn't expecting it. I..." I began to babble, but all the while a warm feeling was growing inside me. Z had *kissed* me. I hadn't known it was going to happen. And now it was over. Would I be able to remember exactly how it felt?

I know I should have been thinking about you, Andrew, about how kissing another guy was wrong. But it felt like a dream. Z in my room. On. My. Bed. So when he pulled me against him and said, "Well, now you *can* expect it. Because I'm going to do it again," I didn't stop him.

I put my fingertips on the stubbly side of his jaw, and when his lips met mine, they were warm and soft and so, so sweet.

I'm not going to say more, Andrew. You don't want to know. But I should have known he would be sweet and decadent. That's the way it always is with forbidden fruit.

CHAPTER 25

Were you aware of a drug problem at St. Ann's?

There's hardly a school in the country that can claim
to be drug-free, but no, I didn't detect it to be an
issue with the students in my classes.

*Did you have any suspicions as to who may have
been behind the theft of the hydrochloric acid
from your lab?*

No, none at all. If they'd swiped it to get high, big
mistake. There are plenty of substances in my lab
for that, but HCl is not one of them.

What happened after the theft?

I received a warning from Principal Cole, and I did
what I had to do. I tightened security. Changed
the locks on the cabinet. No one will be getting in
there now.

—Police interview with Jeffrey Lincoln,
chemistry teacher at St. Ann's

I'M NOT GOING TO GIVE you the blow-by-blow. In the days that followed, my life centered around the Kiss. It had lasted no more than a minute, but it consumed my mind for hours. It was as if it had elevated my life to a greater meaning. I know that's stupid. I should have felt ashamed, like a low-down cheating wreck, but instead, I felt as if I was worth *more*. That's how twisted things were.

I said about two dozen acts of contrition, still trembling in bed, wide awake and feeling the pressure of his lips on mine. Then my phone dinged.

THAT was the sexiest kiss EVER.

Over the next few weeks, I'd get texts like that all the time.

I can't stop thinking about you.

You look hot today.

When can I kiss you again?

And on and on. The weeks went by quickly. I felt as if I were living inside a dream where time was insignificant. What do I remember? We rehearsed *Macbeth* together. It turned out there were no make-out scenes between the Macbeths, but that was of little consequence. Offstage, we made out all the time. We were constantly inventing ways to be alone together, like volunteering to look for props backstage together, or whatever. Whenever we did, Z would pin me against the wall and we would make out for as long as we could without anyone getting suspicious. We both knew the importance of keeping our relationship a secret. There were enough rumors swirling around about Z, and we didn't want to add to the gossip. It was our secret—beautiful, exciting, and all-consuming.

I got lost in him. When I wasn't kissing Z, I was thinking about it, replaying each second in my mind to the point of madness. Like where he'd traced kisses down my chin to the hollow of my throat, how he'd swept the hair from my face, how he'd groaned when he pulled away from me, like he couldn't stand to put any distance between our bodies. Being with him was *all* I ever thought about, so much so that I turned in a chemistry test with an entire page blank. (Lincoln called me back and made me correct it.) I couldn't concentrate on any of my homework. I missed countless dates outside with you. At first I told you I was busy, and I really was—rehearsals were taking up so much of my time. But after a while, I just couldn't face you. You always saw through my lies.

I don't know why I'm telling you this now, Andrew. It can't be good to hear. I guess I want you to know how twisted things were. I was happy, but it was a false happiness, so fragile and easily ruptured. But at the time, I thought that this was meant to happen. Even if Z and I were hurting other people, I told myself that eventually everyone would see that being together was what was best for Z and me. Our feelings for each other were uncontrollable, written in the stars, so beautiful and right that all the angels in heaven were smiling.

God, that's stupid. I'm a horrible, selfish person, Andrew. I knew my being with Z would hurt you, but I never pushed him away. I *should've* pushed him away.

After a week of that, it felt as if the pieces of my life were falling into place. With Z's help, I'd gotten the part of Lady Macbeth down. Acting beside him brought out a different side of me—I felt confident, beautiful, and powerful. My fellow actors seemed to see me, respect me. *Macbeth* was no longer just some stupid school play—it was so much more.

Rachel and Parker even stopped glaring at me. Z seemed to take a day off every so often, claiming to be sick but returning perfectly fine the next day. But when I had to look on with Rachel and Parker in chemistry, they didn't make nasty comments or shut me out. In fact, as I was sitting at the corner of their lab table, bracing myself for their attack, Parker looked at me and said, "Want to try, Victoria?"

I stared at her. She was asking me to help? I took the red litmus strip and stuck it in the green liquid, then pulled it out. We all observed. "Base," Parker said. We wrote that down in our notebooks.

We kept doing that, alternating tries, getting into a rhythm. When we were finished and it was time to clean up, I washed my hands, and as I was drying them, Parker was waiting for me. "Done?" she asked.

I wondered why she was asking, but no sooner had I dried my hands than she had plucked the paper towel from my hands. She threw both towels into the garbage.

Parker Cole was being *nice* to me.

Something was up. She must've been waiting until I had my guard down so she could pounce. But while we were passing the last few minutes, waiting for the bell to ring, she didn't turn her back to me like usual. She sat between me and Rachel, talking as if she was including me in the conversation. She was saying something about texting, and I really wasn't paying attention until I realized she was looking at me. "And so I told her that if she keeps putting winking emoticons on every one of her texts, *of course* guys are going to get the wrong idea."

Rachel nodded in agreement. "Though maybe it's not the wrong idea. Maybe she really *does* want to do all those guys."

They both laughed, and Parker turned to me. "What do you think, Victoria? Does a wink mean, 'I'm just playing around' or 'I want to do you'?"

I was caught so off guard that I nearly fell off my stool. I was no expert in texting, even with my recent experience with Z. His texts were very emoticon-heavy. He constantly winked at me. Did that mean he wanted to get in my pants? From the way we'd been going at it lately, maybe. I pulled my books to my chest. "Definitely."

Rachel squealed, while Parker made a gross-out face. "Great. My dad winked at me yesterday. Ew."

"That's different," I explained.

"Yeah," Rachel said, "Dads are allowed to wink without it meaning anything pervy."

I thought about my own dad, who had never sent a text in his life. "Parents are texting clueless."

They both nodded as if I made sense. I couldn't believe it. I was having a conversation with two girls who, up until this year, didn't even know I'd existed. I knew it was because of Z. Z and me, me and Z—we were a package. Everyone accepted him, and now they accepted me too.

Despite this new development, I still missed Z like crazy. He'd texted me that morning. I think I have the flu. Or maybe

I'm just hot for you? I'd thought about the day before, when he'd cornered me in a stairwell between trig and lunch. We'd made out until Mr. Vargas, the Spanish teacher, walked by on his way to the faculty room and Z pretended he was looking for dirt in my eye.

I'd written back, Great, I hope I don't get it.

And he'd responded, Are you putting yourself off-limits? :(I might as well die.

After that, I resisted the urge to text him, which hit me every two seconds. He needed his rest. The minutes dragged on, and I felt like I might as well die too. I'd take every deadly disease known to man if it meant I could have one more kiss from him. It would be worth it.

CHAPTER 26

Were you friends with Victoria Zell?

Hardly.

And why is that?

She was...different.

In what way?

Well, there were some rumors going around about her. Something about how she'd had a nervous breakdown at her old school.

Breakdown? Had you ever witnessed her behaving oddly?

Um...well, no. She was more uptight. Guarded. High-strung. She kept to herself most of the time, always looking as if she was one wrong look from a panic attack. And then she surprised all of us by auditioning for the play.

Macbeth. Was that at Z's urging?

Maybe. Like I said, he gave people energy, made things happen. And it was obvious she worshipped him, and he got a kick out of that.

Is that so?

Oh yeah. If they were in a room together, it was like no one else was there. They were constantly staring at each other.

So Z was gazing at her too? Is it possible he liked her?

Well, it didn't strike me as gazing so much as sizing her up. He never seemed like the kind of guy who fell in love, you know, like with flowers and poetry and cupids and crap. He seemed to be into figuring her out. I got the impression he prided himself on being the biggest mystery in the room, the one everyone wanted to understand. But to do that, he needed to dethrone her first.

You were in Macbeth too. How was it, working with her?

I think Reese was amazed that she said more than two words in one day. But Victoria was always fading into the background so you'd forget about her, and then doing something that screamed, *Here I am!* It was almost as if she lived most of her life in another world, not ours. Like she just visited here every so often.

—Police interview with Rachel Watson,
junior at St. Ann's

AND THEN THERE WAS THAT night in early November when winter started meaning business in Maine, even though it technically wouldn't arrive for weeks. You came to my front door and knocked in your signature way.

You looked tired and droopy eyed. Your eyes brightened for a split second when I opened the door for you, Andrew. But then you read the disappointment in my eyes, and your face fell. You always could read me so well.

"What's wrong?" I asked.

You shrugged. "Nothing. I haven't seen you in a while."

I stared at you. "I saw you yesterday."

"Two weeks ago, Vic," you said, digging your hands into your pockets. "I saw you two weeks ago. Way before Halloween."

"Sorry," I said, leaving the door open for you and collapsing onto the sofa. "I've been busy. The play."

"Right, I keep forgetting," you said, but I know you well too. You probably thought about that play every afternoon between when school ended and I got home. "When is that, anyway?"

"November twentieth? You're coming, right?"

Your eyes brightened at the invitation. "Of course. Wouldn't miss it." You smiled, and then my phone dinged upstairs. It was a sound my ears had been trained to seek out, but you didn't seem to notice. You kept right on smiling, but my attention was suddenly elsewhere. "We're still on to see Perahia?"

At that point, the conversation becomes blurry. I think I said something like, "Of course! I can't wait. When is that?"

"November thirteenth. My actual birthday. The big one-seven."

"That will be easy to remember then. The date is etched in my memory," I said, tapping the side of my head. "Ironclad."

You laughed, and I gave you a peck on the cheek as I ushered you out the door, making up some excuse about homework.

"Was someone at the door?" my mom asked, coming into the foyer. "I didn't hear—"

I'd already closed the door. "No one. Just Andrew," I mumbled, rushing up the stairs two at a time. In my room, I grabbed my phone. Are you as bored as I am?

I texted back. Totally.

How adventurous are you?

It was Tuesday night, and normally I'd have been happy to snuggle under blankets. But Z had a way of making any proposition appealing. Venturing out in frigid temperatures? Sure. Snorkeling with sharks? Awesome. What did you have in mind?

Meet me at my house. Can you?

I thought about that. I'd have to either steal my parents' car or walk. In the pitch-black. In freezing temperatures. I don't have a car. And my parents won't let me out this late.

Tell them you're going to bed. Can you get to the corner? I'll pick you up there.

I thought about it, my heart already beating hard and fast. There was only one answer I could give. What time?

Ten.

I raced to get myself ready, taking a shower, putting on my mom's passion fruit lotion and a new denim skirt I'd bought to fit my slimmer shape. All the while, I felt like I was at the top of a roller coaster. Scared, thrilled, unable to escape…and wanting it that way. At quarter to ten, while my parents were downstairs watching TV, I climbed out my window, the same way Z had come up, and sneaked toward the street, stopping once to look up at your window. It wasn't lit, Andrew. You were probably… I don't know. I usually knew exactly what you were doing, but this time, I had no clue.

But I didn't care.

I made it to the corner of Spruce Street and Eleventh, which was lit by a single streetlight. A copse of trees and brush effectively hid me from our duplex and anyone looking down the road. I wondered if Z would be late like he always was, but he came right on time. The streetlight illuminated the stubble on his jaw, and he was wearing a rumpled, untucked T-shirt, like he'd just woken up. When I slid into the seat beside him, all I could smell was that intoxicating cinnamon-and-cloves smell that seemed to accompany him everywhere—spicy and sweet. But he said, "Wow. You smell amazing."

"Thanks." Before I'd even slammed the door shut, his hand had found a comfortable place on my knee. But this time as he drove, his hand crept up, higher and higher, until it found its way under my skirt. I gasped. "That's dangerous," I said, breathless.

"I think you like it."

I denied it, but he was right. If I hadn't, I suppose I'd have worn sweatpants. Or I never would've met him on the corner in the first place. I knew he wasn't being protective or brotherly anymore, and I didn't care. I was exactly where I wanted to be.

We drove for a few minutes with his fingers rubbing the goose bumps from my thigh, all the while inching further and further up my skirt. When we pulled into his driveway, his fingers had inched between my legs and I'd parted them.

Sparks ran up and down my spine, threatening to ignite. Suddenly his voice broke through the electricity. "Guess what?" he said, little-boy sweetly.

"What?"

"I was getting ready for school this morning, and I saw something in the woods. Thought it was a horse, but who goes horseback riding at 6:00 a.m.? So I ran out back and it was a moose! A fucking huge moose. It was fucking insane."

I pretended to yawn. "Oh, you people from away. Little Z, there is so much of the wide world you know nothing about."

He grinned, then reached so far up my skirt that I gasped. His fingers were warm, and every inch of me buzzed. "Teach me."

Somehow I was able to steady my knees and climb out of the Civic. His trailer was completely dark. "What about—"

"Bethany's at work," he said, taking my hand and leading me out back. There was a rusting trampoline abutting the tree line. My parents would call it a death trap. He climbed out onto it, then motioned for me to follow. I did, falling back onto a blanket of dead leaves, face to the sky like him. Here you could barely tell where the pines left off and the sky began, except for a few pinpoints of stars fighting their way through the clouds.

The woods behind his house were strangely quiet. The

only sound was the breeze rattling the dying leaves off the trees. I could see my breath in the cold.

"My mom," he said suddenly. "I was six when she left. She told me that if I missed her, all I had to do was look up at the sky because she'd be sleeping under the same one. Like that was supposed to make me feel better."

I said, "It doesn't?"

"The sky's always changing, Precious. There're a billion different skies, and some of them are nicer than others." He was quiet for a really long time while I tried to comprehend what he was saying. Z was the last person I'd expect to wax philosophical on me, but like he said, nothing and nobody are constant. "What's your sky look like tonight?"

I smiled at that. "Um, cloudy?"

"Not anymore. Before, yeah. Not now."

"OK," I said. "Um, what are we talking about now?"

"You." He rolled up onto his elbow. "Why'd you hide yourself from everyone before? Why were you so nervous?" I didn't have time to feel worried about how to answer because he said, "Why would you, when there's this…" He inched his hand under my skirt again, and I giggled and squirmed away.

"I don't know. I just…I don't know." That was the truth. A lot of times when I talked to him, my mind was a complete blank.

"Do you like it?"

"What?"

"You know…*not* hiding."

"Very much," I answered almost too eagerly. "For once, I actually belong."

He reached over and grabbed my hand. It was only when I felt his warm hand that I realized mine was icy. It tingled numbly. "You cold?"

I nodded.

He rolled over me, his face hovering just inches from mine. "There's a way to fix that," he murmured, pushing the hair out of my eyes.

I could barely speak. "How?"

He rocketed to his feet. "Jump." At first there was a tremor, and then he nearly bounced me over the side. I backed away and laughed as he pulled me to my feet. Here I was, sneaking out of my parents' house in the middle of the night and risking their wrath to...jump on a trampoline.

How daring.

He jumped on the trampoline like he did everything else: expertly. He never got out of breath and even pulled off a few flips that I didn't know he had in him. All I could do was bounce, and not too high, for fear of hurting myself or showing off everything under my skirt.

When I was red-faced and panting, he said, "I'm thirsty. Let's go inside." We climbed off, and he opened the door to the trailer. "You're not really allergic to dogs, are you?"

I froze. Great. Now I'd have to tell him about my stupid fear. I was already nervous enough as it was. "No, but—"

"Dog's not here either. OK?"

I smiled, loving that he didn't want me to explain. That he just *got* me. "OK."

He flipped on a light and let me inside. "Home, sweet home."

We were in a small kitchenette. For as run-down as it was outside, the trailer was kind of cute inside. It was old style, with little gingerbread men and wood paneling everywhere, but clean. It even smelled like gingerbread. "Nice," I said, but he wasn't looking for my reaction. The moment he closed the door, he pulled me against him, digging his hands into the back pockets of my jean skirt, and cupping and lifting my backside so that the only natural response was to wrap my legs around his hips.

He threw my whole body into a tailspin. In his arms, I didn't know which way was up or down. There was no tentative invitation like with you, Andrew. From the second his lips found mine, our connection was deeper and more consuming than any kiss—any*thing* I'd ever experienced. I couldn't stop it. I don't think the apocalypse could have stopped us.

I embraced him desperately, hungrily. I felt his legs guiding us through a narrow, dark hallway, bumping knees and elbows as we went. I vaguely knew that we'd arrived in his bedroom, and while I wanted to know what his place was like—oh, I wanted to know everything about him—at that moment, as wrong as it was, I just wanted him.

He finally broke our kiss and stared into my eyes. "I need to be closer to you."

I needed it too. We had gone beyond want. Want implied there was choice. Together, we were completely bound to follow this path that had been laid beneath our feet.

CHAPTER 27

See you tonight.
K. Remember where?
KW?
Yep 12
OK. Don't be late. Place freaks me out.
Under control.
—Cell phone records from November 22, the day of the
murder, courtesy of the Duchess Police Department report

AT THAT POINT, I WASN'T deluded enough to think that
Z was the love of my life. I didn't think we'd break up
with our significant others, get together, and live happily ever
after. No, I saw us as the tragic characters in a play. We were
two best friends who simply couldn't deny or quell the attrac-
tion between us. We were happily involved with other people,
and yet we had this whole secret life together. I was no longer
Boring Victoria Zell. I was mysterious, interesting. While a
small part of me ached to fully be his, mostly I *liked* that we
couldn't be a real couple yet. The pain of being apart was the

sweetest pain I'd ever felt, and when we were together, I was utterly euphoric.

All weekend, I replayed the hours I'd spent with him, shivering with each memory. He'd had sex before, probably a lot of it, with his girlfriend in Arizona and likely others, considering how smoothly he unhooked my bra closure. Considering he knew exactly how to touch me. Considering the package of condoms he kept under his mattress. But that didn't surprise me. There'd been no pain, no awkwardness, no regret. He made it seem only natural to do those things with him.

And as usual, he left me wanting more. Much more. I'd never done drugs, but I could understand addiction. I'd gone so many years smugly thinking that I'd never fall under anyone else's control...and yet, here I was. Fallen. Weak. And totally OK with it. Not just wanting more, but *needing* more.

This was different, I told myself. With addiction, the drug owns you. But we owned each other. Equally. While I was lying in my bed thinking of him, a text came in.

You are the sexiest girl I've ever known.

He was thinking of me too. Yes, beautifully, tragically, we owned each other.

I'm not sure why that wasn't enough for me.

The following week, I walked into lunch and sat alone at my table. Z and I had gone back to pretending we were just casual friends in public. It was so hard, seeing him and knowing about the other night, but he played it off well. When no one was watching, he'd glance at me and mouth, "You look so sexy" or "You're driving me crazy over there." Funny, he never *looked* like he was being driven crazy. He was good at keeping his emotions in check, about holding what we had close to his heart. So I followed his cue and did my best to proceed like it was business as usual.

And then, as I was about to take a bite of my sandwich, something crazy happened.

Parker slid her tray onto my table and sat down across from me. "Can I sit here?" she asked.

Parker and I had been talking more. She'd continued being civil to me, even friendly. As she plopped into the seat, I remembered that Rachel was out sick. But that didn't mean Parker had to sit with me. She had plenty of other friends to sit with. Needless to say, I was a little suspicious.

"Why do you eat here all alone?" she asked, picking a cucumber out of her salad.

She asked as if it was a conscious choice. As if I preferred my own company. I shrugged as she dipped a crouton in a small cup of salad dressing.

"Why don't you eat with Z?"

"All they do is talk baseball," I said, even though he'd never asked. Hanging out with the jocks would definitely make me a sore thumb though, so I'd never minded.

She nodded. "Anyway, Rachel and I were going to go shopping after school for dresses for the dance. But since she's sick, do you want to come with me? I'll drive you back in time to catch the late bus."

Dresses for the dance. I hadn't even thought about that. There'd been a fall dance every year, but you and I never went,

Andrew. We're just not dance people. I couldn't believe she'd think I was. "I'm probably not going," I said.

"Really? I just assumed you were. With Z," she said, surprised.

I shook my head, but I was flattered that she saw Z and I could be a couple. "We're not…" I began, but stopped.

I thought of the way she looked at him. The doe eyes she always threw his way. This was Code Red. She was sitting here trying to get information about Z because *she wanted to go to the dance with him*. That was why she was asking me to go shopping. It definitely wasn't for my fashion sense. She wanted to weasel her way between Z and me, and with her big boobs and her shiny hair, she had a pretty good chance of doing just that.

"You mean, you're not together?" she asked, finishing my original sentence.

"No," I said. "Of course we're together. We're just not really dance people."

It wasn't the most convincing lie ever told. Sure, Andrew, you may not have been a dance person, but gregarious, fun-loving Z was, in every sense of the word. She wrinkled her nose. "Oh. I thought Z said he was going."

I swallowed. He was going to the dance? With whom? I hadn't expected he'd ask me with you in the picture, Andrew. I hadn't wanted him to, of course, because I had you. Was his girlfriend from Arizona coming in for it? My face began to burn. "We haven't really talked about it."

"Then you should come with me. Shopping. Just look around. See what's out there."

"Uh...OK. When is the dance again?"

"The Saturday after the play. Come on. I'll have you back before the late bus leaves."

So that was how I ended up cruising out of St. Ann's parking lot in Parker Cole's red VW on the way to the Bangor Mall. I watched her, wondering what her game was, and whether I was a pawn in it.

The Bangor Mall isn't anything to write home about. Before this year, I'd been there maybe twice. Since September though, I'd been there twice more with my mother to buy new clothes to fit my newer, trimmer shape. There are only about three stores young people can shop in, and Parker and I went to Charlotte Russe. Browsing the racks, I came across the sexiest teal-blue dress I'd ever seen. "You need that," Parker said, inspecting it.

"I don't have the boobs."

"Try it on anyway."

So I did. And when I came out of the dressing room, the salesladies whistled. Parker gave me an approving "wow." And when I looked into the mirror, I knew what all the hysteria was about. I looked older and off the charts sexy. The dress was a halter, with a completely bare back and a short skirt that stopped mid-thigh. I'd never worn anything so bare—even my bathing suits seemed to cover more. But I'd been practicing my posture, and my new exercise routine had given me tone in places I'd needed it.

As I gazed into the mirror, I lost myself in thought. Instead of being a faceless nobody who was ignored, I was a showstopper. In this dress, I looked like someone worthy of Z.

And then I hated myself because I didn't have the money to buy it. It's not like I carry hundred-dollar bills to school with me, and I don't own a credit card. But Parker had her dad's. She was checking out her own emerald-green gown, which was lovely but still nowhere near as hot as mine, and said, "Don't worry. Just pay me back. What are friends for?"

Friends. She considered me her friend. Of course, Parker was the type to throw the word around loosely, since she had so many of them. I thought of that old saying about keeping friends close and enemies closer. I still wasn't sure exactly what camp she fell into, or which one I wanted her to fall into.

"Z is not going to be able to take his eyes off you in that," she said as she pumped the accelerator.

I imagined him drooling when he caught sight of me. That is, until I realized that *I wasn't even going to the dance with him.* Up until two hours ago, I hadn't even planned on going myself. And now—now I knew what I needed to do. I needed to get Z to ask me. I figured I'd tell you that Z and I were going together. As friends, of course. Because he'd asked me. Just as friends.

You see, right, Andrew? It had to be done…if nothing else, to save Z from *her.*

As I was solidifying the plan in my mind, my phone dinged. I pulled it out and read another text from Z. I need to touch you again.

I trembled from head to toe at the thought, and Parker whistled. "Whoa, you've got it bad."

"What?" I asked innocently.

"Who are you texting? You look like a lovesick puppy."

"It's just Z. He sends me texts." I was proud of the volume of messages I'd received from him. When I went back and reread them, they showed the progression of our friendship.

"Dirty ones? Are you sexting?" she asked, raising her eyebrows. "Please don't tell me you're sending naked pictures of yourself to any guy."

"No, it's just…" I smiled some more. I couldn't explain our texting without blushing. So when she stopped at a light, I showed her the screen, thumbing through the hundreds of texts he'd sent me, all of which I'd saved. Some of them were private, some a little dirty, some slightly embarrassing. I'd never delete one. Never, ever. In fact, whenever I was feeling lonely, I'd read through them, analyzing every word and wondering what he was thinking as he'd typed them. And I guess part of me was excited to show someone, anyone, how much he wanted me. How irresistible he found me.

She smiled. "Oh my God. Did he actually say *What are you wearing right now?*"

I shrugged. "He's not the most creative."

She thumbed through the rest of the messages. "He definitely has a texting addiction. Either that or he's just addicted to you."

"Maybe." I smiled coyly, not realizing that this seemingly innocent conversation would destroy everything.

CHAPTER 28

An autopsy found no evidence of fatal injury, illness, or disease. The 40-mg ampule dose of succinylcholine was administered intramuscularly to the victim, possibly causing prolonged apnea, and was considered to be the minimum lethal dose.

—Coroner's report

I HAD FOOLISH DREAMS ALL NIGHT. Z showing up on my doorstep and, like a cartoon character, fainting into a puddle of his own drool at my beauty. Me, leaving a line of dazed men in my wake as Z led me to the dance floor. Everyone in the gymnasium talking about me: "Can you believe that was the girl we used to call a nobody?" and electing me queen of the dance, even though my name was never on the ballot. In my dream it was just assumed that I should get the tiara, considering how drop-dead gorgeous I'd become.

And then I woke up. And by that, I mean *really* woke up, in the worst and most jarring way possible.

I'd convinced myself that going to the dance with Z was

inevitable. It was meant to be. He'd ask me. Or I'd ask him. It didn't matter if we went as friends or as more. We'd been together more than enough for people to start considering us to be a package deal.

So believe it or not, when I walked into Reese's class, I was going to do something I never, ever would have considered only two months before. I was going to smile and say, "Hey, let's go to the dance together." I felt confident, excited.

Weird for me, right, Andrew?

I threw down my bag, slid into my seat, and turned to Z.

I expected him to look up with that brilliant smile of his and say, "Hey, Precious."

But he didn't even look at me.

I cleared my throat. I took out my pencil and tapped it on the edge of my desk. I coughed. Loudly.

And then a sour feeling began to creep in, one I remembered well from my pre-Z days. Those years of isolation. He was the one who broke that mold and changed all that. Desperation surged through me at his silence. If I had to go back to being the outcast again…

No. That wasn't happening.

He was probably just having a bad day. I reached into my bag, grabbed a pack of gum, and leaned across the aisle. "Juicy Fruit?" I asked.

But he didn't look up. "No," he mumbled.

At that moment, I realized I hadn't gotten a gift in my locker in weeks. *Weeks.* With everything else that was happening between us, I hadn't missed them. But now I did. Achingly.

The desperation came again, but this time it rooted itself in the pit of my stomach. I needed to say something to make things right between us. As my mind was racing through the possibilities, Reese walked in. Great. Now it would be forty-five minutes before I could talk to him. Forty-five of the longest minutes of my life, no doubt. The need inside me caught fire until I felt like I was being roasted from the inside out. I was a pressure cooker. Everyone around me was going through the normal motions of the day, while I squirmed in my seat on the verge of bursting.

In fact, I did. I jumped to my feet and shouted in a strong voice I'd never used in class, "Mrs. Reese! I'm going to faint."

Reese stopped writing on the board and whirled around, her eyes wide. An outburst wasn't expected from the old Victoria, but I wasn't that Victoria anymore, was I? I was no longer a little mouse. I was Lady Macbeth. And Lady Macbeth made things happen.

Reese held out the hall pass to me and motioned to Z. "Show your Lady to the nurse, if you would be so kind."

Without a word, Z slid from his desk and sauntered up to the front in his slow, easy way, holding his cell phone in his hand. From the way he moved, it didn't look like he was angry or hurt or devastated like I was. I knew something was wrong, but I was so scared that I could barely put one foot in front of the other. When we stepped out of the classroom, he started to walk a few steps ahead of me, all business. No typical Z sauntering. No sly grin.

"What's wrong with you?" I asked.

He dug his hands deep into his pockets and turned to

me, giving me this narrow-eyed, *What the hell is your problem?* expression, as if there was something very wrong with *me*. At that moment, I felt very wrong. More wrong than I had in my life. "Nothing," he snapped.

We walked a little further, and all I could think about was the number of times he'd pulled me to him for a secret kiss in this hallway or reached under my skirt, his fingers trailing up my thigh as he gave me his innocent altar-boy look. The thought of that never happening again terrified me in a way nothing ever had.

That *couldn't* happen. I knew I would die first.

The door to the nurse's office came into view all too quickly. I stopped. "No, tell me."

The disgust didn't leave his face. "Are you sick, or what?"

Sick? He looked down at me like I was gross, diseased. I suddenly remembered the excuse I'd manufactured to get us alone. "Um, no. I made that up."

He rolled his eyes and reversed direction so quickly that you would have thought he *lived* for Reese's class, Andrew. "I've got to get back," he said.

I clamped my hand on his. I hadn't meant for my hand to be so quivery and slick with sweat against his bare skin. He looked at it as if I had seven fingers. He didn't shake me off, but the way he stared at my hand was enough. I slowly stepped away. "Look, you need to tell me."

His face brightened. It was as if the curtain had gone up and he'd gotten into his character. The Z character that I knew so well and loved so much. He smiled at me. And for a second, I thought, *Yes, we'll be back to the way things were by the time we're back in English*.

Instead, vile words floated through that pleasant smile of his. "You told."

"Wh-what?"

"Did you show Parker our texts, or not?"

My stomach dropped. Of course. Of *course* she would tell. Parker Cole never met a secret she didn't want to share with the world.

I opened my mouth to speak, to do damage control, but he silenced me. "I'd thought those were just between us."

"They were," I started, but I couldn't backpedal out of this. I'd screwed up royally and betrayed him. *You are the only person I trust.* "I'm sorry. I should've... I'm sorry. I won't ever do it again."

"Again?" He let out a snort. I was trembling, and he just stared at me, calm and nonchalant. I felt like a toddler being berated by her mother. "You did it before. You told Parker and Rachel how my mother had me when she was thirteen and ditched me. You know I didn't want anyone to know that. Why did you?"

Oh hell, I had. All this time, he'd known I'd told them, and he never said anything. The way he'd held me, the way he'd kissed me and whispered my name and groaned with need as he entered me, completing me, completing us... Never again. It was over. We were over.

And I would never be whole again.

In that heartbeat, my life went from perfect to meaningless. "I only meant to defend you," I whispered.

"Right, and showing Parker our private texts is the perfect way to do that."

"No. I did that because—" I broke off, my eyes flooding with tears, much to my embarrassment. I told myself I'd never be that person again. The one who cared, the *only* one who cared.

Of course he wouldn't understand how hard it was to be the outcast. He watched me cry for a moment, really sob, then waved his hand in the air. "Forget it. It's over and done with."

I looked up. I thought maybe he'd forgive me, and we could move on.

But he *hadn't* said he'd forgiven me.

He'd only said it was over.

I swallowed and wiped my eyes. I gestured to a poster for the Fall Dance. "Are you going to this thing?"

He nodded. "You know me, I'm a dancing machine."

I cleared my throat. "Are you going with your girlfriend from Arizona?"

He shook his head. "We broke up a while ago. I asked Parker last night."

I gagged. *He* asked her? "What? But…what about …?"

He put a brotherly hand on my shoulder. "I figured you were going with your fabulously talented boyfriend. Right?"

The smile he gave me… I can't explain it. Wholesomely wicked? Sweetly vile? As if he knew exactly how he was twisting my insides, and worse than that, *he didn't care*. He walked back to Reese's classroom, leaving me staring after him with all the walls crumbling around me.

CHAPTER 29

Murder has rocked the small town of Duchess, Maine to its core. Named for an exiled aristocrat who found refuge there in the early 1800s, the town is secluded and small, home to roughly 1,500 people. It's a place where everyone is a neighbor and people aren't afraid to let their children walk alone to the community park. Nestled among the tall pines, Duchess has been largely insulated from the troubles of everyday America. That is, until one cold autumn night.

—From a primetime news special, *Death in Duchess*, air date unknown

I TOOK THE MAXIMUM DOSE OF my anxiety medication that night. Little good it did. It didn't even make me drowsy enough to sleep. Instead, I lay in bed, thinking about the Zahir. The more the character in the story tried to get rid of the coin, the more he became bound to it. The man realized he was in too deep and tried to save himself, but all that did was make him more the coin's slave, until he was so completely tied to it that it consumed him.

Was I Z's slave? Was I bound to him? If he left, would the pain lessen, or would it grow and fester like an open sore until it consumed me completely? Would I die fifty years from now, thinking of him and only him?

Yes.

No. *No,* I needed to get hold of myself. Move on. I was never his, and he was never mine. I'd always known that. I had someone else. I had you, Andrew. And you and I—Andrew, *we* belonged. Not Z and me. That was an illusion, a fantasy that had come to an end.

If our relationship was truly, truly coming to an end, that was how it was meant to be.

I told myself that sweet little lie until I drifted off to sleep.

CHAPTER 30

Who do you think took the hydrochloric acid?

No one.

Someone had to have stolen it.

I understand that. But this is a small school. Everyone knew everyone else, since kindergarten. No one would do something like that.

But you didn't know Z. He was new to the school, correct?

Yeah. Still, I don't get it. Why would he do that? And to poison another classmate? I can't believe he'd have anything to do with that. There wasn't a vengeful or hurtful bone in his body.

So you never caught him doing anything dangerous or illegal?

You mean drugs, right? No. He didn't touch that stuff. He was a pretty serious athlete. And he was friends with everyone, from the popular kids to the losers. Hell, sometimes he'd play tic-tac-toe with a first-grader in the hallway during recess. He was friends with everyone.

And Victoria?

Who?

Victoria Zell.

The mouse. She was new to the school too. I don't
think I've heard her say more than two words.

What do you know about her?

Nothing. I mean, she'd be cute—hot, even—if she
weren't so uptight. Suspicious, you know? Everyone
wanted to meet her when she first arrived. But a
few of us tried talking to her and it was like...she
was a fortress, you know? She didn't even throw us
a bone. So eventually we gave up.

Were Z and Victoria friends?

Z? Hell, yeah. Like I said, he was friends with everyone. He was good, man. He came in, guns blaz-
ing, and infiltrated her fortress. And he was proud
of that.

Proud?

Yeah. He had access to her the rest of us had been
denied.

*Do you think he may have taken that access a little
too far?*

No. I mean, who can say? But my gut tells me no. He
liked to joke around, yeah, but not in a cruel way.
If he found a way to break down her walls, it wasn't
with the intention of hurting her.

—Police interview with James Burney,
junior at St. Ann's

O BSESSION IS STRANGE. ONE MOMENT, you think you have control. And by the time you realize that you've lost your free will, you don't even care. You are happily lost in oblivion.

Until your obsession gets taken away from you.

Then you'll do anything to get it back. Anything.

At that point, my schoolwork went to pot. Sleep only happened in an Ativan-induced haze. I kept myself sequestered in my bedroom, staring at all the old texts he'd sent me. Nothing mattered if it didn't involve Z.

St. Ann's isn't exactly a hotbed for drama, but there was a curious incident during that time. Even that failed to interest me. Someone had stolen a vial of hydrochloric acid from the chemistry lab. Normally calm Mr. Lincoln went on a *serious* warpath. First he told us that if the responsible party returned it, there would be no questions asked. When thirty sets of eyes stared blankly back at him, he told us all that the "perpetrator"— whoever it was had been elevated to "criminal" status—would be swiftly expelled from school if he or she was caught.

Sure, nutty James Burney had a penchant for trying to take up-skirt pictures of the girls, and Parker Cole and Rachel Watson offended the dress code daily, but that was the limit to our criminality. The juniors had grown into a dysfunctional family. Everyone knew everyone else's quirks and their potential, having been in class together since kindergarten. And nobody in the class had ever done anything so bold as to steal from the school.

So it should have been obvious who the responsible party was.

And yet, it wasn't. Everyone looked equally mystified.

Z was so smooth under pressure. He looked as relaxed as ever. I stared at him, waiting for him to show his guilt, but he didn't. He turned to me and raised his eyebrows, like, *What do you want from me?*

Parker had gone back to ignoring me. That much I could accept. But Z? He knew how to push the knife in and twist it until you screamed for mercy, as if he'd been practicing the move since the day he was born. That morning, when he'd sat down beside me, he smiled cordially at me and said, "Hey, Vic."

That was it. No Precious.

He offered a few friendly, inconsequential niceties, as if *we* had never been a *thing*. By the time we'd separated for lunch, a lump the size of Nebraska had formed in my throat.

I'd been reduced to being one of his casual acquaintances.

In other words, overnight, I'd become nobody again.

When we met up in science, I'd almost wished he'd completely ignore me or totally lose his cool. At least then I'd know that what'd happened between us had mattered. But he'd let my betrayal roll off his back too easily.

Someone as cold as that could have easily stolen the hydrochloric acid.

That fact became clear to me as I sat there in science class that afternoon. Like a veil had been lifted from my eyes. Z was so secretive. He'd stolen my locker combination. He'd stolen my notes. Of course he'd stolen the vial from the chemistry lab. And yet no one could see past his charming facade.

Except…

As Lincoln expressed his disappointment in all of us, his gaze swept the classroom. When he said, "If any of you have information, I urge you to come forward at once. At. Once," he focused on Z.

Lincoln's stare was so intense that I think other people noticed it because a few heads turned to follow his line of sight. Z cleared his throat and looked down at the lab bench.

At that moment, discomfort flashed on his face. It was a *blink and you miss it* moment, something only I likely noticed, but it spoke volumes. Guilty as charged.

After Lincoln's speech, Z's shoulders relaxed. It was back to normal. A person with a cold, dead heart wouldn't let anything worry him for long.

During lab, we were all business. He did the work and I took the notes. The worst part though was that Parker kept looking at him and smiling flirtatiously. Z would always smile back. Every once in a while, he'd stop and call over to them, "How are you ladies faring?" or "Can I interest you ladies in a sodium-chloride milk shake?" It was always "you ladies," and it was always met with a fit of giggles. That and the chemical smell were making my stomach queasy.

While I observed and noted the results of our experiment, Z meandered over to Parker and Rachel's lab bench. It took me a moment to realize that Lincoln had left the room. Obviously Z had been waiting for his chance. I watched Parker and Z flirting out of the corner of my eye.

And then I saw it.

He put his hand on hers.

Z was a touchy-feely person. Every time he talked to a girl, he'd put a finger on her arm or smooth a stray hair. But this time, he left his hand there long enough to cross the line from casual to meaningful.

Seven one-thousand, eight one-thousand, nine one-thousand... It was still there.

He was taking her to the dance, I knew. Fine. But were they going out now too?

My queasy stomach turned into a rumbling volcano, threatening to spew. I had to stop this.

"Zachary Zimmerman."

Every face turned to the door. Lincoln stood on the threshold, arms crossed. Z cringed.

"Back to your station. I'm sure you'll have time for advancing your love life later."

The class erupted in laughter. Laughter usually followed Z. But this was the first time others were laughing *at* him, not with him. Z wordlessly slid onto his stool, looking as close to having his tail between his legs as I'd ever seen him.

Good, I thought.

I continued to scribble observations in my notebook, but I wasn't observing the experiment so much as him. He perched on the stool, rigid, like a scarecrow in a field. I could see the muscles of his arms tensing in his short-sleeve polo. He always wore short sleeves, despite the near-frigid weather. It was almost frightening, the intense way he was staring at Lincoln.

"You want to record the next phase?" I asked him.

He didn't answer. His stare hadn't softened. If anything, it had grown harder.

I wanted to strike at him, to wound him more. He was not going to flirt openly with Parker, take her to the dance, and then use me for my science genius. Not happening. *See? You don't own everyone. You think you do, but you're wrong. You don't own Lincoln, and you don't own me.*

I gathered my courage, then waved a hand in front of his face. "Don't think you're going to copy my lab report."

He blinked, then scowled at me. But only for a second. Then he smiled. "Got it all under control, Vic."

I gnashed my teeth as I hunched over my notebook, wishing just once someone or something could send his world spinning. I didn't know when I'd gone from adoring him to reveling in his humiliation, to *wanting* his suffering, but it happened in a heartbeat. It's a hair-thin line between love and hate, Andrew. But you already knew that, didn't you?

CHAPTER 31

Did Victoria ever talk to you about an Andrew Quinn?

No…no. I don't know anybody by that name.

*She never mentioned that she was taking him to
the dance?*

No, that doesn't ring a bell. Sorry.

*Did you observe anything out of the ordinary at
the dance?*

Z was upset at one point.

Over…?

No clue. I mean, Z wasn't there for most of the dance.
He left with Parker for a while. When he came back,
he was…not quite pissed. More like shell-shocked.
I remember thinking it was odd because he's usually more together than that. Something really had
him freaked out.

—Police interview with Rachel Watson,

junior at St. Ann's

Unfortunately, Z *DID* HAVE IT all under control. I stopped leaving my lab reports in my locker so I'd be sure he wouldn't "borrow" them. I desperately wanted him to come to me on his hands and knees, begging for help. But he didn't. Maybe Parker let him copy her labs. Regardless, he didn't need me.

Not the way I needed him.

I couldn't breathe without him. It wasn't the intimacy as much as the friendship, his mere presence in my life. He all but ignored me at rehearsals, so I'd go home afterward, pop more Ativan, and just lie in bed, writhing, physically spent, and wishing I could wake up from this nightmare.

You showed up that night in a rented tuxedo. You had flowers, pink carnations, my favorite. When I opened the door, you were holding them out in front of you, and your face was distorted, fighting back a sneeze. You're allergic to carnations, but you still got them for me.

When you saw that I was still in my sweats, you startled and the sneeze erupted from your face. "Ready to go?" you asked, your voice so fragile.

I just stared at you, dazed. "What?"

"To see Perahia. We planned months ago…" Your voice trailed off, and your eyes filled with disappointment. "You forgot?"

It was your birthday. I always made a big deal of your birthday. Remember the year I'd bought you a giant piano-shaped cake from Shaw's? It was gluten- and sugar-free because of your allergies and diabetes, and was horrible, worse than those cardboard cookies your mom makes. But we had the best food fight in my backyard, grabbing chunks of it off the platter and throwing them at each other.

But this year, you received no Happy Birthday, no cake, no card…nothing.

Sweet Andrew, I am so sorry. My mind was so muddled that I'd forgotten what day it was. November 13 had always been Your Day. But I'd gone the whole day and not made the connection once. Things I knew by heart were lost to me because my heart was diseased.

My diseased heart could not bring itself to care about your disappointment. My own was so deep that it drowned me. I had these images in my mind of Z, of all the good times we'd shared. And somehow they had all just crumbled. The absence of our friendship was nothing to him. But I had lost my heart. And it wasn't fair. I wanted him to miss me, and I wanted to destroy something the way I'd been destroyed.

So I lashed out at the person closest to me: you.

"If you get changed real quick, we can make it," you said. "My mom's warming up the—"

I cut you off. "I'm not going."

You swallowed. "Um. What? Are you OK?"

I was so angry at you. In that moment, I hated you. Hated you for not being more like him. "I don't want to go on a date with your mom because you don't have the guts to drive us yourself," I snapped.

"But I—"

"You screw up everything, Andrew—tonight, your life, all

of it. You could've been great—really great—and what did you do? You wasted your talent, your whole life, because you're afraid. Because you wouldn't grow a pair. You're pathetic!"

By this time, I was screaming. Screaming and crying and acting utterly insane.

But the worst part was that you did nothing.

You stood there, clutching the stems of my flowers, and let my words sink in.

I didn't mean what I said—don't you see that? You were already great. *I* let you down first. I was the one dragging *you* down. "Victoria?"

I turned, chest heaving. My mom was staring at me. Disappointment and shock leaked from the corners of her eyes. "Leave me alone!" I screamed at her, vising my head in my hands. "Go away. Just…all of you…go away!"

Then I slammed the front door and ran to my room, satis-fied that I'd ripped a hole in someone's heart that was at least as big as the one Z had ripped in mine.

CHAPTER 32

You went to high school with Victoria Zell when she
   attended Duchess High, yes?
We went to school together from kindergarten to
   freshman year.
What kind of person was she?
She was nice. We didn't hang out or anything, but she
   seemed smart. Not the most popular student, but
   not the most unpopular either. She was kind of
   quiet and secretive, didn't like talking much about
   herself. She was a little nervous that last year. We
   all figured it was the pressure of adjusting to high
   school. I mean, we were all stressed out.
Did she ever behave erratically?
I once saw her in the ladies' room after she'd had a
   good cry, but heck, we all had moments like that.
And...
You mean the geometry legend? I was in that class,
   so I know the truth. We had our big final exam.
   She didn't freak out like the rumors said. She just

stood up in the middle of the test and walked out. She was completely calm and under control. There was no tantrum, no hysterics. It was actually kind of awesome the way she just got up and left. She never came back to school after that.

So that didn't seem like a nervous breakdown to you?

Nervous? No, she'd been nervous before. It was like she'd made peace in the war going on in her head. A surrender. Like, "Hey, stress? Screw you. I'm done here."

—Interview with Alison Dunham,

junior at Duchess High School

I DIDN'T TALK TO YOU FOR nearly a week after that, Andrew. I should have felt bad, especially since what happened the night of Perahia had been simmering for weeks before. You were the only consistently good thing in my life. Being your girlfriend fed my sanity, made me whole, and I couldn't see it.

I see it now.

Too little, too late, right?

I know you can't forgive me now. But you forgave me then, didn't you? You always forgave—your mom, your step-dad, everyone. If only people were as gentle with you as you were with us. None of this would have happened. I probably wouldn't be in this ditch right now, wondering if I still have all my brain matter. I'm thinking of that picture of us on my phone. That confidence you had with your arm securely over my shoulder... That could have been you all the time.

You could have been great, Andrew.

I know it's not all your fault.

But some of it *is* your fault.

"What is going on with you, Miss Zell?" Reese asked me for the third time during the dress rehearsal. I stood center stage in a heavy velvet gown, with Rachel kneeling in front of me, scowling. Everyone seemed to scowl at me now. Reese had begun to soften during our rehearsals, but in recent days, some of the demonic Reese had returned. And today I'd tripped over my lines, forgotten stage direction a dozen times, and omitted an entire soliloquy. "You had this down last week."

I nodded. "I'm sorry. It must be…allergies."

It was the best excuse I could come up with. I cleared my throat and sniffled for effect. My dutiful lady-in-waiting grimaced and snapped, "You're going to ruin the play."

I swallowed. "No, I won't."

She stood up and whispered, "You suck. You should just call in sick and let your understudy do the part."

I turned on my heel, then hurried offstage for my water bottle. Tears stung my eyes. The theater spun around me. One more day and the gymnasium would be packed, and I'd be onstage with Z as my husband.

After what I'd said to you about growing a pair, there I was, scared to death, Andrew. I'd never wanted this. I was never an actress. The only reason I'd auditioned was so Parker wouldn't be up there with—

In the quiet of backstage, I heard someone giggle. Whispers came from behind a giant foam background. That was where Z and I had frequently gotten comfortable. I inched my way over and peered between the curtains. Z was wearing his velvet Macbeth cape. He'd pinned Parker against the brick wall, something he used to do to me. Her face tilted up toward the dull amber stage light, eyes closed in bliss as he buried his face in her neck.

I stumbled back, then over to the ledge where we kept our water bottles. Reese had gotten them for the entire cast. They were red and said "St. Ann's Future Stars!" on them. I found the one that had the masking tape on it with my name, then pulled it open and started to take a sip.

I froze as the liquid touched my tongue. It tasted sour. The smell was overpowering, acrid, bringing tears to my eyes.

Rachel skipped over to me and grabbed her bottle from the ledge.

"Somebody put something in my water," I whispered.

She looked at me like, *yeah, right*. I shoved it under her nose, and she sniffed. Her eyes widened. "Mrs. Reese!" she screamed. "Oh my God! Mrs. Reese!"

A small circle began to form around us, and Mrs. Reese appeared a moment later. Rachel thrust the bottle under the nose of just about everyone who came near. The reaction was almost exactly the same: disgust, then eye-popping fear, then a scramble to test their own bottles. "Somebody poisoned her water bottle!" Rachel cried, and it practically became a chant.

Mrs. Reese was momentarily speechless for once when Rachel stuck my water bottle under her nose. "Give that to me," she snapped, and then pulled out her cell phone. Principal

Cole's booming voice echoed through the line as Z broke through the crowd.

Z didn't ask what had happened.

He didn't have to.

It didn't matter that his lips were rubbed red from being suctioned by Parker's mouth. When Z put his hands on my shoulders, I forgot I'd nearly been poisoned. "Did you drink any?" he asked.

In the middle of my thank-you prayer to God—Z was looking at me again, touching me, caring for me!—it occurred to me that I had to formulate a response. "Just a…a few drops."

With Reese still on the phone, Z took control of the situation. "Move away. Let's sit her down." He put his arm around me to guide me to a chair. Someone handed him a cup of cold water. "Drink this," he said. After I'd downed the whole thing, he asked, "How do you feel?" I managed a "fine," when really, I felt nothing short of bliss. My tongue didn't burn; my esophagus didn't tingle. I felt no pain in my chest…just this enormous giddiness.

He had left Parker to care for me. To sit by my side.

Well, of course he had. Z thrived on being the center of attention. And this was the center. For now, anyway.

The next thing I knew, a new chant rose over the cast, emanating from where Reese was hunched over, finger blocking one ear as she talked into her cell phone. *She's calling the police!*

My throat seized. I looked at Z. Again, he didn't appear worried, but when had he ever?

"Miss Zell," Reese called, "I'm having them send an ambulance. Hold on."

Z spoke up. "I'll take her to the emergency room. I can get her there quicker."

I melted. Although he'd pretended I was invisible for the past week, he did care. He helped me gather my books. As he walked me out of the gymnasium, I caught a glimpse of Parker staring after us, ready to spit fire, even though I was the one who drank the acid. I smiled as he held open the door to his Civic like a total gentleman. When he drove out of the parking lot, he turned. We weren't heading south toward Eastern Maine Medical Center. Instead, we sped off north toward Duchess.

"What are you doing?" I asked him.

He smiled. "Don't give me that. I know where you want to go."

Damn him. "Are you kidding me? My esophagus could be corroding as we speak."

"But it's not," he said very surely.

I refused to give in so easily. He'd driven me absolutely nuts the past few weeks, acting as if I didn't matter at all to him. I wanted to hurt him so that he'd never ditch me again. "Fuck you," I growled. It was the first time I ever said such a thing. I crossed my arms. "Turn around."

He didn't. He shifted and pressed on the accelerator.

"Do it," I demanded. When he didn't, I reached over and pulled the wheel.

That got him. "Hey!" He overcorrected and we careened into oncoming traffic. The driver coming at us laid on his horn, its sound echoing in my ears as the car swerved and narrowly missed us. Z shook his head and then pulled into the nearest parking lot, for a Presbyterian church. He cut the ignition and stared at me. "You're crazy, you know that?"

"We're even now. You tried to kill me. Just returning the favor."

"What? You mean the acid? Dammit, Vic." He pounded the steering wheel with the palms of his hands. "Why would I do that? Oh yeah, I'm an evil genius who goes around killing high school students for the fun of it. You're out of your mind."

We stared at each other for the longest time.

Then he shook his head and bowed it, and when he looked up again, he was laughing. I laughed too. His moods were always so contagious. I'd just been poisoned, and yet we couldn't stop laughing our asses off.

"Why did you do it?" I asked him.

He narrowed his eyes at me. "Come on, Vic. Don't tell me you don't have any clue who stole the acid."

I studied him. "I don't."

He just stared. "Tell me. Is your wide-eyed innocence an act?"

"No. I have no idea who did it. Do you?"

He leaned back in his seat and raked his hands through his hair, then stared out the windshield. "I am in league with some crazy, crazy bitches," he mumbled.

I sighed. "You don't seem to mind Parker's craziness. You're with her a lot these days."

"What? Is that jealousy?" he asked, a playful smile on his face. "You're something else, Vic. *You* have a boyfriend you haven't been faithful to. *You* told people details I told you in confidence. And then you go and put on this innocent 'poor me' act, when *you're* the one who made this bed."

My face started to heat. He'd always been the one who played dangerous, not me. How had I become the bad guy? I reached for the door. I'd walk home, if I had to.

Z didn't try to stop me. He knew I wouldn't dare leave. He adjusted his rearview mirror and said, "You told me I can't trust anyone. And you're right. I don't. Not anymore. I'm a lone wolf."

"Some lone wolf," I mumbled, sinking down into the seat to let him talk.

His face turned serious. "I'm doing what I need to do. Chemistry is the only class standing between me and college. Lincoln has it in for me. He's threatened to fail me on more than one occasion. Parker told me that she often does a little 'repair work' on her grades, and she could help me once the teachers submit them in December."

"Z! Parker might be able to get away with it, but *you* could get expelled. Not to mention, there are easier ways to pass chemistry. Why don't you just talk to Lincoln? He'd give you extra credit or—"

"I've tried everything. He has it in for me."

I stared at him, unable to believe that someone was immune to Z's silver tongue. "No, he doesn't. He's not some—"

"What can I say? I have no power over the guy. I don't look half as good in a skirt as you girls do. Come on. You really think I *want* to be with Parker?" he asked, scowling. "Give me more credit than that. She's hot, but she will not shut up for a second. She's annoying as hell."

I didn't know what to say. Finally, I mustered, "You're the one who agreed to go to the dance with her."

He sighed. "Don't remind me. Hey, you're going too, right? With that fabulously talented boyfriend of yours?"

"I, er…" I started. I'd planned to leave that perfect dress hanging in my closet. I couldn't ask you to withstand that kind of social torture after what I'd done the night of the Perahia concert. But now, with Z looking at me, hopeful…maybe… "I could go alone."

"No, that would be weird. But if I drove you and your boyfriend, like a double date, then I wouldn't have to be alone with her."

"No," I said, twisting my hands together. "I mean, Andrew and I were thinking of doing something else. But…" Oh God, I couldn't say no. Not with the way he was looking at me. "Maybe we could go to the dance for a little while. If you really didn't want to be alone with her."

He nodded vigorously. "Yeah. Yeah, I don't." He reached over and started to play with the lock of hair near my ear. His other hand snaked over the center console and somehow found my knee under layers of the thick velvet of Lady Macbeth's dress. He grinned. "They did not make it easy to get it on back then."

"Not happening," I said, pushing his hand away, surprised at how resolute my voice sounded. If he asked again, I knew I'd be a goner.

He conceded. "Are you feeling better, Lady M?"

I nodded.

Then he drove me home. He didn't try anything, which I half hated, half thanked God for. I climbed up the stairs to my bedroom and hung my dress on a hanger for tomorrow's performance, then raced back outside.

You were sitting in our space. The sky was spitting little icy pellets, and yet, there you were, propped up against the fence, still as a statue. Funny, I couldn't remember the last time I'd come out here to meet you. And yet, there you were.

"Hi!" I said too brightly.

"Vic?" you asked.

"Yeah, I'm here. So...you come out here even when I don't? Even when it rains?"

Your voice was soft and somber. "It helps me to think."

I slid down against the fence, my sweater catching on some stray splinters. I didn't care that my spot of ground was damp. I didn't care that it was cold. I didn't care because life was finally going right again. "Do you hate me?"

I heard you pop a bubble. You passed me a stick of Juicy Fruit and said, "I could never hate you, Vic."

I tried to think of something to say to that, but I couldn't. Because sometimes I hated you so fiercely I thought I would die. The last night we'd spoken, on your birthday, I'd told you how much I hated you, how I wished you would man up and stop being such a wimp. I'd become your stepfather, the person you despised most in the world.

And yet you still didn't hate me.

I shivered in the silence, rubbing the goose bumps from my arms. Finally, you said, "I'm looking forward to seeing your acting debut."

I smiled. "You're still coming?"

"Of course. Wouldn't miss it."

I cringed, remembering I'd said the same thing about your birthday.

"Hey," I said. "Maybe we can do something on Saturday night?"

Excitement crept into your voice. It had been a long, long time since we'd done anything together as a couple. "Really?"

I swallowed. "Yeah. There's this dance at school."

A long silence followed. I knew what was going on in your head, Andrew. *We never went to dances before. You know better than to ask me to a dance. All those people. All that dancing! All that awkward social interaction. No thanks! We used to be on the same page about this.* But I also know you were thinking about my "man up" speech. You wanted to please me, you adorable, wonderful person, you. "If it would make you happy, Vic," you said quietly.

"It would."

"I returned the tuxedo already."

"That would be overdressing. You can wear whatever you want, really."

"I'd have to ask my mother if she could drive—"

"Someone will pick us up."

Excuses gone, I could almost feel the panic gripping you. I reached between the slats and tried to grab your hand and reassure you, but couldn't find it. "It'll be fun."

My mother appeared at the back door, silhouetted in the light from the kitchen. Her voice was an octave higher than normal. "Victoria. There's a policeman here to see you."

I stood up and wiped the wet dirt from my backside.

You said, "What's going on?"

"Someone put something in my water bottle at rehearsal."

You stood up. Your voice was concerned. "They did? What?"

"Oh, I'm sure it was a prank. Just some hydrochloric acid."

"*Acid?* Prank? Are you sure?"

I nodded. "Obviously. Who'd want to hurt me?" I smiled, desperately trying to add levity to the conversation, since you were about two steps from freaking out. "You know how sweet and innocent I am."

"You're not all that sweet and innocent," you countered, craning your neck for a look at the strange car parked in the driveway.

I smacked you. "Shut up."

You massaged your arm. "Ouch. All right, you're pure as the driven snow. With a really deadly right hook." You dug your hands in your pocket and rocked back on your heels, like you always did when you were thinking. "Um, well, OK." You said it like it was obviously not.

"What?" I said.

You shook your head. "I was just wondering why that wasn't the first thing you told me. Because someone almost killing you is kind of a big deal."

"It was just a joke," I said. "And I'm kind of…in shock over it."

Admit it, Andrew. I'm the most horrible liar ever. I should have cared about the poisoning, but it meant nothing to me, not after my conversation with Z. Not like I could tell you that. My mother was standing in the doorway, twisting her hands nervously. I would have to endure about a thousand questions from her and the police officer, and I dreaded that almost as much as I dreaded the third degree from you.

"So…dance. OK?"

Do you remember what you said, Andrew? You said, "Are you sure you don't want to go with someone else?"

"Who else would I go with?" I asked. "I want to go with my boyfriend."

"And t-that's me?" you stuttered.

I blinked. You never stuttered with me. I made myself answer right away, so as not to call attention to it. "Of course it is. Why even ask?"

You waited a long time before you spoke. "I feel like you're moving away from me."

"Never. I'm here. I'll always be right here," I told you, and I meant it. I still mean it. Sometimes friends move apart, but the best ones always come back.

CHAPTER 33

How was the performance?

It went off without a hitch.

Z was good?

He was competent. But...

But?

But everyone was on edge. The theater group at St. Ann's is like a family within a family. And we knew there was a cat among the pigeons. Moreover, it felt like... We all felt as though the acid incident was a prelude, and the real tragedy was yet to come. We were all holding our breath, waiting for something to happen. But I don't think anyone guessed how bad it would be.

—Police interview with Quincy Laughlin,
senior at St. Ann's

I T ISN'T RIGHT TO HAVE one person mean so much. At rehearsal, when I thought Z hated me, my words came out in a jumble. I could scarcely remember to breathe. But then, everything fell into place.

During the performance, I kept looking out from the wings to try to spot you. It was too dark though. I figured you were likely in the very back, since you hated sitting next to strangers. But the thought of you, watching me and smiling, buoyed me. Even with a thousand eyes on me, I hardly felt jittery at all. After the performance, there were three curtain calls. Reese floated about backstage, calling the cast "inspired" and "a revelation."

And I understood because that's what Z was to me.

I was hugged and congratulated by people I didn't even know. But I didn't care about them. There was only one hug that stood out in my mind, and it was the first one I received, the second the curtains swung closed. Z wrapped his arms around me, kissed me on the ear, and whispered, "You're a fucking acting maniac, Lady M."

How could I not love him after that?

Not that I didn't already love him.

I mean, as a friend.

Of course, Z was incredible. I doubt classically trained actors with years of experience could have churned out as moving a performance. Still, he went around, congratulating every last actor, every last stagehand—from Quincy, who'd been a perfectly acceptable MacDuff, to someone's twelve-year-old little sister who was in charge of making sure no one tampered with the water bottles again. He made everyone feel important.

News of the water-bottle incident had spread like wildfire and definitely rattled the quiet student body of St. Ann's.

Principal Cole gave a speech before the performance about how they were taking what had happened very seriously, determined to get to the bottom of it, et cetera, et cetera. According to Rachel, the police had come after Z and I left. They'd questioned people, searched the gymnasium, and found the empty vial in a nearby trash can. They took the vial in for fingerprinting. But really, the only person who got a strict tongue-lashing was Lincoln for not taking more care in storing his chemicals. In fact, rumors swirled that his job was on the line.

No doubt Z loved that.

After the performance, I spent as long as I could backstage. Nobody ate the *Great Job!* layer cake from Shaw's supermarket—partly because, as you know, layer cakes from Shaw's are always crappy and partly because everyone feared it was poisoned—but we all stood around it, congratulating one another. Parker hadn't been onstage, so she just kind of slinked into the background. Tonight was my night, for once. I'd never felt so adored, so a part of the St. Ann's family.

Being onstage must release endorphins because I was pumped, and so was Z. He looked hotter than I'd ever seen him. After we changed, he came out of the dressing room wearing his jeans, a raggedy T-shirt, and the immaculate, royal Macbeth cape. He held it in front of his face, like Dracula. I giggled. Then he reached into the garment bag I was holding, which had my costume I was returning to wardrobe, and pulled out my regal red cape. He swung it over my head and tightened it at the neck. "I vant to suck your blood," he said.

"Not if I suck yours first," I said, making my pointer fingers into fangs and wiggling them in his direction.

He grabbed for me, and I shrieked and ran away. Laughing, he chased me all the way out to the hallway, where I stopped short. He caught up to me and threw his arm over my shoulder. I could feel his breath on the back of my neck. I swatted him away.

Because my parents and your mom were there.

I looked for you, and my heart sank as I realized you hadn't come. I knew it was a long shot to ask, what with your anxiety. Still, I'd hoped. I know you didn't want to let me down.

But you did. I understand why, but it hurt me not to see you there. I suppose after what I did to you at Perahia, I deserved that little turnabout, didn't I?

I introduced Z your parents, and they all told me how wonderful I'd been. Then they heaped their praise on Z. Your mother told me she was so happy for me and hugged me tight.

I told your mom, "I'm sorry Andrew couldn't be here."

My father cleared his throat. My mother hooked her arm through mine, as if expecting me to collapse like a house of cards. But all I was thinking was that maybe it was better this way. You were where you wanted to be, and I was where I wanted to be.

Oh God, you could cut the awkward silence with a knife. Their eggshell smiles told me everything. They'd watched Z chase me out into the hallway and grab me, coming in close enough to kiss me.

They knew I'd betrayed you.

The only person who wasn't awkward was Z. He smiled and tossed his cape over his shoulder, wordlessly taking it all in. Then he told me he'd swing by my house at seven the next day for the dance, and I nodded and waved goodbye.

He turned on his heel and sauntered down the hallway and out to the parking lot, still rocking that cape of his.

I suddenly felt goofy in my cape, so I untied it.

He had no one. Not a single person from his family had come to see his brilliant performance.

And yet I still envied him as he escaped into the cold November night.

CHAPTER 34

Who do you think was responsible for the acid incident?

Who would do that?

If you had to pinpoint anyone...

Probably Victoria.

Victoria...you think she poisoned her own bottle?

I know it sounds out there. But I could see her doing
    something like that. I mean, there were all these
    rumors about her from her last school, that she'd
    gone berserk. So yeah, I wouldn't put it past her to
    poison her own water bottle to get attention.

So Victoria had acted out before to get attention?

She tried out for the play. Does that count?

You did too. You were her understudy.

What? Are you saying I poisoned Victoria so that I
    could be in the play? Yeah, no.

Were you upset you didn't get the part?

A little, but I wouldn't hurt anyone for the role. I
    mean, that's crazy. But Victoria has a shady history.
    Nobody quite knows what's going on with her.

My boyfriend's last girlfriend went to Duchess and said she'd break down crying for no reason in the middle of math. Plus, she totally had the motive. What can I say? She was jealous of me. She wanted what I had.

What you had?

Yeah, duh. My boyfriend. Z, I mean. Not the guy I'm dating now.

OK, but if Victoria had it in for you, why did she poison herself? Why not sabotage your water bottle?

Because then I would've been the center of attention. And she didn't want that.

Would she have had the opportunity?

Totally. She could've done that anytime she wasn't in a scene.

Did the stunt have the desired effect?

The second he heard the news, Z was at her side, volunteering to take her to the hospital.

So obviously he didn't think she'd done it to herself.

No. He always thought the best of everyone. He even offered to give her a ride to the dance.

So they were friends?

Friends, yeah. Maybe even more. I don't know why. He was the only person she talked to, really. He managed to get her to open up, and I think he liked how that made him special. He might have felt sorry for her, but I think he enjoyed protecting her. They were both the new kids. But it was sickening, really, how quickly he'd drop everything the second she needed him. Z lived for secrets, for mysteries. He gravitated to them. And she was one of the biggest mysteries in school. So, whatever.

You sound a little jealous.

I don't get jealous. And I don't get even either. Victoria was weird. And there was no mistaking that she was vengeful too. Especially after what she did at the dance.

—**Interview with Parker Cole, junior at St. Ann's**

THE DANCE. I THOUGHT ABOUT it literally every second of that day and, because of that, allowed myself too much time to get ready. Every step in the process was like part of a sacred ritual. I started with a long bubble bath, then washing and curling my hair, and slathering on passion fruit lotion. I think brides probably spend less time getting ready on their wedding day. Even so, I was ready before six.

You are so like me, Andrew. You must have been carrying on your own rituals in your house because a little after six fifteen, you knocked on my front door. Your hair was slicked back with gel, and you were wearing your old, too-tight chinos and a carefully pressed white shirt and tie. You trembled, your face as somber as if we had a date with the executioner. You had a little plastic box with a corsage in it, which you dropped the second you saw me.

"Oh God," you whispered.

I looked down at myself. "Do I look bad?"

"No. Just…" And then you started to stutter. "I-I d-didn't kn-now it was you, at f-first."

I pulled you inside. You were always comfortable with my parents, but there was a strange silence in the room when my parents came in. My father said, "Are you sure this is a good idea? It's going to sleet later. The roads may be slippery," but I just waved him off and told him that it would be fine.

By the time seven rolled around, I could practically see your heart beating out of your chest.

What was it, Andrew? Why were you scared of me? I'd like to think you were struck speechless by my beauty, but it was something else, wasn't it? Did you know then that you couldn't go through with it?

When Z came, he honked from the driveway. They didn't get out. I could see Parker's blond hair and lipstick-magnified scowl through the dirty windshield of Z's Civic as I navigated down the cracked driveway in my new high heels.

But when I turned to wait for you, you weren't behind me. You were standing on the porch between our two front doors, looking more frightened than ever.

"Come on," I beckoned.

You bowed your head. "I can't do this."

"Really?" I said, looking back at Z's car. I had this frantic feeling. "You can. I promise. It'll be fine."

You were sweating despite the cold air. I could see little droplets on your forehead, illuminated by the porch light. "Go on without me."

"I can't do that," I murmured, picking my way back up

the steps, taking your hand, and tugging you toward me, all the time knowing that I could, and I would. I'd have gone in that car even if flaming meteorites were crashing down all over the earth. Z needed me.

But you were resolute. "Really. Go. I'll be fine."

And well, you know, I did. I had to, Andrew. I had promised Z.

"Hi," I said when I slid into the backseat.

"Zup," Z said, looking at me when I closed the door. "What about your boyfriend?"

I was so wrapped up in wanting, needing Z to say more, to look me over and whistle or say I looked nice, that I didn't answer. When I realized he wouldn't be pulling out of the driveway without an explanation, I said, "He's not feeling well. It's just me tonight."

Parker looked up from her phone and let out an audible groan. Z mumbled something about that being "too bad," then threw the car in reverse and looked back at me as he pulled out. Had he not done that, I might have waved at you or watched you as we pulled away.

He grinned mischievously, which made every hair on my body stand at attention.

We rode to St. Ann's without conversation. Z cranked up the volume on the radio because "Dope Hit" by the Young Freaks was playing. I watched Parker. She wasn't wearing the expensive green dress she'd bought with me. This one was silver, like the wrapper on a Hershey's kiss, and looked even more expensive. Her hair was twisted in an elaborate updo. At one point, she turned to me and slurred, "No date. Isn't this *convenient* for you?"

I peered over the seat back and saw one of those travel cups between her knees. She lifted it, took a sip from a straw that was rimmed in red, and then dug into her purse to reapply her lipstick.

"Do you think you could bounce us around a little more?" she complained as Z went over a pothole. "I really want to have this gloss up my nose."

He looked over at her, his lips a straight line. I think if she hadn't been Cole's daughter, he might have deposited her on the side of the road to fend for herself. Instead, he slowed down.

When we pulled up at the school, Parker insisted on being dropped off in front. The decorating committee had put up an arch of gray and burgundy balloons in the front doorway to the school, and a group of classmates was huddled under it, talking. When Parker tottered out of the car and nearly tripped up the curb, I finally realized why.

She was drunk or high, or maybe both.

"Do you need help?" I asked as she wavered on her heels in front of the school, trying to get the small strap of her purse over her head.

She practically snarled at me as Rachel approached. "No, thank you." She grabbed onto her friend's arm and shrieked, "Let's get this party started!"

Rachel looked horrified. She mouthed to me, *Is she on something?*

I shrugged, and Parker led her into the fray. Ordinarily if

someone showed up to a school function in that state, she'd be suspended. But this was Principal Cole's daughter. I assumed she'd be fine.

I wanted to wait for Z, but he was parking the car in no-man's-land and it had begun to rain. So I tried to push through the crowd, to find some place where I wouldn't feel like a total third wheel. But the weirdest thing happened. People stopped me and said hi. They opened their circles to let me in. They all knew me now because of the play, because of Z. I chatted with all of them, and even though I didn't know these people well, they acted like I'd been a part of their circle their entire lives.

When they asked me who I came with, I told them my boyfriend was sick.

Twenty minutes later, I saw Z. He moved through the crowd with ease, talking to people, giving high fives, laughing.

We both orbited the room, but in different paths. Eventually, I knew that like two ions with opposite charges, we'd collide.

After I made the rounds, I managed to snag a seat at one of the tables. I exhaled an enormous breath as I settled down with a basket of popcorn, thinking that would be my date for the night. I'd never been to a dance before. I'd been so wrapped up in getting you to go with me and trying to look beautiful that I hadn't realized I had absolutely no idea what to do at one of these things. I trembled, feeling a little of what you must feel every time you step out of your house.

I looked across the dance floor. Z had somehow found drunk Parker. She scowled at him, shaking her head belligerently. He seemed to say some calming words to her. He leaned over and kissed her forehead, then looked in my general direction. I swung my head around and realized his eyes were fastened on the exit behind me. Two seconds later, I watched him escorting her toward the back hallway. Great. I collapsed against my seat and wondered if I should have stayed home with you. You wouldn't dance even if you were here, but I missed you. Alone among the folding chairs, I felt fear vining its way up my spine. *You don't belong here.*

No.

It was Z's voice I thought of then. *Vic, calm down. Relax, all right? You're perfect.*

Before I knew it, I'd made my way from the empty chairs to join the throng. I was surprised that the kids on the dance floor welcomed me in. The newest song from Young Freaks was playing, and though I didn't know the words, it seemed like everyone else did. The mob on the dance floor began to throb in time with the pulsing of the strobe light.

I danced. I danced wildly for once, without caring or worrying what everyone else would think.

Even though I kept my eye trained on the doorway that Z and Parker had disappeared through, I got caught up in the dance, the beat, the rhythm. I'd never felt so free. Parker wasn't the only one who'd been drinking because I could smell the alcohol in people's sweat, and everyone was going wild. But I felt drunk too. Maybe it was the strobe light. Or maybe it was Z reappearing alone. He stood on the sideline and scanned the room, then proceeded to make a beeline my way.

He grabbed me by the hand and danced up next to me.

I know he'd been joking, but he *was* a dancing machine. He hooked a finger and beckoned me close to him. I leaned my body toward him. He gyrated against me, and I had no choice but to match his movements with my own. I smelled his scent, that heady, cloying cinnamon that made me feel crazy enough to want to lick his jawline. Then he whispered, "You think your boyfriend would mind if I borrowed you?"

I shook my head.

Of course you'd mind.

But that was beside the point.

At that moment, I was dying to be alone with Z.

He took my hand and led me toward the hallway. "Where's Parker?" I asked.

"Sleeping it off in the nurse's office," he said dismissively, leading me toward the front offices. We went past the guidance counselors' offices, and sure enough, the one open door was to the nurse's office. I thought we were going to check on her, but Z kept on walking.

"Is she OK?"

He nodded. "She's bombed, but she'll be fine. Come on."

I followed him into the secretary's vestibule, where we stopped at a thick paneled door with "Principal Cole" written on a polished brass placard. He smiled at me and held up a key.

"Where'd you—"

He shushed me, then twisted the key and let me in. Before I knew it, he'd made himself comfortable behind Cole's ornate, antique desk. He leaned back in the executive leather chair and put his feet up on the blotter, as if he had all the time in the world.

I cast a nervous glance into the secretary's office. "Can we go now?"

Z shook his head and smiled. "Relax."

"But what are we…"

He reached down and riffled through a drawer, pulling out a Sharpie, which he hung from his lip, like a cigar. "What do you think, kid? Zachary Zimmerman, leader of the free world. I like the sound of that." He put his hands behind his head and stared up at the ceiling.

"Really, Z," I told him. "What's this all about? I mean, first you poison me, and now you're begging for more trouble."

He gave me a questioning look, like *I* was the one who was up to no good, even though he was the one with both hands in the cookie jar. "It wasn't me. I didn't do anything to your water bottle."

"Then who?"

"My sweet girl," he said. "You and I are the same. Why would I ever hurt you?"

I melted right there. He could've called me his little sack of dog poo, and I would've swooned. Being called his *anything* always got me. "You never told me who did it."

"Who else? Parker. She's jealous as hell of you."

My mouth dropped open. "Me? Why?"

He tossed the key up in the air and caught it. "Why else? Because you have me."

I…*had him*? It certainly felt the other way around. I opened my mouth to tell him that, but he stood up and strode over to me. He grabbed my hand and pushed a lock of hair out of my face. Then he put a finger on my chin and gently lifted it. "What does that mean?" I murmured.

"Come on, Precious." He pulled me flush against him, and his fingers trailed down my bare shoulder blades, making me shiver. He found my zipper and tugged playfully at it, then brought his mouth to my ear, close but not quite touching.

I knew if he asked anything of me, I would cave. It took all my strength to push him away. "No way. I'm wise to you and your snaky ways."

"Break my heart," he said.

If his heart was broken, you wouldn't know it. He collapsed back into the chair, puffing on his imaginary cigar. I collected myself enough to remember where I was. "Z," I begged. "Why are we even here?"

"Ah, my sweet, innocent Vic. What will it take to turn you to the dark side?" Then he stood up and motioned me toward him. "Come on. You've always wanted to sit behind this desk, haven't you? Do it. Just once."

Begrudgingly, I stalked over to the big leather chair and slumped into it. "Happy?"

He'd already skirted to the file cabinet near the window. He stuck another key in the lock and twisted it, much to my horror. My voice broke as I said, "What are you doing now?"

He shrugged, grinning, and started to leaf through the files.

"Those are Cole's private files. You could get expelled… arrested!" I whispered hoarsely. When he didn't answer, I pushed out of the chair and stalked to the door. "I'm leaving."

But, of course, I hesitated. He knew he had me on a string, so my threat did nothing to stop him. By the time I got back to the main hall, I felt foolish. I stood there for a moment, already missing him and replaying his words: *Because you have me.*

I turned around.

I went back.

We collided in the doorway as he was coming out of Cole's office. He jumped back, eyes wide. Then he exhaled. "Hell, Vic."

"We need to—"

He silenced me by planting his hands on my shoulders, bringing his face to just inches from mine. His eyes bored into mine, as if searching for some hidden truth. His voice was no longer playful. "Why didn't you bring your boyfriend?"

"What?" His gaze was too intense. I had to look away. "Andrew was feeling sick, and—"

"Why didn't you bring your boyfriend, Vic?" he repeated, louder this time.

I shrunk back. He wanted me to admit that I'd left you at home so I could be alone with him, that I'd planned this all along. But that wasn't true. *You* bowed out on me. I opened my mouth to speak, but stammered. "I-I don't know. I…"

My eyes trailed behind him, to the cabinets near the window. One of them, the one on the very bottom, U–Z, was slightly open. "Wait. Whose files were you going through?"

But the answer was written all over his face.

"You went through *mine*? Those are private!"

"Last night, after the play…I had to know the truth."

I scowled at him. So *this* was why he was risking expulsion? If he had gone through my files, all he would've found were the details about my dull meetings with Leary. Hardly the stuff of good investigative journalism. "What truth? That my grade point average is a three-point-three?"

He put a hand under my chin, twisting my face to meet his. "Say it," he murmured. "Come on."

I started to quiver, and tears flooded my eyes. His intensity scared me.

"Then don't say it," he whispered as I closed my eyes, feeling his eyelashes fluttering on my face. "Just know that I know. It's OK. I won't tell anyone."

"I don't know what you mean," I answered.

"You and me. We're both so fucked up, so afraid that one wrong move will send the house of cards crumbling to the ground. I get you, all right? *That's* what I mean."

The anxiety. Yes, sometimes, that crumbling feeling was all I felt. But I'd been rendered mute by a combination of fear and desire. As he pressed his body against mine, I lost myself again, right there, in the tragedy of us. There were so many forces working to keep us apart, and yet we always wound up together. *Binding energy*, Lincoln would've said. It had a definition in chemistry class, but right now, the only definition I could think of was the two of us.

I thought Z was going to kiss me, so I relinquished control and tilted my chin up to meet him. But he stopped. He didn't jump; he didn't back away; he didn't do anything to convey we were in danger. Instead he uttered a listless, "Zup."

Dazed, I followed his line of sight to the door.

Parker had cleaned herself up. Her hair was down but brushed, and her makeup was flawless. The only ugly thing about her was her expression. "What are you doing, Z?" Parker snarled.

Z backed away from me. "Look, Parker, it's—"

She scoffed. "Not what I think it is? Really? You're going to use that line on me?"

His voice was uncharacteristically soft. "No, it's exactly what you think it is. But what you don't get is—"

Her eyes blazed. "What? That you're a real asshole, Z? No, I get that." Tossing her hair, she turned and stalked out the door.

My heart was in my throat. "Do you think she's going to get us expelled?"

I could almost see the gears in his head turning. "Not if I can help it." He adjusted his tie and raced after her.

A strange calmness settled over me as I fixed my dress and closed the office door behind me. This was Z. He'd find a way to fix it. I didn't doubt that one bit.

CHAPTER 35

Description of Head Injuries: Multiple contusions on back of skull and fracture associated with blunt force trauma. Multiple punctuate scratches were present over the bridge of the nose. The left cheek was contused and edematous, with an overlying two-inch contusion. The lips were abraded. The mucosal surfaces of the lips were contused and slightly edematous, with multiple superficial lacerations. Four-inch area of abrasion along left mandible region.

—Coroner's report

Z MANAGED TO COAX PARKER INTO leaving with him. I saw them slip out the front doors together, and they drove home without me. I didn't mind. The ride home would have been *very* uncomfortable.

I caught a ride home with Marcus Poplin and Ava Brice, a couple of seniors who live in Milo. I made small talk with Marcus and Ava, and they went on and on about how well I did in *Macbeth*, but I wasn't thinking about that. I was thinking about Z. I wondered what he was saying to Parker. I wondered why knowing him was like trying to decode the most baffling of riddles. Why had he been so intent on breaking into Cole's office? Just to go through my files? If that was the case, he didn't have to risk our expulsion. I would've told him whatever he wanted to know.

But that was Z. He thrived on danger.

I sure didn't.

When I got home, my pulse was still pounding, and I was shivering because my dress was damp with cooling perspiration. You were waiting on my front porch, the collar of your lumberjack flannel pushed up to your ears to ward off the cold. I wiped my mouth and forced my best smile as you took my hand. "How was it?" you asked me.

"Not so great," I mumbled. "I wish you'd been there."

That was the truth, incidentally.

"You know I can't do those things, Vic."

There was an unusual fierceness in your eyes. I tried to head to my door, but you held on to me. Then you pulled me to you and kissed me.

I like the way you kiss, Andrew. You and Z are a study in opposites. He takes control, and you do everything tentatively. But this time, there was no hesitation in your kiss. It was as if you'd been psyching yourself up to do it. You never quite know where to put your hands or how to move your tongue, but you're sweet and gentle and you taste good. And you let me be an equal participant in the kiss.

I was tired of Z being so complicated and volatile. I wanted easy, safe. One boy and one girl in love forever. Enough of this bouncing around between Z's whims. I wanted the comfort and stability only you could offer me.

After a few seconds, you tried to pull away, but I wouldn't let you go. You felt too good.

"We can continue this," I whispered, coaxing your body toward mine.

I was going to suggest you come to my bedroom, but you shot down the idea before I could get it out. "We can't."

I pouted, then leaned in and kissed your ear. "I want to."

You backed away and looked at the ground. "*I* can't. Jeez, Vic."

I stopped.

Your voice was harder than I'd ever heard it. "You know this. You know it's impossible. You…you need to get a good night's sleep, Vic. Whatever you want me to do, it can't happen. I know I'm not the person you want anymore. That's *my* fault. I accept it. You…you still have a chance to find that person. The person who'll make you happy." There was disappointment on your face. Had I ever disappointed you before? "If I come to your bedroom, I'll only make things worse."

You may have been scared, but you had no reason to fear me. I didn't see what we would have done as tearing us apart—I wanted us to building something beautiful between us. Except nothing I did drove you wild enough to abandon all reason. While at times I thought Z had a cold heart, often I thought yours was even colder. Sometimes you made me feel *so wrong*. Why couldn't I get you crazy with desire? Why couldn't I get you to lose inhibitions, Andrew? Why did you have to be so damn *well-behaved*?

I dropped your hand and ran into the house without another word.

CHAPTER 36

Ms. Cole, was Z agitated the night of the dance?

Yes.

Do you know what he was upset about?

We'd had a fight. About Victoria. She came without
a date and proceeded to glom on to him, taking
up all his attention. He was my date, and yet he
couldn't say no to her. Like I said, sometimes he
was too nice for his own good. I think he liked
having her hanging on his every word. She was his
groupie. I told him he needed to man up and tell
her to get her own life. At first he agreed, but then
he started acting really strange.

But he still drove you home.

Right. Well, not home. We went to an after-party. But
he apologized, and everything was fine between us.

So he didn't drive Victoria home.

Right. Victoria wasn't invited to the after-party at the
hotel because it was just three couples, so it was
never the plan to take her. But something was on

Z's mind. On the drive to the hotel, he was quiet.
Then he banged his hands on the steering wheel
and told me he needed to fix something.

What?

Who knows? The world. That's Z. He dropped me off
at the hotel, saying he was sorry but he'd make it
up to me, then he sped away.

And you have no idea where he was going or
what he needed to fix. Do you think it involved
Victoria?

I don't know. Yes, maybe. He wouldn't tell me. Like I
said, Z loved a good mystery, especially one star-
ring him.

—Police interview with Parker Cole, junior at St. Ann's

I WANTED TO BE WITH YOU that night, Andrew. Just so
we're perfectly clear: it was supposed to be you.

I told my parents the dance was boring but fine and headed
straight to my room. Z texted me as I was getting ready for bed.
U make it home OK?

I texted back: Yep, no thanks to you. ;) Then I texted him
what I was really thinking: What happened with Parker?

He came back with: Nothing good. Doghouse. Population
me. With a little emoji of a black dog with a pink tongue.

Serves you right. You ARE a dog. Will she tell Cole?

He quickly responded: Nah.

Really? I thought we were doomed for sure.

I waited a long time for the next text. We need to talk. Alone.

I'd gotten to be an expert at texting—and expert at many other things, thanks to Z. But my fingers trembled over the screen: That depends. Will you break up with her?

His response made my stomach drop. What about him?

I swallowed. I didn't want to break up with you. I love you, Andrew. Always, unconditionally. What we had was like coming home after a long adventure. Z was that adventure. I'd been unfair to you. You deserved so much better. If I broke up with him...then what???

He wouldn't let you go.

I stared at those words. You and I are close, Andrew, but Z didn't know you. He didn't know the gentle soul you were. If I broke up with you, you'd go. You'd hate it, and it would destroy you, but you'd leave me be. And God, I didn't want to destroy you. I never wanted that.

Never.

Vic. Stop. You have to stop pretending.

I would rather die than break your heart, Andrew. You and I...that was all I knew. We were a given. Maybe that was why I took our relationship for granted. But the possibility of there no longer being an "us" was more terrifying than thrilling, like losing a limb. I know.

Then I typed: Come over tonight.

I smiled at his response. Thought you'd never ask.

I opened the window and let the cold air in. I was warm with anticipation, my face flushed. Every part of me ached to be filled by him. As I stood in front of the window, taking in deep breaths of frosty air, I saw that little orange fireball near your house. Your stepdad's cigarette. He was out in the backyard, muttering curses into the darkness.

It was after midnight. I thought about how you'd turned me down, Andrew, how it could've been you in my bed that night. I heard noises that could've been your mother crying. Your stepfather was probably pissed at you for coming back so early. He probably called you a faggot again. Am I right?

Z must have been driving toward my house when he texted, too hyped up to go home, because he showed up only a few minutes after your father went inside and slammed the screen door. Z scaled the side of my house and said as he threw his leg over the windowsill, "I thought that guy would never leave. Angry man."

"That's Andrew's stepfather," I explained. I started babbling about your stepdad, about how he didn't do anything but work and drink and drag you on hunting trips, but Z silenced me with a finger across my lips.

"I don't want to think about *them*. Just you."

He kissed me, uncharacteristically tenderly and softly. He led me to the edge of my bed as if it were *his* room and sat down with me between his legs, staring up at me with such little-boy innocence, as if I held his whole world in my hands. He slowly slipped my zipper down my side.

"We don't have to do anything," he whispered. "I just want to be close to you."

I nodded and pulled my dress down the rest of the way, then helped him remove his shirt. Just thinking of his body made me suck in a breath and tremble—but getting to touch it again? Taste it? I tentatively traced a finger along the rise of muscle just under his collarbone. His skin was so smooth, like sculpted marble, with a little coarse, golden hair. He wasn't a boy. He wasn't a man either. He was only a hair-breadth from immortality.

We got into my bed, under my ruffled comforter, and pressed against each other. He was so warm, and I could feel his heart throbbing against mine. He held me, breathing softly on my shoulder for the longest time. "This feels perfect," he murmured. "You know, you're perfect."

It *was* perfect. Ours was a study in inevitability. That night, we didn't make love. I'd always thought that phrase was corny. No, we made more than that—we made each other. We didn't rush. We bared everything to each other, as was meant to be. As was right.

The sky began to lighten. He held on to me, his chest against my back. His lips nipped my ear as he whispered, "I don't want to leave you."

The thought instantly hollowed me. "Then don't. Stay with me, and let's do this forever."

He kissed the top of my nose. "Think your parents would have something to say about that?"

I sighed. I knew they would.

"It's like a different world here, a fantasy world." He pointed to the window. "I don't want to face what's out there. I know you don't either."

I know he didn't mean it, but he pointed at our spot. And

the second he did, guilt overwhelmed me. I stiffened, then wiggled out of his arms.

He sat up and looked at me. "What?"

"I… Nothing."

"Tell me," he said, tracing circles on my knee. "If you don't tell me, how am I supposed to help you?"

I shook my head. That's one thing Z never got; sometimes things couldn't be fixed. "I… Forget it."

"You're an enigma wrapped inside a conundrum, you know that?" He sighed, throwing up his hands.

"You're one to talk! You're a riddle shrouded in a mystery."

He chuckled, conceding. "OK. But what was the first thing I told you when we met? To ask me. Ask me anything."

"What, so you could make a joke in answering?"

For a second he looked stricken, but he nodded. "Fine," he said. "You want secrets? I'll tell you all my secrets. But only on the condition that you tell me yours."

I sighed. "But I don't have any."

He stared at me as if I'd sprouted horns. "Yeah, you do."

"You went through my files at school. What did they say about me?" I asked. "I get the feeling you already know all my *secrets*." I whispered the last part because it was kind of ridiculous. Even if my file contained notes from my talks with Leary, that information wasn't juicy. I took anxiety meds. So what? So did a million other people. I had nothing to hide.

Z motioned to zip his lips, and I lunged at him and playfully pulled the imaginary zipper back. I so desperately wanted to know him. "OK, fine," I said. "We trade. You go first. Shoot."

He gripped handfuls of my pillow. He didn't look at me. "I... Oh hell. Here goes. The rumors about me and Bethany? They weren't lies."

I don't know why I was so shocked. Z never did anything halfway, so I should've known his secret would be huge. "You mean..."

"After my grandparents died, there was all this back-and-forth about where I was going to go to finish up my schooling. I came here from Arizona over the summer, not knowing anyone, not knowing what the fuck I was going to do. The only person I knew was Bethany. She picked me up at the airport, and well...she's hot and she was nice to me. Really nice, and not in the way an aunt would be. She and I..." He paused for a moment. "It was like we were playing house together, isolated from everyone else. We were both lonely people who ended up drifting together. And then she told me she had to register me for school. I didn't know why, at first. I figured I'd get my GED and get a job, but she was insistent. I thought it was all a joke, me going to a private Catholic school like St. Ann's on the state's dime, her acting all mom.

"The next day, she introduced me to this boyfriend I didn't know she had. I quickly figured out why she'd agreed to have me stay with her. I'm her meal ticket. She's collecting money from the government as my guardian—you know, to feed and clothe me. But it doesn't go to that; it goes into their pockets. Will, her boyfriend, is a fucking a-hole. He told me that if I didn't want to be thrown out on the street, I'd better start earning my keep. Dealing to the rich kids at school and stuff. You know, like the bowling alley. *That* is why I'm at St. Ann's, and why I'm so popular there. So…I don't know, Vic. My life is fucked up beyond recognition right now."

I stared at him for the longest time.

He'd said his life was fucked up a million times. He'd said I was too sweet to be corrupted by him. I thought he was just saying those things.

But yeah, his revelation was more than I expected. Suddenly, every one of his unexplained absences and mood swings made sense. All those times he'd been unable to meet me to practice his lines.

"Oh my God, Z," I whispered. I could feel a tremor in his body. He was scared. For the first time, he didn't have his life under control. "You need to leave. You can't stay with them."

"And go where? I told you. In another year and a half, I *will* leave. But I've got to get into college first, earn a baseball scholarship or something. Otherwise I have nowhere to go." He hung his head. He looked so different, so young.

His facade crumbled, and I saw Z for who he really was, for what they'd made him. He'd let them puppet him, tell him what to do and where to go, and he was just going to let that continue? For how long would he be able to put up with that? He could get arrested or killed.

No. Not acceptable.

"So?" he asked.

My turn.

I said, "Wait. Back up. You have to do something. Don't let them push you around."

His eyes widened with surprise. "What would you do?"

The first thing that came to mind shocked me. *Kill them. Kill them before they kill you.* My hands shook—where'd that kind of violence come from? Instead I said, "Go to the police."

He said, "And then I wouldn't have anywhere to live. I spent three months in foster care after my grandparents died. It's hell."

We were silent, unable to come up with a better plan. Then he nudged me. I'd put my turn off long enough.

I mumbled, "I was going to break up with Andrew. I almost did last night."

I waited for him to say something encouraging. Instead, he said, "Buzz. Wrong."

"What?"

"What kind of secret is that? I mean, it's not even true."

"Yes it is," I said, indignant, my face heating as he studied me.

"Something tells me you'll keep saying that you were *going to*. Never that you did. You can't, can you? Why don't you admit you're just as messed up as I am? We can't move forward or backward. We're both stuck."

He was right. I'll never be able to leave you, Andrew. Never. You're all I've ever known. You may not make my heart beat faster the way Z does, but you're responsible for it beating steadily. For it beating still. And I love you more than anything.

Instead of telling him that though, I said, "Speak for yourself." Then I cleared my throat. "I have anxiety. Which is why I have those pills." I pointed at my night table.

His gaze traveled over to them without much interest. He didn't seem satisfied. I was about to tell him I was all out of material when he grabbed my wrists in his hands, pinning me down with his weight. Those brilliant blues worked their hypnotizing action. "The whole world is for shit, Precious. But not this. No matter what is going on outside this window, *we* still matter. I wish we could just leave them all behind."

A crow flitted across my window, startling me. I thought about that old wives' tale, about how a raven outside one's window signified the approach of death. The sun was starting to poke over the horizon, casting pale-yellow rays. It would be hard for Z to escape unseen if he waited much longer. He started to pull on his boxer briefs, and I threw myself into his arms, desperately raining kisses over his face as if pressuring my lips to memorize every feature. It's like my lips knew that this would be our last time.

"So what do you want to do? Run away together?"

I said it as a joke. But he nodded slowly. "Bethany has a stash of money. Easily more than a thousand dollars. We could, you know."

Fear gripped me. Fear of leaving home, of leaving you, Andrew. I thought of all the times you tried to escape, and look how that turned out. "But I…"

"We can do it," he said. "Throw the past away. Get away from all these demons that haunt us. Start fresh. That's what we need."

I laughed bitterly. It would never work. "I… What would we do? I mean, what would my parents and—"

"Andrew." It was the first time he actually said your name. His eyes narrowed, and he exhaled. "Dammit, Vic, let your enormously talented boyfriend fight his own battles for once. Look, let's meet tonight. In the Kissing Woods."

I shuddered. "You mean the Killing Woods. Why?"

His finger trailed lightly down my chest to my breastbone, and when his gaze met mine, it was there again. That adoring, more-than-the face-of-God look that told me *this* was the moment all the others were leading up to. "Because I need to show you something. Maybe then you'll be able to leave it all behind."

So, of course, I agreed to meet him. Before he climbed out my window, he touched my lips with his finger, and even before he pulled away, I ached to have him back.

He climbed outside and gracefully scuttled onto the grill and out of the yard, leaving me smiling goofily after him.

Until I saw you. You were still wearing the same outfit from before, like you hadn't slept all night, staring up at my window from our spot by the fence. You didn't move. You didn't even seem to breathe. For the first time, looking into those eerily calm features of yours, I had no idea what was on your mind.

And for the first time, Andrew, you scared me.

CHAPTER 37

I KNEW I NEEDED TO MAKE a choice, and that choice would completely alter the course of my life. I'd weighed the pros and cons. I had safety in one column, adventure in another. Love versus lust. Sanity versus madness.

So in the end, I closed my eyes and jumped.

I didn't meet you at our spot in the backyard last night, but I don't think you expected me to, did you? You were different now too, harder, more suspicious. Not just because of me. I wasn't the first person to hurt you, Andrew, but I'd probably hurt you the most.

The look on your face while you were standing in the yard scared me. You were more than just disappointed in me. You were enraged.

But here's the truth: I thought about you and me more than you probably realize. I thought of how blissfully simple everything had been before. And, oh Andrew, my Andrew, how I wished we could go back in time. As deeply as I'd fallen for Z, part of me wished I hadn't changed, that I was still the person who wanted nothing more than you.

I wanted you. I never stopped wanting to be with you, do you understand?

Never.

You were the one who gave up on us.

I invited *you* in first. It was supposed to be *you* with me that night.

Instead, *you* gave up on me.

Last night, while my parents dozed watching a football game in the living room, I went out to the street and broke into a run. I'd thrown on one of my dad's running jackets, pushing up the collar to hide my face, and pressed a black skullcap over my hair.

The frosty air felt good on my bare skin, freeing. Z was right on time again. He pulled over to the side of the road in his Civic, leaving his headlights on. I shone my flashlight at him. "What's with the disguise?" he said.

"It's not a disguise. I'm cold."

His breath came out in a white cloud. When he came around the side of the car, he collided with me, lifting my body off the ground and kissing me hard.

I took him by the hand and led him into the woods. As we crunched over dried leaves, our heavy jackets caught on bare branches, and animals called to each other in the distance.

Z pressed me against a white, knotty cedar tree, tilting my face up to the stars. Those big eyes were wild. He seemed so strong, so powerful, that my fingers weakened and I dropped the flashlight.

He took my hands between his own and restored feeling

to them. We spent much of the time before midnight reverting those woods back to their original name, as we desperately raced our cold hands under layers of clothing, seeking the blissfully warm skin underneath. "Trust me, you have to trust me," he whispered to me again and again, as his fingers and lips touched every inch of flesh they could find.

I told him I trusted him, but part of me was just saying what he wanted to hear, what I wanted to be true. Like I told him, I'm beyond trusting and being trusted now. Trust can be repaired and regained, but I think sometimes it gets so beaten from you that it shatters into a zillion pieces. Then it becomes nothing more than a word.

When we pulled apart from each other, breathless, I whispered, "Why did you want to meet me here?" I pressed my forehead against his.

He looked at me for the longest time, as if willing the answer into my head. "You know, don't you? Tell me you know. Tell me you remember the last time you were here."

I shook my head fiercely, but as I did, a memory loosened in my mind, falling into place. The wet, earthy smell. The leaves crunching. The air biting. The night wind. It was a night like this.

You and me, Andrew. We used to come here. Not to make out though. We were just kids then. Best friends.

How many times had you tried to run away? Right down Route 11, headed for Bangor. This was as far as we ever got. Sometimes you'd say you'd never been able to make it even *this* far without me. We'd stay out here, huddled together, barely talking, waiting until your stepdad had calmed down enough so that you could venture home.

I whispered your name.

Z opened his mouth. His eyes pleaded with me. "You remember?"

I nodded. "We have to go."

He held my hand. "No. *No.* Listen, Vic." He took my head in his hands, bending down so that his eyes were level with mine. "Come on. You need to remember this."

He was scaring me. I wrenched away from him and snapped, "I don't want to." When he reached for me again, I held myself rigid in front of him. "Why…why are you doing this?"

"Because I want to help you, Vic."

"Me? You're the one with all the problems. With the fucked-up life. Why don't you help yourself first?" I turned away from him, heading toward the street. As I started to climb the embankment toward the road, he grabbed at me. I reeled back and smacked him. He blinked, stunned, then rubbed his raw cheek.

"Don't touch me. I've got to go."

"You know what happened," he said. "He's dead. Andrew's dead."

I stopped. I whirled. "You're out of your mind."

"What happened?" Z asked. His voice sounded distant, drifting in and out on the wind. "You found him here in the woods. He'd killed himself, right? You were what…fourteen?"

"I have no *fucking* clue what you're talking about," I spat out.

You'd warned me, Andrew. You'd said, *Forever. This time,*

I mean it! But you said that *every* time. Every time he beat you down, every time he made you feel worthless, you'd come to our spot and tell me you didn't know how much longer you could take it. You'd tell me you were running away, hitchhiking across the country until he'd never find you. I heard that at least a thousand times. How was I supposed to know this time was different? Did you always carry a vial of that stuff from your stepfather's hunting cabinet? Did you always carry an extra insulin needle with you? Did you? Why didn't you tell me?

I saw you leave. I heard your father screaming, *Faggot!* and watched you storm out of the house, slamming the screen door behind you. You looked up at my window and hefted your blue backpack onto your bony shoulders.

You wanted me to come out and save you.

I watched you march in the direction of Route 11.

I didn't rush out like I should've. It was early spring, and you know how I hate the cold. The first weeks of mud season suck. Patches of depressing, half-melted snow clotted with sticks and soft earth were everywhere. All of the green buds and little creatures that make springtime happy were still too afraid to come out and face the world. How many times had I joked with you that I wished you'd time your efforts to run away more for midsummer?

I knew exactly where to find you. I threw on my jacket and headed after you, walking at a leisurely pace and wishing I lived in Miami. I imagined the pines above me were palm trees. I told myself that when we were grown, we'd live somewhere with palms and sweet, flowery breezes.

When I got to the woods, I followed your footprints in the muddy snow. I found you sitting on the ground, slouched against a tall pine. You smiled when you saw me, and the first thing I thought was, *All is well. Thirty more minutes, and we can go home. In time, this storm will blow over too.*

But then your head lolled like a puppet on a string.

Remember what you said, Andrew?

What took you so long?

You tried to sing to me. *Someday, when I'm old and gray,* those stupid made-up lyrics. But your lips were slack, and the notes came out all garbled and wrong. That wayward tongue of yours was getting its last laugh, I guess.

I couldn't breathe.

Then you told me you loved me. Well, you said, "I love…" but you couldn't make your mouth form the last word. Good thing I know you, Andrew. If anyone else had said it, I would have thought they meant "I love puppies" or "I love steak and onions" or "I love the Payless BOGO special," never that it was about me.

It was the only time you ever said that to me, but still, I knew. I always knew. My heart stuttered in my chest like it wanted to beat for both of us. I crouched in the mud beside you and touched your hand. It was unnaturally cold.

Damn you, Andrew. I knew everything about you, but I didn't know *that*. And it was an egregiously huge omission. My future had a lot of what-ifs in it, yet it always, *always* included you. But your somedays never included me, did they? All those times you sang to me, you never planned on being old and gray. You never planned on escaping to palm trees and warm breezes. Instead, *this* was your plan. *This* was what you day-dreamed about. Not me. Not us.

Do you remember the last thing you told me?

You told me it would all be over soon.

Liar. The worst was just beginning.

Your face was ghostly pale. One of your diabetic needles lay on the ground, a little vial too.

I shook you, trying to get you to wake up. I punched your chest, willing your heart to keep beating. I promised you that if you didn't leave me, I'd never leave you.

But that didn't work. You closed your eyes.

I called you stupid. I called you an idiot. I told you that if you hurt me like that, I'd curse your name, never talk to you again, walk away and never turn back.

I lied, of course.

And now Z was standing before me, going on and on, trying to urge a confession out of me, begging me to trust him, but I've heard that before. Everyone is always telling me to trust them, that decisions they make are for my own good, but good doesn't exist in my life anymore. Not since you left, Andrew.

But Z just kept pressing, shaking up all those bottled emotions inside me. I wrestled him off me and screamed, "Stop it!" so loud that the trees shuddered around us.

I took a breath, but bile rose from my throat. I huffed out, "I don't trust *anyone* anymore. I hate you. I hate him, and I hate you."

My limbs were frozen. I couldn't even think to move them.

He slinked beside me, holding me steady against the trunk of the pine tree, whispering soft words of comfort. I even allowed him to kiss me, but meanwhile, everything inside me had begun to rebel. His hands and lips and body smothered me. I lashed out, biting hard on his lip.

"Fuck!" He bent over, collecting blood in his palm. "Vic, what the fuck?"

I licked his blood from my lip. God, I'd *bitten* him. That was crazy. I started chanting in my head, "I'm not crazy. I'm not crazy. I'm not…"

Z wrapped his arms around me, whispering, "You're not."

I hadn't realized I'd said it out loud.

I blinked. The last time I spoke to you, Andrew, was after the dance. You were there with me outside our duplex. I'd seen you, felt you, kissed you. *You were there.* I whispered, "He's not dead."

"I get it. It was a shock, Vic. He meant a lot to you," Z said to me, his arms still wrapped around me. "But you can get it back. *We* can get it back."

But you knew me better than that, Andrew.

"He's not dead," I repeated, pulling out of Z's embrace. "You think you can fix everybody? Try fixing yourself. I won't leave him again."

Before I could run for the road though, I heard branches snapping. Footsteps pounding closer.

That's when you came in.

You were a force, Andrew. You were anger and desire and hate personified, leveling that entire forest with your rage.

Fight and flight instincts warred inside me. Someone screamed my name, but I wasn't sure whose voice it was. You and Z have such similar voices, you know? I remember a scuffle, punches thrown, leaves cast into the cold air, faces twisted in agony. I remember splinters from the heavy branch I pried from the frozen ground digging into my palm.

I remember Z saying, "Why, why, why," over and over again. Asking first, then pleading. It was the first time I'd ever seen fear in his gorgeous blue eyes.

The first, and the last.

The truth was, I wanted to help. I wanted to save you both.

But, Andrew, I meant what I'd said before, while I cradled you in my arms that night when we were fourteen.

I told you I was sorry. I told you I'd protect you. I told you I'd never let you down again.

And this time, I didn't.

CHAPTER 38

THE SKY IS LIGHTENING. I can't talk anymore. I'm so tired. My throat hurts. My battery is almost dead. But, Andrew... if you hear this, then, well, you'll know the whole story.

You'll know that I never meant to hurt you.

You're gone. You left me. And it's been hours. You've never been gone this long. I don't know if I'll see you again. Is this really the end of us? I thought you came to the Killing Woods tonight for me so that we could be together. I thought you'd finally found your courage. But maybe you've given up. You're angry at me.

You have every right to be.

But my conscience is finally clear. In the end, I chose you. I wish we could go back to that night when we were fourteen. Of course I'd do things differently. I'd prove to you how much you mean to me, and you'd never doubt me again.

Oh, fuck it. It doesn't matter. You're gone and I'm here, and hindsight's a massive waste of time. Some things are inevitable.

CHAPTER 39

What word would you use to describe Z?

Kind. He was always thinking of others. He used to
    leave me gifts in my locker. Stupid, silly little things
    like stickers and candy. He liked to give the impres-
    sion he was a bad boy, but down deep, he was a
    puppy dog. He lived to make people smile.

When was the last time you saw Z?

After the dance, when he drove me to the hotel.

After your fight.

Yes. When he had to "fix" something. But I don't know
    if he really could have. He was…

Yes?

Always trying to help, whether he could or not.
    Shortsighted. That's another word for him.

As in…

He'd give and give of himself until there was noth-
    ing left.

Who do you think wanted to hurt Z?

I can't believe anyone wanted to hurt him. Maybe they

just wanted him. That's the person he was. But there was only so much of him to go around.

—Interview with Parker Cole,
junior at St. Ann's

I T'S BEEN EIGHT DAYS SINCE they found me.

I am walking again. I only had one break, a compound fracture of my thighbone, and though it aches through the pain medication, it's healing. But parts of me never will. I am whole, but only on the outside. Inside, my thoughts are black, tortured, consumed.

The hospital room where I've spent the last week is depressingly void of color. A vent blows hot air onto my face. My throat is dry, my mind awhirl with thoughts of that night in the Kissing Woods with Z. Lips and hands and intense desire. The darkness, the bony tree limbs scratching at us, the desperation.

The death.

"Victoria," a voice says, luring me back.

I blink. Father Leary is looking at me. He's been at my bedside presiding over me these past few days, murmuring prayers to the Holy Father while I pretended to doze. My parents hover behind him. We are all good at pretending these days. My mother pretends to read a magazine, and my father seems acutely interested in something on his fingernail, but I know they are both hanging on my next words. "What?" I croak.

"The police need to talk to you about what happened in the woods."

I close my eyes. At first, my parents said that I was too fragile to relive those moments. At first, they defended me. They said that their daughter wasn't capable of hurting a fly. They said that yes, Victoria may have had some mental confusion, but she'd never resort to violence. But the police have become more and more persistent, my parents more and more doubtful. Now, my parents don't look me in the eye.

Leary turns to my parents, then back to me, a troubled look on his face. "I'm sorry, Victoria," he says, his voice flat. "You can't put them off any longer. You're going to have to talk to the police."

They want me to tell my story, but I get the feeling they already know it. One version, anyway.

The room is crackling with tension. When my mother takes my hand, I expect a jolt of electricity, but her hand is cold. She and my father volley their meaning-fraught glances over the bed before my mother opens her mouth to speak. Then she closes it. She leans over and brings my hand to her cheek. She doesn't have to say a word, and I don't want her to. I don't want to hear those words out loud.

I know she will tell me that you've been dead for nearly two years. She will say that you're just in my head, Andrew.

And of course, you won't be here to back me up. To share in the responsibility with me. Just like *I* wasn't there for you.

What a bitch payback is.

They will say that what happened to Z is all my doing.

They will say that I swung that tree branch at Z, while he raised his hands to shield himself, asking me why I would do such a thing.

They won't understand when I tell them that I *couldn't* stop. That you needed me to protect you.

I will defend you, Andrew. I will always defend you.

Because how many times did I tell myself I'd rather die than disappoint you again?

CHAPTER 40

How well did you know Z?

He was in the play with me.

Were you friends?

Yes.

Were you romantically involved?

…What?

Did you have a romantic relationship with Z?

…

Miss Zell?

I have a boyfriend, sir.

And who is your boyfriend?

He has nothing to do with any of this.

Who is your boyfriend, Miss Zell?

That's… Why does it matter?

It's important information. This is a criminal investigation.

Well, he's… His name is Andrew. He's really shy. He's
    agoraphobic. I…I've known him since I was little.
    He lives next door. He's homeschooled. He's a
    brilliant pianist.

Were you cheating on him?

...

Miss Zell, were you seeing Z while you were involved with Andrew?

...

OK, let's try a different question. When was the last time you saw Z?

On the night of the dance. So, Saturday?

November twenty-first. And what were you doing on the evening of Sunday, November twenty-second?

If it was late on Sunday, I was probably sleeping. My parents don't let me out late on a school night.

And what did you do that morning?

I went for a run. I always run along Route 11 in the morning, before school.

Did you see the Honda Civic belonging to Z on your run?

Yes. It was parked on the shoulder of the road.

Did that strike you as odd?

Yes, but I assumed it broke down or something. It was an old car.

What happened while you were on your run?

I was jogging. I must have slipped and fell, and I guess I tumbled down the slope. I don't remember a lot. When I woke, I was lying in a ditch and I could hardly move.

So you never saw Z while on your run? Not at all?

No. I... No. I've said this before.

> *We found some text messages from you on his*
>   *phone that said you were planning to meet him*
>   *that night, in the exact place where he was killed.*
>   *Can you explain that?*
> *...*
> *Miss Zell.*
> I... No. Honestly, I can't remember. I-I went for a run.
> **—Police interview with Victoria Zell, junior at St. Ann's**

W HEN I'M RELEASED FROM THE hospital, Mom and Dad
take me out to dinner. They say I need it.

Skin and bones, that's what they call me. I used to be
strong, a long, long time ago. Now they say I am on my way
to becoming a walking skeleton. I nibble at my salad; I haven't
eaten much in more than a week. What I do manage to get
down always comes back up.

But food won't fill me. From now on, for the rest of my
days, I will be empty.

Back at home, I wander out to our spot. My parents never
took down the purple lights. They haven't hung Christmas dec-
orations or shoveled the snow from the walk either, almost like
their world ended that night too. Piles of snow drift against the
place I used to sit, leaning against the peeling paint of the picket
fence. I crouch down, boots slipping on the slick, silver surface
of old snow. I think of the shimmery satin dresses blinking in
the colorful strobe as we swooshed through the dimly lit gymnasium, of *Macbeth*, of those eyes. Those big, blue eyes that were
my world.

Are my world.

That can never change, can it, Andrew? Even now, we can never undo what's been done.

I reach out and scrape at the paint on the fence. It's badly in need of rehab. You used to be the one to paint it, since your stepfather never did. I wonder if it will ever see a paintbrush again. Your stepfather has come outside on more than one occasion, drunkenly using this fence as target practice. Some of his arrows are still buried in the wood. I wonder if the shape of the digs spells your name.

I start to pull our silver gum wrappers from between the slats. There are dozens. I pull them out one by one, opening them and setting them flat. They're damp from snow. I reach into my pocket and pull out a lighter. Then I light a corner, watching each paper burn. They burn to embers, drifting through the air.

Like fireflies.

They extinguish themselves on the snow. As I look down, I see the tip of another silver wrapper poking through the slats of the old fence. I take the piece of gum and unwrap it, folding it into my mouth. "Thanks, Z," I whisper.

He laughs softly. "Any time."

"Andrew left me. I haven't seen him since…"

"Ah, Precious. Well, you can't trust anyone. You were the one who taught me that."

I smile. I suppose I did. "The police interviewed me at the hospital. It was horrible. They think it's me. I can tell. They think that *I* did those horrible things to you." I chew for a moment, but it doesn't do much to calm me. My voice is hardly a breath. "They don't understand."

He doesn't say anything, but I can hear Z chewing too. I start to chew in unison with him, hoping the rhythm will lull my nerves.

"I'm worried," I finally say, shredding the wrapper in my hands.

"I know."

"You do?"

More laughter. "Aren't you always, Vic? But don't. When they come for you, you won't be going alone."

"I won't?" I ask, and once again, I know he will tell me the very words I needed to hear. Z has always been the master of knowing exactly what to say. I don't even have to ask my next question. It's like my body trembling is a sign only he can read.

"It's strange. I understand everything now. Before, the blinds were closed and I could only see part of the truth. Now, I see it all."

"That's like the Aleph," I whisper. "From Reese's class."

"Yeah."

"You see the truth about me?"

"Yeah, I see it all. I've been inside your head, Vic. I know it was you with the acid. I know you had no choice. You were afraid. You'd already lost so much."

My teeth chatter in my skull. I am all contradictions again, warm yet shivering, scared yet thrilled. "You understand why I did it, Z?"

"I get you, Precious." He reaches out and finds my hand

with his cold one, squeezing my fingers. He's still wearing the same bulky sweatshirt he'd worn when I last saw him. That sweatshirt made it impossible to tell the exact moment when his heart stopped. I'd had to put my hand under it to feel his chest, beautifully muscled and warm, twitching before it stuttering to a halt.

But Z's much stronger now, eternal. He bears no bruises or welts or pain, no fucked-up life with no home, no future. Z is strong, resilient. This is the Z I know and love. His eyes twinkle like ice-blue stars, just like they had as they stared lifelessly at the full moon…but they're wider and brighter and more breathtaking than ever before.

"You don't hate me?" I ask nervously.

"No. We're perfect." He pushes a lock of hair behind my ear and touches my temple. "In here, no one can disappoint us, can they?"

I swallow hard, liking the sound of that. "Don't leave me. You won't leave me, will you?"

"You can never rid yourself of the Zahir, Vic. I'm still here. More than ever. I'm still here. Lady M said it best." The smile that breaks out on his face is enough to light the entire darkening sky. "'Out, out, damn spot,' huh, Precious?"

He leans over and kisses the top of my head. His lips are cold as ice and light like snowflakes, but he's still the same Z. The same, only better. He's *my* Z now. Only mine. The Z that will never leave me, even in the hell I've built for myself.

I pull Z beside me. Silently, shoulder to shoulder, we let the darkness stretch over us like a blanket, insulating us from the blind, blind world.

HUNDREDS ATTEND FUNERAL FOR SLAIN TEEN

Bangor, ME—Approximately 800 attended a funeral service on Tuesday for a murdered Duchess teenager.

Zachary Zimmerman, 17, was remembered at St. Ann's Church in a service celebrating his life. Zimmerman was found beaten to death in a wooded area off Route 11 in Duchess at about 10:30 a.m. on November 23. That unsolved crime has sent shock waves through this small, tight-knit community.

The service had a number of youths in attendance, including students from St. Ann's High School where Zimmerman was a junior. Zimmerman was a member of the baseball team and had recently portrayed Macbeth in the autumn play.

Duchess Mayor John Richardson spoke at the funeral, praising Zimmerman for being a model student and a helpful friend, and calling for action to help address violence in the community.

"It's been different in the week since he died," St. Ann's junior James Burney said. "Z always put people in a good mood. Half the time we've been expecting him to show up and tell us it was all a joke."

Police believe that Zimmerman was targeted by someone he knew. They are still investigating several leads.

Zimmerman's death prompted a public meeting last week with county and law enforcement officials and church and community leaders to discuss ways to combat violence in Central Maine.

"Zachary's death has had a tremendous impact on us all," Father Leary said. "Having lived in Central Maine all my life, I'm shaken. Shaken that something like this could happen to someone who never did anything but try to help others to better themselves."

ACKNOWLEDGMENTS

I am deeply indebted to so many people who helped to draw *Unnatural Deeds* out of my head and into your hands.

First and foremost, all the hugs and kisses go to Mandy Hubbard, my agent and writing BFF, who can always be counted on to read my first drafts and suggest edits to elevate it to a creepiness beyond anything I could've come up with on my own.

Secondly, much love to Annette Pollert-Morgan, my wonderful editor, for taking a chance on this crazy little book and whipping it into shape. A big thank-you goes out to Elizabeth Boyer, Nicole Komasinski, Danielle McNaughton, and the entire staff at Sourcebooks. I am deeply appreciative to everything you've done!

Unnatural Deeds would still be hanging out on my computer if it wasn't for the encouragement and insightful critiques from these wonderful ladies: Margie Gelbwasser, Lynsey Newton, Charlotte Bennardo, Jennifer Murgia, Cindy Sorenson, Tara Goodyear, Sara Bennett-Wealer, Gryffyn Phoenix, and Jen Nadol. You are all rockstar writers and I adore you!

I also have to thank everything that has ever made me feel

out of control with desire. It's because I know that feeling so well that I felt compelled to write about it. I'm looking at you, chocolate-marshmallow ice cream, *Sherlock*, and the two weeks of vacation I get every year.

As usual, I saved the best for last. Thank you to Brian, Sara, and Gabrielle for everything. No contest, you three are my true obsession. I love you most.

YOU'RE NEVER REALLY

ALONE

Don't miss this new spine-tingling novel from Cyn Balog

CHAPTER ONE

**Welcome to the Bismarck-Chisholm House—
where murder is only the beginning of the fun!
Stay in one of our eighteen comfortable staterooms.
You'll sleep like the dead. We guarantee it...**

SOMETIMES I DREAM I AM drowning.

Sometimes I dream of bloated faces, bobbing on the surface of misty waters.

And then I wake up, often screaming, heart racing, hands clenching fistfuls of my sheets.

I'm in my bed at the head of Bug House. The murky daylight casts dull prisms from my snow globes onto the attic floor. My mom started collecting those pretty winter scenes for me when I was a baby. I gaze at them, lined neatly on the shelf in front of my window. My first order of business every day is hoping they'll give me a trace of the joy they did when I was a kid.

But either they don't work that way anymore, or I don't.

Who am I kidding? It's definitely me.

I'm insane. Batshit. Nuttier than a fruitcake. Of course, that's not an official diagnosis. The official word from Dr. Batton, whose swank Copley Square office I visited only once when I was ten, was that I was bright and intelligent and a *wonderful young person*. He said it's normal for kids to have imaginary playmates.

Where it gets a little sketchy is when that young person grows up, and her imaginary friend decides to move in and make himself comfortable.

Not that anyone knows about that. No, these days, I'm good about keeping up appearances.

My second order of business each day is hoping that *he* won't leak into my head. That maybe I can go back to being a normal sixteen-year-old girl.

But he always comes.

He's a part of me, after all. And he's been coming more and more, invading my thoughts. *Of course I'm here, stupid.*

Sawyer. His voice in my mind is so loud that it drowns out the moaning and creaking of the walls around me.

"Seda, honey?" my mother calls cheerily. She shifts her weight on the bottom step, making the house creak more. "Up and at 'em, buckaroo!"

I force my brother's taunts away and call down the spiral staircase, "I *am* up." My short temper is because of him, but it ends up directed at her.

She doesn't notice though. My mother has only one mood now: ecstatically happy. She says it's the air up here, which always has her taking big, deep, monster breaths as if she's trying to inhale the entire world into her lungs. But maybe it's because this is her element; after all, she made a profession out of her love for all things horror. Or maybe she really is better off without my dad, as she always claims she is.

I hear her whistling "My Darlin' Clementine" as her slippered feet happily scuffle off toward the kitchen. I put on the first clothing I find in my drawer—sweatpants and my mom's old Boston College sweatshirt—then scrape my hair into a ponytail on the top of my head as I look around the room. Mannequin body parts and other macabre props are stored up here. It's been my bedroom for only a month. I slept in the nursery with the A and Z twins when we first got here because they were afraid of ghosts and our creepy old house. But maybe they—like Mom—are getting used to this place?

The thought makes me shudder. I like my attic room because of the privacy. Plus, it's the only room that isn't ice cold, since all the heat rises up to me. But I don't like much else about this old prison of a mansion.

One of the props, Silly Sally, is sitting in the rocker by the door as I leave. She'd be perfect for the ladies' department at Macy's if it weren't for the gaping chest wound in her frilly pink blouse. "I hate you," I tell her, batting at the other mannequin body parts descending from the rafters like some odd canopy. She smiles as if the feeling is mutual. I give her a kick on the way out.

Despite the morbid stories about this place, I don't ever worry about ghosts. After all, I have Sawyer, and he is worse.

As I climb down the stairs, listening to the kids chattering in the nursery, I notice the money, accompanied by a slip of paper, on the banister's square newel post. The car keys sit atop the pile. Before I can ask, Mom calls, "I need you to go to the store for us. OK, Seda, my little kumquat?"

I blink, startled, and it's not because of the stupid nickname. I don't have a license, just a learner's permit. My mom had me driving all over the place when we first came here, but that was *back then*. Back when this was a simple two-week jaunt to get an old house she'd inherited ready for sale. There wasn't another car in sight, so she figured, why not? She's all about giving us kids *experiences*, about making sure we aren't slaves to our iPhones, like so many of my friends back home. My mother's always marching to her own drummer, general consensus be damned, usually to my horror. But back then, I had that thrilling, invincible, first-days-of-summer-vacation feeling that made anything seemed possible. Too bad that was short lived.

We've been nestled at Bug House like hermits for months. Well, that's not totally true. Mom has made weekly trips down the mountain, alone, to get the mail and a gallon of milk and make phone calls to civilization. We were supposed to go back to Boston before school started, but that time came and went, and there's no way we're getting off this mountain before the first snow.

Snow.

I peer out the window. The first dainty flakes are falling from the sky.

Snow. Oh God. Snow.

My mother appears in the doorway, her body drowning out most of the morning light from the windows behind her.

She'd never be considered fat, but *substantial*, tall and striking. Mom is someone people intrinsically want to imitate. She was one of the most popular professors last year at Boston College. My father used to say all the young men in her lectures were in love with her, and all the young women wanted to be like her. She can make a glamorous entrance even when stepping out of her car to get gas. That—and her size—are what separate us, people say. I'm short and rail thin, and people don't usually pay attention to what I say or do.

"Why the sourpuss?" Mom says airily, twirling her blond curls into an elegant chignon at the base of her neck. "Is it because we're not going back just yet?"

I don't know how to respond. She says *just yet*, but I hear *ever*. The snow only cements the word in my head. My mother loves changing plans. She doesn't let other people's schedules dictate what we should do, which is why I've always missed lots of school. My mother will get these crazy ideas for adventure, like crabbing in the bay or going off to Sturbridge Village for a candle-making seminar, and we pick up and go. Like I said, life experience. *Books and the inside of a classroom can only teach you so much*, she says. It's part of why her students love her.

"It's only a little longer, all right?" she says, surveying the foyer in a lovestruck way. "We're very close to having a buyer for the house."

She's told me that before, but plans have changed a dozen times since June. I hate to think of what will happen if they change any more. *Fun* is what my friends used to call my mother. Except that that brand of "fun" can wear you down.

"But…" I trail off, a million buts dying on my lips. But *everything*. It's one thing to live in such a remote place during the summer, when the surrounding landscape is bursting with color and the birds are singing. But in the winter?

What are you complaining about? Sawyer asks me. *People like you shouldn't be part of the general public.*

And maybe it's true. Maybe being alone with my family on the side of a mountain will keep everyone from finding out what is going on inside my head. That *he* is there, always threatening to take over. Maybe, without the outside world to intrude, Dr. Maya Helm's crazy daughter can just go on being crazy.

Not that I can tell my mother that. No, to her, Sawyer was my fictitious childhood playmate who has long been forgotten.

But the thing is, Sawyer had been coming to me more and more since we came here. He's always in the back of my head, that little voice spurring me to be a little wild whenever I want to hold back and play it safe. At first, I thought everyone had a Sawyer, like when he told me to throw a binder at Lucy Willis for calling me ugly in third grade or touch a hot radiator when I was two. Gradually though, I learned Sawyer's voice was something to keep quiet. Still, back home in Boston, I had distractions to drown him out. I had studies and color guard and friends.

Here, he is front and center in my thoughts, twenty-four seven.

And Sawyer likes it this way. Even though my head is screaming that we need to get as far away from this place as possible, one part of me, the part of my stomach that's supposed to get queasy and unsettled, feels warm. Comfortable.

My mother comes up to me and swipes a stray lock of hair from my face. I flinch. "Don't."

"Everything's OK, love." She gives me a convincing smile, even though the world might as well be crumbling around us. "I know you're bored to death here, but I promise, we'll be back home soon."

I *wish* it was just boredom. I swallow and nod, then slide the money and keys in the pocket of my sweatshirt and head out the door before the kids can notice me. If this weather continues, I can't delay. The mountain road we live on is no joke. Our van nearly slid into a ditch during a light rain, so snow won't be any better. Not that I've ever been here in the winter.

The van creaks to life, and I pull out of the decaying three-bay garage and down the winding driveway, pinging gravel into the air behind the car. The snow looks almost pretty, landing delicately on the windshield.

It's twenty miles to Art's General, the closest store. I listen to the radio part of the way, but the only station we get is all static-filled talk about the blizzard that's coming. Twenty inches expected, at least. I switch off the radio and try to ignore tension in my hands from gripping the steering wheel so tightly. I concentrate on the tree-lined road. Of course I'd noticed the days getting darker and colder, but I thought it was only September. I'm losing track of time now, ever since Dad checked out in the middle of the night without so much as a goodbye.

August 31. Three days before the official start of school. That was the last I saw him. The details are hazy, like a dream. Sawyer sees to that. But the outcome is the same. Dad's gone.

And we are alone with Mom and her whims. This early in the morning, the parking lot at Art's is empty. Not that it's ever crowded. When I lived in Boston, weather like this packed the stores with frantic people stocking up on bread and milk and toilet paper. But there simply *are* no people to pack Art's. It's a wonder the store stays in business, but a good thing it does. Otherwise we'd probably starve to death.

I navigate around the old snowblower carcasses he has for sale on the sidewalk, then push open the heavy door. When the bell over the door tinkles, Elmer, who took over after Art died, stares at me like I'm a ghost. "Seda?"

I give him a wave.

He cranes his neck to look out the window. "Your mom with you?"

That's the most he's said to me, ever. Elmer's never been a talker, so if I go about my business, he should leave me alone. "Not today," I say, then turn to my list. It's a mile long and has things like hot cocoa and canned vegetables and bottled water on it.

Either she's way overestimating our appetites, or this is a *We're not going back to Boston* list.

I slump against the canned goods display, then startle at the horrifically loud crash as half a dozen tomato soup cans go scattering and rolling in all directions. Elmer just scowls and picks up his crossword puzzle. I fish after the cans and restack them quickly. As I'm piling items into a basket and trying to decide whether I should buy the kids SpaghettiOs as a treat, the bell dings again and I hear a sound that makes me freeze.

Laughter.

Art's store likely hasn't had this much noise, this much life, ever. Peeking around a tuna fish display, I watch as a group of teenagers piles inside.

They shine. They're all wearing bright, heavy coats and hats—and sunglasses, despite the lack of sun. The two girls wear meticulously applied makeup, with masses of hair heavy with styling product. The dark-haired one has devil horns on her head, and the other has her blond hair tied into ponytails with pink and blue ribbons and a giant, black heart painted on her glowing cheek. One of the boys wears a hideous mask with a long, bumpy nose, and the other has vampire fangs. They're my age, maybe, but the difference is, despite trying to look scary, they're lovely.

I can't help but stare as they start to pile gum and Twinkies and frosted doughnuts into their arms. My mom would flip if I even touched the packaging of that stuff. Elmer glares at them like they're subhuman, but do they even notice? No. They're confident. Unbreakable. Untouchable. I remember that look of invincibility from my friends, back in Boston.

Boston seems a million miles and years away right now. It's hard to believe I was there only four months ago.

One of the boys—the tall, lanky one who keeps popping his fangs in and out his mouth—scans the shelves as he saunters down the aisle toward me. He's wearing a hat that says *Panthers* and a school letter jacket that says *Wit* on the breast. I step back when his eyes focus on me.

He notices and narrows his eyes, curious at first, then amused.

I blush. I push my hair behind my ear, then look down at my Boston College sweatshirt. It has a crusted brown stain on the front. Stew, from...three nights ago? I forget.

I cross my arms in front of me and, for the first time, realize I'm not wearing a bra. I used to wear one all the time in Boston, even years before I really needed one, but they've been folded in my underwear drawer since the end of July. He comes up very, very close, smiling, and I inhale the scent of detergent, fresh and clean.

My heart is beating faster than it ever has. I'm in the process of filling my lungs with that glorious smell when he says, "Excuse me."

I am standing in front of the refrigerated case. I scuttle aside, and he reaches in and pulls out a Mountain Dew.

My mother says that's cancer in a bottle. But I'm not sure anything could kill this boy. He cocks his head at me and sidles down the aisle toward the register, where his friends are waiting.

I can't stop gawking. Another guy, who's short and has one of those little GoPro cameras, has been filming the whole thing. "That your inbred trailer-trash girlfriend?" he says, smiling at me.

Letter Jacket Kid looks over his shoulder at me, then says, "She's better action than you've ever gotten, Li." The two girls giggle as the cash register dings. When they leave, the store slides back into its tomb-like silence, and I drop the SpaghettiOs in the full cart and head to piling the items on the Pick-6 mat in front of Elmer. He rings up my purchase slowly, studying me over his bifocals as I pretend to be very interested in the Marlboros behind him. "Haven't seen your mom a while. She OK?"

I nod. God, he does everything at slow speed. I help take cans and boxes out of the cart so I can move him along.

He nestles them, one by one, in a paper bag. "And the kids?"

I nod. "Good." I start turning the prices toward him, so he can ring faster.

"Your father?"

I cringe. I've practiced this answer, and I'm happy to say it because I know it's guaranteed to shut him up. "He left us."

As I expected, he stares at me, his grizzled jowls working, trying to come up with a diplomatic response. *I'm sorry* is what you say when someone tells you their father died, not when he doesn't want to be with you. Mom tells me he never wanted to live in the country, and that if he were still moping around, he'd spoil our fun. At least, that's what she says when she's putting on her brave face. But I know why she has me babysit the kids while she drives to Art's every week. She calls him. That's why every time she comes back, she seems a little more defeated.

On the ride home, I can't stop thinking of those kids—real, normal people my age, who live in the outside world. I have a van filled with plastic bags of food that tell me that's no longer my life. It's just me, my mother, and my siblings. Forever.

You have me.

And Sawyer. I can't forget Sawyer.

Ever.

CHAPTER TWO

**Live—and die!—your dream.
Welcome to the most haunted mansion in
Allegheny County. Legend has it that everyone
who visits succumbs to the disorienting effect of
Solitude Mountain. Can you survive the night?**

S AWYER CHIDES ME AS I pull into our long, winding driveway, where the snow is blanketing the gravel. *Your jaw was
open so wide, you could've been catching flies.*

He's right, but I couldn't *help it. I'm almost sixteen. I should
be planning a sweet sixteen party. But right when my life is supposed
to be beginning…it's all ending. Those days of staying up all night and
texting my best friends are gone. In fact, I haven't talked to Juliet or
Rachel for weeks. Bug House is in a dead zone for cell phone service.*

*To think, my family used to be so "with it." My mom was a
media arts professor with an actual social media presence and tens of
thousands of followers. Her class on the modern horror film had the longest wait-list of any at the whole university. My dad played the electric
guitar in a band, and I was officially the coolest kid in school because my*

mom let me stay up late to watch him play at all these trendy bars in the city. At Bug House, we don't even have a television set or a telephone. We have an old film projector and a bunch of reels of old horror movies, but my mom uses those for the book she's writing.

Before I left Boston, my friends and I used to hang out at Rachel's brownstone all the time since her parents were never home. The day before I left, Rachel told me that Evan Bradley, who I'd been in love with since I started kindergarten, liked me. She'd given him my number because he'd wanted to *text me over the summer,* she'd said in an excited squeal, her eyes glistening.

I knew my parents would never approve of him. He had a reputation for being a troublemaker and always having smart-ass replies in class, but I didn't care. He was dreamy, and we'd bonded in bio because he sat behind me and would crack jokes. He always told me how smart I was, so I started moving my test sheet to the corner of the desk to let him copy my answers. Being around him was a rush. So when I got the news, my best friends and I jumped up and down and hugged.

A day later, after we'd crossed the border into Pennsylvania, I discovered the outside world couldn't quite reach this far up Solitude Mountain.

It's like my entire life got put on hold that day. I've never made out with a boy or smoked weed or done any of those foolish things that are a part of being a teenager.

And as long as I'm up here, separated from my friends and other kids, I know I never will.

Sawyer will see to that.

Bug House is really the Bismarck-Chisholm House. I

don't know who Bismarck or Chisholm were, and I'm not sure anyone else does either. Their only legacy is having their names attached to this rotting monstrosity, so I'm sure they're spending their afterlife rolling in their graves.

We live in the main part of Bug House, the heart of it, the part that isn't completely falling to ruin. A few decades ago, my aunt and uncle, the former owners, bought the house and ran it as a murder mystery hotel. It was pretty groundbreaking at the time, and people would come from all over the country to stay here. Some of the most famous and glamorous people in the world visited for themed weekends. They actually paid serious cash to have the crap scared out of them. But then the idea caught on, and you didn't have to drive hours into the middle of nowhere to stay at a place like Bug House. Murder mystery events could be found on practically every street corner, so my aunt and uncle shut the place down shortly before they died.

And we're supposed to sell it. No one wants this place though. Those who do want to demolish the building. Mother refuses to sell to a buyer who'll "ruin it," which also seems to include making it a normal bed-and-breakfast or house. Even when people like the Gothic architecture and decor, the mannequin body parts in seemingly every closet, brownish fake bloodstains on the wallpaper, and nooses hanging from ceilings aren't the kind of characteristics anyone wants to preserve. All the stuff of nightmares is housed here.

Supposedly, long ago, Bug House was a regular, stately home, but wing upon wing were added over the years. Six of them, to be exact, all stretching out in different directions in a maze of aging hallways and secret passages and history. One of the old brochures had an aerial shot of the grounds, and the mansion looks like a bug, with my big, round attic room as the head. Which is how Sawyer gave Bug House its nickname.

Despite what he tries to tell me, Sawyer isn't alive. I'd say he was dead, but I'm not sure he was ever living. My mother has a womb for twins. That's what she told me when I asked why my four younger brothers and sisters came out in pairs. I was little at the time and didn't get why I didn't have a match, and she said I did, once, but I'd absorbed him in the womb. A few days after that, I started to think that maybe the wild voice speaking inside me could be him. So I guess you could say that if he lives, he lives inside me.

When I was five or six, I found a baby name book in my mother's dresser with two names circled: Seda and Sawyer. Seda, my name, means *Spirit of the Forest*. Sawyer, of course, is the woodcutter. Sometimes I envision him, tromping around with an ax over his shoulder. Sometimes I feel him in my gut, pushing against my stomach as if with the head of an ax, testing to find a way out.

Like I said, I don't tell people about him anymore. At first, when I told my mother about Sawyer, she laughed and said I have a *real good imagination*. But I wasn't imagining him, and eventually, Sawyer started asking me to hurt myself. Then others. It was just a suggestion, but he'd wanted me to stick a kid in fifth grade with a pair of scissors.

I managed to fight off that suggestion. And though I never

told a soul about the scissors, I did tell my mom some of the other things Sawyer talked about. Thus, Dr. Batton. But when I got the distinct impression that Sawyer's intrusion in my life was supposed to be lessening with age, not growing, I decided I had to deal with him on my own. So I've let her think that I've outgrown him. Now, when we talk about Sawyer, it's always as a joke, like he's my old imaginary friend I cast off years ago. We laugh and say, "Ha ha, remember the time Sawyer wrote all over the hallway with red crayon?" as if he was such a pleasant, quirky part of my childhood.

At least at Bug House, I never have to worry about Sawyer giving me suggestions. My siblings—Adam and Avery, who are six, and Zoe and Zain, who are just four—are my heart. Sawyer's too. I can tell by the warmth in my stomach every time I look at them. Still, my mother is wrong about me having an overactive imagination. My twin is a little...no, *a lot* of an asshole. He's bitter that I'm the one who was born. And what scares me is how much he's been with me lately. Like it's only a matter of time before he takes over.

I sneak in the back door, which leads directly to the kitchen. Shaking snowflakes from my ponytail, I stuff our purchases into the cabinets. The kids are running around the dining room table when I come in. As usual, Zoe's cries are eardrum-shattering, her energy like that of the sun. My mother is dancing about the room, setting vegetarian sausages on their plates as if she's posing for a *Better Homes & Gardens* article.

All kids think their mothers are beautiful, and I suppose I still do, despite the way this mountain has changed her. She used to be the mom who'd show up at my parents' nights at school, and every harried Boston mother would whisper, "How does she do it?" She had the most perfect arched eyebrows from meticulous plucking and wouldn't be caught dead without her tawny-colored lipstick. Now I'll walk into a room and she'll be wearing a sweater she'd packed away, which will still smell like her $200-a-bottle vanilla perfume you can only buy on Newbury Street. But when she moved out here, she transitioned seamlessly into the crunchy, fresh-faced, natural mom without skipping a beat. Those harried Boston mothers would probably still be envious.

When the kids see me, they rush over, circling my waist and nearly toppling me to the ground. "Seda! Seda! Seda!" they shout like gunfire.

"Sit and finish your breakfast," I mumble affectionately, ruffling their silky locks.

Adam, Avery, Zain, and Zoe scurry to their seats. We've never cut their hair—it's a total sin to think of putting a scissor to it, as shiny and ethereal as it is. They don't like to bathe either, so they look like wild children, street urchins. They're skinny, so mostly corn-silk ringlets and knobby, bruised knees with Band-Aids. Zain crawls under the table, complaining that he hates sausage, and Zoe sings "Your Baby Has Gone Down the Plughole" to her one-eyed old doll in a voice that's never any less annoying than a whine. Avery chases her brother, and Adam stops, reads a line of his favorite novel, and shovels a forkful of eggs into his mouth every lap around the table.

I part the lace curtains and press my nose against the leaded glass, fogging it over. The lake beyond the rotting fence is so still that it's almost like on a postcard. And totally covered with snow.

"I want to play outside," Zain says from under the brocade tablecloth. Zoe bangs her doll's head on the table concussively and agrees, as usual. He could say he wants to jump from the top of a very tall building, and she'd be all in.

"You'll be sick of the snow in a week," I mumble. Turning toward the table, I take in the three links of sausage on his plate. Each has a single nibble taken out of it. I push up the tablecloth and frown at him. "And you could've saved a sausage for me."

He sticks out his pink kitten tongue.

"It's freezing out there," I tell him, grabbing a half-eaten sausage off his plate and eating it anyway. I show him my still-red fingers. "Trust me."

Adam glances up from his book, *Charlie and the Chocolate Factory*, his favorite. "He won't be able to stand the cold for a minute." He emulates someone shivering and crying at the same time. It's a very good imitation. Adam's the actor in the family.

Zoe pouts. Zain points his tongue at his brother. But Adam's right: Zain hates the cold. And this is the wrong place to be if you hate cold.

Two hundred inches.

That's how much snow Solitude Mountain got last year. I can almost imagine it burying half the house. I know this detail, because I googled it back when we lived in the outside world. I told my mother that, but she just smiled and told me we'd be back in Boston before the snow.

But it's not the snow that's bothering me. I love snow. Well, used to, when it meant ski trips and ice-skating with my friends.

Staving off a hundred little arguments and tantrums, I shovel cold eggs into my mouth and wash them down with orange juice. My mother is oblivious to it all. "Just look," she says, sitting across the table from me. "The landscape is so beautiful! The winters here must be lovely. I bet city slickers would love to come here to escape, once the estate is back in business."

Oh God. My mother actually still believes someone will want to buy this place and run it like her aunt and uncle did. She mentions potential buyers all the time, but the deals always fall through. A couple of times, she even mentioned moving up here full-time and running the murder mystery mansion herself. As I look around the room, I cringe. My mother's aunt and uncle must have been really macabre, because the dining room resembles the Haunted Mansion at Disney World, with heavy velvet drapes, giant wrought-iron candlesticks, and ornate, high-backed chairs. All we need are gossamer forms in evening dress waltzing around us to complete the picture. I can't see people coming here to escape. This is a place to escape *from*. "Mom. No."

"Oh, you are such a negative Nelly." She smiles brightly, wadding up a napkin and tossing it right at my face. "Well, of course not *now*. A little elbow grease is all the place needs."

"All the elbow grease in the world couldn't save this house, but whatever," I grumble.

She opens her mouth to reply, but nothing comes out. Instead, she rolls her eyes as if I've told an amusing and slightly inappropriate joke. She thinks I've been a spoiled, disengaged teenager because I lost my iPhone.

She is so wrong.